93

Titles by Todd Borg

A DARK ROAD SUSPENSE SERIES:

WILDERNESSS VACATION
WILDERNESS JUSTICE
WILDERNESS PUNISHMENT
WILDERNESS THREAT

THE TAHOE MYSTERY SERIES:

TAHOE DEATHFALL
TAHOE BLOWUP
TAHOE ICE GRAVE
TAHOE KILLSHOT
TAHOE SILENCE
TAHOE AVALANCHE
TAHOE NIGHT
TAHOE HEAT
TAHOE HIJACK
TAHOE TRAP
TAHOE CHASE
TAHOE GHOST BOAT
TAHOE BLUE FIRE
TAHOE DARK
TAHOE PAYBACK
TAHOE SKYDROP
TAHOE DEEP
TAHOE HIT
TAHOE JADE
TAHOE MOON
TAHOE FLIGHT
TAHOE RESCUE

WILDERNESS VACATION

Josie Strong
A Dark Road Suspense
Book 1

by

TODD BORG

THRILLER PRESS

Thriller Press First Edition, July 2024

WILDERNESS VACATION
Copyright © 2024 by Todd Borg

ISBN: 978-1-931296-75-5

Cover design by Keith Carlson.

Manufactured in the United States of America

For Kit

ACKNOWLEDGMENTS

I owe a great deal to my editors, Liz Johnston, Eric Berglund, Christel Hall, and my wife Kit. They find and fix countless mistakes. They make much-needed suggestions for improvements. If my book reads well, they get the credit.

Graphic maestro Keith Carlson produced a spectacular new look for this new series. So beautiful I want to keep staring at them. I can't thank him enough.

Kit also serves as initial reader, story coach, last reader. She has an unerring ability to find and take out my misjudgments. I can't thank her enough.

PROLOGUE

Josie Strong was holding a fork when it slipped from her fingers and clattered to the floor. As she leaned over to pick it up, she heard the tink of breaking glass and the explosive ringing of a loud bell. The sound was startling and made Josie jerk. She felt something like sand hitting the back of her neck. It took her a second to realize that the window next to where she was sitting had shattered. One of the panes no longer reflected the yellow glow of the kerosene lantern. Instead, it was a square of black night punctuated at the edges by two triangles of broken glass.

The ringing of the bell slowly diminished. Josie turned toward its sound. Her daughter Samantha was already staring at the opposite wall of the log cabin's kitchen area. A few cooking pans hung from hooks. One of them was swinging wildly.

Josie didn't understand. Then she did. She yelled at her daughter. Her voice was a ragged, loud whisper.

"Sam! Get down on the floor! Someone is shooting at us!"

ONE

36 Hours Earlier

When Josie Strong saw the man at the Minneapolis-St. Paul airport, her first thought was that he looked like a sniper she'd recently seen in a movie. He was big and hard and had short red hair cut off in a flat top. His hair was crimson enough that it drew attention away from his huge, reddish nose. He reached down onto the baggage carousel and picked up a metallic case with solid locking latches. Maybe it contained goods for a salesman, high-tech coffee machines or something. Or maybe it contained component parts for a specialized rifle.

Such thoughts wouldn't normally occur to a Southern California professor who lived in the world of research papers and textbooks focused on the Middle Ages. But Josie's daughter Samantha had watched a movie two nights before in their Santa Monica condo. It was a thriller that featured a sniper team, a group from the Navy SEALs. They were big men with huge muscles. Their necks were so thick that their heads looked unnaturally small. Josie had no idea if real Navy SEALs looked like that. But the Hollywood version was obviously compelling to a 14-year-old girl like Samantha. Samantha had seemed especially interested in the Black team member, a man the filmmakers contrived to show shirtless most of the time. Josie couldn't tell if her daughter's focus on the man was because he was sculpted and beautiful, or if she paid attention because he was black like them.

Now, two thousand miles away in Minnesota, Josie felt like she was seeing someone from that movie. The big man glanced at them and walked away toward the tram that took passengers to the rental car counters. His metallic case caught the light.

Josie and Samantha waited until their roller bags came down the chute. They were easy to see because Samantha's was bright purple, her favorite color until the month before when one of her friends was murdered and dropped off a beach cliff in the middle of the night. Samantha had withdrawn. She refused to go to school and didn't speak a word for two weeks, a trauma that the school psychologist thought should ease up over time.

As Samantha eventually re-engaged with the world, she took up with a goth group of white girls at her school and started wearing black clothes and black work boots she'd gotten at the Goodwill store. Samantha was tall and skinny, and when she wore her black hoodie shadowing her face, she brought to mind the grim reaper.

To Josie's horror, Samantha pierced the upper rims of her ears without asking permission, and hung large safety pins through them. She began using heavy black eyeliner, which, on her brown skin, looked vaguely threatening.

Samantha had also decided she hated purple. Apparently, Goodwill didn't have black goth travel bags, so Samantha had begged her mother to get her a different bag, something like one she'd seen on a goth website, shiny black with a gothic cross logo. When Josie refused and pointed out that, if the purple bag was her dream travel item just one year ago, it would probably suffice now, Samantha reacted by plastering a dozen large skull stickers on the purple bag.

As mother and daughter wheeled their bags away from the baggage pickup, Samantha steered a weaving course through the crowds, bumping into people as she watched her phone more than where she was going. Several times, people glared at Samantha as she careened into them.

Josie had explained that they wouldn't have phone reception where they were going and that they'd have to actually speak to each other. Samantha had been sullen ever since.

"How long 'til the guillotine drops?" Samantha asked as they walked. It was her phrase for losing cell reception.

"It probably won't happen until we get near the Canadian border. The Airbnb description said the lake we'll be on doesn't get cell reception." Josie didn't tell Samantha that lack of phone service was the very reason why she chose to rent the cabin.

"Do people live on this lake?"

"No. The Quetico Wilderness in Canada is like the Boundary Waters Wilderness in Northern Minnesota. They only allow people to stay for a limited time. There might be campers. But we'll be on an island in the lake. According to the description, the island is the epitome of seclusion."

"What's the point?" Samantha sounded incredulous. "They can't stream anything, right? No music, no movies, no TV."

"Right. No cable and no electricity, either."

"Then what do we do for lights?"

"They have some battery-powered lights. And we'll have flashlights. But the batteries won't last the whole week. We'll have candles, and we're going to learn how to use kerosene lanterns. Imagine how cozy and fun it will be to read a book by an old-fashioned lantern."

Samantha made an exaggerated turn of her head and stared at Josie. "My books are on my iPad." She swerved her roller bag.

Josie wondered if it was true.

"So where do we get food?" Samantha asked. "Is there a restaurant or store?" Samantha was chewing her gum with an open mouth, something she did when she was irritated.

"No. We carry our food to the island in the canoe, and we cook it ourselves on a wood stove," Josie said. "We bring our own food, supplies, everything except water."

"How do we get water?"

"Out of the lake."

Samantha stopped chewing, her jaw open. "If we can't get bottled water, then why not just drink out of the faucet?"

"There is no faucet. The cabin has no plumbing. No running water."

"Then how do we go to the bathroom?"

"The rental description says there's a very nice outdoor john."

"What's that?"

"An outhouse. A hole in the ground."

Samantha stopped walking, and her eyes opened wide. Several people behind her had to stop. "You go to the bathroom in a hole in the ground?" she said, her voice loud enough to be heard by everyone nearby. "You must be joking!"

"The hole in the ground is covered by a small platform with a toilet seat. It might be inside an outhouse. The website didn't make it clear. But it said that there is a great view for performing one's morning constitution."

"What's a morning constitution?" Samantha asked, still not moving, holding up the passage of a dozen people behind her.

Josie started walking and gestured at Samantha to follow. "It's a euphemism for going to the bathroom."

Samantha walked with her head bent down as if she were inspecting the floor for a lost safety-pin earring.

"Anyway, I'm not going to drink lake water. That's gross and unhygienic." Samantha said it with no sense of irony that she hadn't referred to an outhouse the same way.

"The water's very pure," Josie said. "This is a wilderness. It hasn't been spoiled by people. All we have to do is run the water through some kind of filter. The outfitter will explain how it works."

They got out of the tram and walked to their rental car counter. The man with the high-tech case was at the next counter. He was just signing the form. Samantha stared at him.

Josie thought that it must be the man's muscles that drew Samantha's attention, because the man was otherwise quite unattractive. His oversized nose was bulbous and he had some kind of bad eczema. His flat-top hair seemed to angle one way at the front and the other at the back. Despite his general aura of robust health, his skin looked sickly, with a rough texture and ridges that probably came from some past injury or disease. Josie thought the flat-top hair style was especially unattractive because she could see the skin of his scalp. Even his brown eyes were a bit foggy, the color less intense than was usual.

The man glanced at Samantha and saw that she was looking at him. "Hey, hon," he said. "Sweet equipment hanging from your ears."

Samantha suddenly glared at the man. "My earrings are none of your business. Concentrate on your own equipment."

"Will do, hon. I've got lots of that."

Josie didn't like that at all. Samantha was tall and attractive underneath the goth exterior, but she was obviously just a skinny kid. A kid did not need the attention and inuendo of a muscle man twice her age.

The man gave Samantha a smile that was half-sneer and walked away.

Josie signed the rental car paperwork, got the key fob, and they were on the freeway a half hour later.

"This car's got full navigation," Samantha said as she brought up menus on the touch screen.

Josie had often thought the use of touch screens was Samantha's single significant skill.

"The robot lady will tell you where to go," Samantha added.

"I've told you, Sam. We use maps. We figure out where we're going ourselves. If all you do is turn right when a synthetic voice says to turn right, you never learn the territory. Navigating with maps builds spatial analysis and critical thinking skills."

"Who cares about learning the territory?" Samantha said.

"Apparently not the people who just watch celebrities on TV," Josie said. "What do you want to learn about?"

"I already know everything I need to know. Music. Videos. Movies. Fashion."

Josie was about to reply with a comment about Samantha's fashion sense but had the wisdom to stop herself. "You can stream music if you want, at low volume, but please leave the navigation off."

"You never get tired of being the professor, do you?" Samantha said. "You don't even know how to kick back and relax. Everything has to be about learning. It's never about just living."

Josie thought about it as she drove. What Samantha said was true. Josie didn't know how to relax. If she wasn't doing something productive, she felt like she was wasting time. Even watching movies with Samantha, or taking this vacation, was something that Josie justified as a mother-daughter bonding exercise, not as entertainment or relaxation that was worthwhile for its own sake. Even as she had the thought, she realized that she hoped both of them would learn a great deal about the wilderness. Josie had read the great naturalists. Darwin, Muir, Leopold, Thoreau. Josie fully expected that she and Samantha would develop a serious appreciation for the flora and fauna of the woods, the rhythms of the forest, and what Thoreau referred to when he said that he went into the woods because he wished to confront only the essentials of life.

Yet, despite her desire to escape fluff and trivia, Josie had often wondered if her focus on productivity was a big mistake. Maybe she'd get to the end of her life and wish she'd learned to enjoy watching sports or playing video games or simply hanging out in the park and barbecuing with friends.

But it was her work ethic that drove her to escape a difficult childhood and go to college and then graduate school at UC Davis. It took great persistence to complete her Ph.D. and teach for years as a tenure-track assistant professor at UCLA. While teaching, she wrote and published dozens of articles before eventually becoming an associate professor. One day, she hoped to earn a full professorship.

It hadn't been a perfect life, but it was pretty darn good. Best of all was finding Samantha, and Josie loved Samantha more than she could say. Josie believed that her focus and drive made their life good.

TWO

They drove north from Minneapolis and St. Paul up Interstate 35. Two and a half hours later, they came to the city of Duluth, which sat at the western tip of Lake Superior, which, by surface area, was the biggest freshwater lake in the world. During the drive, Josie had seen why Minnesota was called the land of 10,000 lakes. The state was mostly flat. Water couldn't easily run off. So it had pooled into countless shallow lakes.

From the northern end of Duluth, the highway crawled northeast along Lake Superior's North Shore. The coast was beautiful and rugged, and the lake, as large as an inland sea, shimmered an intense blue, set off by stands of birch trees that had already turned yellow gold in the cold fall temperatures of September.

They drove through several small towns and, 100 miles later, came to Grand Marais, a town, Josie had read, that grew as a terminus for the fur trade in the 18th century.

"Grand Marais sounds French," Samantha said, as she read the sign at the entrance to the town.

"That's very perceptive of you. It was settled by French Canadians back in the seventeen hundreds. "

"Just because I'm not a stuffed-shirt bookworm doesn't mean I'm not smart."

"Of course," Josie said, trying not to let what sounded like an insult bother her. She told herself this was the nature of mother/daughter relationships. Josie did her best to make her voice sound cheery. "I read that beginning in the eighteenth century, French

Voyageurs plied the Boundary Waters by canoe."

"So what are these Boundary Waters?" Samantha asked.

"It's a huge network of lakes laced through a wilderness forest. The boundary between the United States and Canada goes right through it. The Quetico Wilderness is just north of the Boundary Waters. Before the eighteenth century, the only people were Native Americans, the Ojibwe. Then came the French voyageurs. Native Americans, and some voyageurs too, were trappers, and they placed traps throughout a large stretch of the wilderness. They would make a regular circuit, hiking and canoeing through the forest, visiting all of their traps by memory."

"Go ahead and say it, Mama. They knew the territory."

"Now that you mention it, yes. Thousands of square miles of wilderness. No GPS to tell them where to turn."

"What did the trappers do?"

"They caught animals in their traps?"

"What kind of animals?"

"I think most of the animals that live in the forest. Beaver and rabbits, otters and fox and lynx. Probably even bear and wolves, too."

"Oh, I get it," Samantha said. "I read about that in the Sierra Nevada Mountains. They trap problem bears, then release them far away where they can't bother people."

"Yes, I've read about that, too. But the wilderness trappers didn't release the animals. They killed them."

Even though Josie was concentrating on her driving, she could sense Samantha making a face of disgust.

"Does that mean they ate the animals?" Samantha asked.

"Well, I suppose they ate some of the meat. But mostly, they wanted the animal skins to sell for upscale clothing. So they skinned the animals, cleaned the skins, and packed them in the large canvas packs they carried in their canoes."

"Oh, my God, that's terrible!" Samantha paused. "Is that

where fur coats come from? Skinned animals? I can't believe it!"

"Yes, I agree. That's why synthetic furs are popular now. But back then, the skins were quite valuable. Wealthy people in Europe would pay large sums for fur coats and beaver hats. So the voyageurs paddled their cargo across the Boundary Waters. When they wanted to go from one lake to the next, they would carry their canoes and ninety-pound packs of fur on their shoulders over the portages."

"What's that mean? Portages."

"I think it's the French name for the trails that go from one lake to the next. Eventually, they brought their furs all the way to Lake Superior. From there, the furs began the trip that would go through the Great Lakes. The fur trade from North America to Europe was one of the biggest industries in the country."

They drove through the town of Grand Marais.

Josie stopped for gas. Then she drove down the main street of Grand Marais, looking for a motel she'd found online.

From their motel, they walked across the street to a cafe to get some dinner. Josie was a non-rigorous vegetarian who avoided all salt because of her blood pressure. But everything on the menu was some variation of beef. They ended up ordering meatballs and gravy on mashed potatoes. It came with green beans that were out of a can. So much salt, it was like drinking sea water. Josie could barely eat it. But when in Rome…

In the morning, they turned inland and drove up a winding road called The Gunflint Trail. Several times while checking her rearview mirror, Josie noticed a white car a good distance behind them. She couldn't tell the make, nor were there any distinguishing marks. But something about it caught her attention. Maybe it was because it looked like their own rental car. But she realized that she'd seen a similar car following them from some distance as they drove up the North Shore of Superior the day before. It didn't alarm her. In fact, she was glad to see a white sedan for the simple reason that her fears of predatory men stalking women always included the image of the bad men in pickup trucks. In fact, nice as most pickup drivers were, Josie had nevertheless noticed that unsavory men usually chose vehicles that telegraphed toughness. By contrast, small white sedans seemed less menacing.

When they were about 60 miles into the forest, they came to a sign that said Bear Trap Lake. There was an arrow that pointed to a narrow, gravel road that wound off to the right.

"This is our turnoff," Josie said as she turned onto a road with two rutted paths for the tires. The center portion of the road was high enough that its grass scraped the bottom of their rental car. A short distance in was another sign that said Northern Lights Canoe Outfitters—2 miles.

They bounced and rocked and shook their way along the bumpy road.

"I'm curious," Josie said. "You said you read about how they trap problem bears in the Sierra. Where did you read that?"

"I was just curious about them. When you first planned this trip, you said we were going to bear country. It made me think about how we have bears in the mountains around L.A."

"Yes."

"So I figured I should know about bears if we're gonna be camping in their backyard."

Josie nodded. "I'm so pleased to discover that you pursued a curiosity that took you away from your phone."

Samantha made a show of turning in the seat and staring at Josie. "I used my phone to read about bears."

"Oh." Josie said, her dismay probably obvious.

"Books and stuff are good resources whether you read them in paper form or digital form, Mama."

"Yes, you're right." Josie was still disappointed. She would be thrilled if Samantha ever read a physical book.

Ten minutes later, they approached the end of the bumpy, rutted road. Just ahead was a lake, a rustic lodge, and some cabins and parking lots for canoe-tripping campers who were off on long-distance trips. Josie had considered such a trip, but realized that carrying a 70-pound canoe and 30-pound packs across portages was far beyond Samantha's and her physical capabilities. At 46 years of age, Josie still felt physically vital. But she was no athlete, and she carried extra weight on her bones. Better to go a short distance so she and Samantha could get the experience without taking too much of a risk.

They parked and got out. Josie was struck by the freshness of the air. It was crisply cool, and heavy with the scent of pine. It smelled different than the mountains of California. Was it the blue trees she'd read about? Spruce? Or maybe it was the rocky earth. The sun seemed warm for the middle of September at such a northern latitude. But the air was cool to the point of feeling like frost on the skin.

They walked into a building with a Canoe Outfitters sign. Josie introduced herself and said she had an appointment to rent equipment and hire a guide.

The man behind the counter checked an appointment book, then called out toward a back room. "Hey, Bill? Your nine-thirty is here."

A man carrying a clipboard walked out through a doorway. He was a fit-looking, gray-haired man with weathered skin and a long gray moustache. "Josephine Strong?" he asked, reaching out his hand. "I'm Bill Masenrud."

"I'm Josie, and this is my daughter Samantha." Josie shook the man's hand. She worried that he'd crush her bones with his grip, which had too much power for women, children, and old people. But she realized he probably dealt primarily with young men. A vice-grip handshake said, 'Pay attention, don't dismiss me, I'm in control.'

Bill smiled warmly, then gave a quick look at Samantha, probably noticing that her urban goth look was nothing like what he normally saw up in the canoe wilderness. "Says here you two are from L.A. Long way to come for canoeing."

"Yes," Josie said. "We were looking for an experience that is the opposite of our daily life."

"Oh? What would that be? A serious job that you need to escape?"

"She's a professor," Samantha said, drawing out the words as if to mock her mother. "Exercise is carrying pencils. Blackboard chalk is pumping serious iron. Canoeing will be so totally butch compared to that, you should give us, like, the baby-steps gear."

"Well, then, I think you found the right place," Bill said, not reacting at all to Samantha's obvious abrasive attitude. "Let me ask, what kind of camping equipment did you bring? We can fill in as needed."

"Actually, we didn't bring anything except our clothes," Josie said. "We pretty much need everything."

"Got it. I'm your specialist. Any chance you've obtained a wilderness permit?"

"Yes. We did it online. We watched the video, took the test, everything."

Samantha said, "Mama doesn't get the form fields, so I helped. She says it's her eyeglasses. I say it's her prejudice against data mining."

Bill nodded but didn't respond. "Follow me as I pull gear. I'll explain as we go."

Bill took them into a large back room.

"Look, Mama!" Samantha said. "A dog!"

THREE

Samantha went over to a medium-small dog that was lying on top of a large cardboard box. The dog was a deep tan color with a saddle of black and a beige chest. There were black patches on its snout and a black area around its right eye, which was brown and contrasted with its left eye, which was a pronounced blue. The dog had small floppy ears, and its fur was medium long, scruffy on its head and smooth on its back. "Can I pet him?"

"Her," Bill said. "Yes. Her name is Unknown."

Samantha reached out and tenderly pet the dog. "Hi, Unknown."

"Evocative name, Unknown," Josie said. The dog turned its head past Samantha and looked over at Josie.

"She just showed up one day, identity and origin unknown. Probably, some people lost her when they were camping. She's very self-contained. Nice, but no enthusiasm. Patient. Never gushy. Doesn't bark. Totally reliable. Perceptive, too. Just look at her. You can tell she's thinking things about us."

"Isn't it interesting," Josie said, "that we believe we can judge a dog's perceptual abilities by the look on their face. It's probably true."

"Just like people," Bill said. "Some just sit and stare. Others pay attention. Unknown doesn't miss anything." Bill started around the perimeter of the room gathering equipment and supplies. He sized Samantha and Josie for paddles and handed one to each woman. "Hold them like this when you're paddling, one hand on the grip at the top, one hand on the throat just above the blade's shoulder. If you lean a paddle against a tree or something, turn it upside down so the tip of the blade doesn't get damaged on the rocks." He ran his fingers along a blade. "As you can see, these paddles are wooden and very strong. But the edge of the blade is actually quite thin." He pulled out a third paddle. "Here's a spare in case you lose or damage one." He next got them flotation vests, packs, a camp stove, and pans and utensils for cooking. There was one wall with bins full of dried foods. It was like the box-dinner aisle in a supermarket only with each meal sized for two and packaged in flexible vacuum packs that wouldn't crush the way boxes would.

Samantha seemed to enjoy picking out her choices. Josie tried to conceal her horror at realizing that every selection was basically a powder concoction full of salt and sugar. Except for the oatmeal packets, nothing seemed to contain any fiber. And the few dried vegetables comprised just a tiny portion of each meal.

"Basically, you stir these into boiling water," Bill said. "The ingredients slowly rehydrate. Each packet says how much water to use and how long to cook."

"Are there no fresh vegetables?" Josie asked.

Bill frowned. "You have to carry all your food for a week. There's no refrigeration. This time of year, it freezes at night, but it gets quite warm during the day."

It took a moment for Josie to absorb what the man said. She felt foolish for not having realized it when she first started reading about camping in the wilderness. She turned, thinking, and looked out the open door toward the forest and lake beyond.

There was a sudden movement. Something moving behind some trees.

Josie walked to the door and stared out at the woods. Nothing moved. Nothing seemed out of place. She remembered that Winston Churchill said, 'One should never run away from anything. Never!'

"Mama, they have stacks of dark chocolate bars!" Samantha said.

"Good energy source," Bill said. "We also have granola bars, but they actually have more sugar than semi-sweet chocolate. Take as many as you want."

Samantha looked at Josie.

"It's okay," Josie said. "One per day max."

Samantha grabbed a handful of chocolate. "Unknown's watching me."

"You should know that any significant quantity of chocolate can be poisonous to dogs," Bill said. "Unfortunately, they like it same as us."

After they picked out the food, Bill went over all of the different cook gear and utensils.

He pulled out two large, Army-green canvas packs. They were basic large bags with a flap top and leather straps with buckles to close them. There was no padding on the shoulder straps. They were nothing like high-tech backpacks. "These are called Duluth packs."

Samantha frowned. "Some neighbors took me backpacking. Their packs had padded metal bars to fit your back."

"Canoeing packs have a different design focus. The design is all about a wide, squat pack that will sit low in a canoe and keep a low center of gravity. They don't have frames like hiking backpacks because the frames would catch on the canoe thwarts. It might not be as easy to carry Duluth packs on the portages, but the carrying part is relatively short distances."

Samantha silently mouthed the word 'thwart.'

"Thwarts are the structural cross bars that go across the canoe," Bill said.

He set the packs on their gear pile and turned to them. "You're staying at the Johnson cabin, right? Up on Lac Falls on the Quetico side of the border?"

Josie nodded. "Do you think that was a good choice?"

"Sure. In fact, it's one of the only choices for Quetico cabins. This is tent country because you can carry tents in a canoe. But because you're not taking a distance trip, the Johnson place is perfect. A few mice, of course. Can't avoid them."

"What?!" Samantha said. "Did you hear that, Mama? I'm not living with mice!"

Josie had the same thought, but she didn't say anything.

"Don't worry," Bill said. "The cabin has two bunk beds, so it sleeps four people. They changed out the bunkbeds some time back. The new ones have smooth metal legs. And if you don't leave fabric hanging off the edge, mice can't climb up. That's why the bunks are moved out from the walls, too. Best to leave them where they are. One woman moved one of them next to the window to enjoy the night breeze. She woke up to find a mouse family reunion on her bed."

Samantha gasped. She turned and stared at Josie.

Bill continued going down his list. He pulled out two small bottles of bug repellent. "One bug juice each. Unless you're like some other Californians we had who didn't like bug juice because it has chemicals with really long names. Your call. But I put it on first thing in the morning and use it before I go to bed, too. However, we've already had a hard freeze, so that killed most of the biting black flies."

Josie took the bottle and looked at the ingredient label with suspicion. "A great deal of very fine print," she said.

Bill watched her as if she confirmed what he thought about Californians. Then he walked over to a wall of cabinets with large doors. He opened one and pulled out two green sacks made of nylon and secured at the top with a special clip. "These are sleeping bags, insulated with washable polyester filling. Each bag gets washed and then sealed in this breathable stuff sack. When you get out of bed in the morning, sealing your bag into the sack is how you make your bed. Mice can chew through it, of course. But if they do, the hole will be obvious, and you'll know to check it over carefully before you climb inside."

Samantha inhaled sharply.

Bill pulled out a canoe country map and spread it out on a table. "This map shows the lake you're going to as well as the nearby lakes and portages." He opened a drawer and took out a compass. "Do you know how to navigate with a compass?"

"In principle," Josie said.

"I'm good on my phone," Samantha said. "But there's no cell reception here."

Bill gave her a patient smile. "I've heard from other canoers that even though GPS works here, most mapping apps can only use it in conjunction with cell reception."

"You better show us the best way," Josie said.

"First rule is to always know roughly where you are. If you're completely lost, things get hard. But if you know your starting point, it's easy to track where you're going. Right now, we're here at the outfitter's lodge." He pointed to the location on the map. "The top of the map is north. And a compass points north, right?" He held out a compass and they all watched while the needle turned to point north. "So all you do is rotate the map until the top of the map faces north. Presto. The map is now oriented to the real world." He set the compass on the map so that they could see that the top of the map faced north.

"For example, look at this island in this lake. Now look at where the road comes and stops at the outfitter's lodge on this point. That's where we're standing right now." He put two of his fingers on the map to represent the locations. "You can see on the map that if you go from the point of land that's straight out and a little to the right, you'd come to the island."

Samantha drew an imaginary line with her fingertip. "So if we look the same direction on the landscape, we could probably see that island." She looked out across the water. "There it is!"

She turned to Josie. "See, Mama? I don't need a digital assistant. I know the territory!"

"Very good," Josie said.

"Let's look at where we want to go this afternoon," Bill said. He pointed to the map. "This lake here. So where is it in relation to where we are now? The outfitter's building is here. By looking at the map, you can tell that if we walk out of this building and go the direction the map indicates, we're going to hit the water."

"What about magnetic declination?" Josie asked.

Bill raised his eyebrows. "Wow. What are you... Oh, that's right, a professor."

Samantha was staring at the ceiling.

Bill said, "It's true that a compass points toward the magnetic pole and not the geographic pole. But here in the Boundary Waters, the magnetic pole is pretty close to the same direction as the geographic pole. So you don't need to worry about it. The compass will get you where you need to go. Now if you were out in Seattle, or worse, up in Alaska, then the magnetic declination is very large. Out there, if you aim for what you think is north, you'll end up closer to Iowa than the North Pole."

Josie nodded.

He moved his finger. "We'll paddle across the lake toward this next lake. The two lakes are connected by a portage, the trail where we'll walk and carry our gear. At the second lake, we'll stop at the customs' station, then head into Canada. After that, we have just one more portage and we'll be on Lac Falls, which has a very nice falls coming into it on the west side."

"You need a few more items," Bill added. He went to yet another rack of bins. "Here's two waterproof containers of wooden matches. They float. They're the kind you can strike anywhere, so be careful of them. Don't drop the container."

"I don't get it," Samantha said. "If they float, what difference does it make?"

"Actually, you can drop the container on the surface of the water. But if you drop them on hard rocks, the jolt can be like a strike and light them on fire. Losing your source of fire can make for a very cold night, not to mention, cold food." He pulled out a roll of newspaper. "This is your firestarter. Keep it dry and use it sparingly. You know how to build a fire, right?"

Josie shrugged. "A little newspaper, a little pile of twigs, some bigger branches, and so forth, right?"

Bill nodded. "And only in the wood stove or the official fire ring outside."

Josie nodded.

Next he pulled out a metallic cylinder. "This is a water filter. Takes out all the nasty stuff that's too small to see. The key is not to contaminate the water you've filtered by letting unfiltered water drip into your clean supply. The filter works by depressing this plunger, here. The filtered water comes out this outlet tube. Lac Falls, the lake you're going to, is very clear. In fact, the main reason to use the filter is to catch giardia, which is mostly found near shore. We don't recommend it, but if you paddle out into the lake where the water is deep and still, you are very unlikely to get giardia or anything else other than some water bugs in your water bucket."

"Water bugs in our water?!" Samantha's voice went up in pitch.

"Most bugs are harmless," Bill said. "Think of them as protein supplements."

"Then what's giardia?" Samantha asked.

"It's a microscopic parasite that comes from beaver poop. If you accidentally drink it down, it will grow in your system and create havoc and make you very unhappy for a long time."

"We'll filter very carefully," Josie said.

"Another thing you'll want is some line." He pulled out two coils of thin, synthetic cord. "These are each one hundred feet. You won't likely need them. But camping presents a lot of situations where you can use line. Lashing something into your canoe. Hanging up clothes to dry."

Bill pulled out two large jars made of see-through plastic. "These are bear canisters," he said. "You put all food in them. To open them, you depress this button, then unscrew the top. Because you aren't taking more than two little portages, you have the luxury of being able to bring as much food as you want. I'll send you out with two bear canisters, so you don't have to struggle to fit your food into just one."

"Bears can't open them?" Samantha said.

Bill grinned. "When they see these, they head on over to the next lake."

"I thought you said this cabin was on an island," Samantha said. "How would a bear get to it?"

Bill made a small smile. "Bears can swim better than we can."

"And they like to eat powdered, dehydrated food?" Josie asked, not meaning to sound sarcastic.

"They like to eat anything. And if they smell food, they will get serious about getting it if it isn't in the bear canister." He turned and looked at Samantha. "So you wouldn't want to get any idea about bringing a chocolate bar to bed with you. A bear might decide to tear off the cabin door and come into bed with you."

Samantha tried not to react. "Can a bear really tear off doors?"

Bill paused. "Let's say you weighed three hundred and fifty pounds and had two-inch claws and were strong enough to scamper up trees…"

Samantha made a single slow nod. "Got it," she said.

"Last item," Bill said, "is a camp knife." He pulled out two large knives in leather sheaths with belt loops at the top.

"This is to fight the bears when they come for the chocolate?" Samantha said.

Bill grinned again. "No. You don't fight bears even with guns. Having a knife is like having a coil of line. A knife is a basic tool that is used in a hundred ways. No camper should be without one."

Josie and Samantha each took one. Samantha unhooked her belt buckle and slid the sheath onto her belt.

"You don't have a belt," Bill said to Josie.

"No."

"So there's a use for the line. You can braid it and make a homemade belt. Something to hang your knife on."

Bill looked out at the water.

"One more thing. Are you both good swimmers?"

"I am, she's not," Samantha said.

Bill turned to Josie. "If you fall in and you're wearing your flotation vest, will you be okay? Or will you panic?"

Josie paused. "Somewhere in between. Even if I have a flotation vest on, it would still be good if I didn't fall in. If I don't have a flotation vest on, you don't want me near the water."

"Understood," Bill said. "There's also another reason not to fall in. It's the middle of September, so the water is already very cold. If you were to fall in, you'd need to get out fast. Otherwise, you'd succumb to hypothermia."

"What's that?" Samantha asked.

Josie answered. "You know. We've talked about the Pacific surf in the winter. Even if you can tolerate the feeling of cold water, it will gradually pull the heat out of your body, paralyze your muscles, and make it so you can't swim."

"And then you drown," Samantha said.

"Correct."

"This sounds like a great vacation," Samantha said.

FOUR

"You follow the rules," Bill said, "it'll be the best vacation of your life." He pointed at the map, "We'll put in at this point across the road."

"What does that mean, put in?" Josie asked.

"Oh, sorry. It's where we start on the lake. It means putting the canoe in the water and putting our packs and gear in the canoe. We'll head out a narrow bay to the main body of Bear Trap Lake. You two will be in one canoe. I'll take one by myself and come back here after I leave you at the island. There's no major wind expected for the next few days, so you won't have to worry about big waves."

He moved his finger on the map. "When we get to this point, there's two very short portages of only fifty rods each."

"What's a rod?" Samantha asked.

"Isn't it a medieval term of measurement?" Josie asked.

"It goes way back as a farmer's measurement, so probably yes," Bill said. "A rod is sixteen and a half feet. People disagree on exactly why we use it in canoe country, but it's probably because a rod is about the length of the average canoe."

He moved his finger on the map. "After the first portage we'll come to Lac Le Grande, which is where the customs station is. After that, we come to the second portage. That takes us to this river, which flows out of Lac Falls." He pointed with his big finger. "Your island is this one. It's about one hundred yards wide by two hundred yards long. The Johnson cabin is at the west end, perched for great sunset vistas. And the latrine is here, which is a pretty good hike from the cabin. If you can manage not having to get up at night, you'll appreciate that."

"A closet that covers a hole in the ground," Samantha said with disgust.

"You could call it that," Bill said. He handed them a booklet. "There are lots of rules for the Boundary Waters and the Quetico. They're all in that book. Memorize them and obey them. If a ranger comes by and finds you in violation of any rule, you can get ticketed. If it's a flagrant violation, and you're convicted, you can go to jail."

Josie thought that Bill's effort to sound stern was probably for show. The more he could convince canoeists to do things the right way, the less trouble for all.

"What kind of laws would you have to break to go to jail?" Samantha asked.

"Stuff like you have to carry water for washing dishes far back from shore to dump it. You can't dump dish water close to the lake. You can't build a campfire on the shore. You can only have a fire in an official fire ring. You have to put out your fire with water and stir the embers until they are wet and dead out. This is leave-no-trace country. If you litter, the governor will call out the National Guard to clean it up and charge you a quarter million dollars for every hour they spend on the project. You can't put anything into the latrine but your body waste and toilet paper. You toss one of those pre-moistened towelettes down there, the ranger will dangle you by your feet, down into the hole, until you pull it out."

While it was obvious that Bill said the words just to make an impression, judging by Samantha's reaction, it seemed to be working.

"Let's go out on the dock, and I'll show you the basics of paddling."

He had them kneel on the dock boards and hold their paddles down into the water.

Unknown sat nearby and watched.

Bill got down and demonstrated how to do a basic stroke, front to back.

"This is called the forward stroke. It's your basic power stroke, the way to drive the canoe forward. The person at the bow just does the forward stroke. So if you are at the bow, Samantha, you are going to be the main power source of this expedition."

Samantha made a big smile.

"The person at the stern helps power the canoe but also steers. A portion of the stern paddler's effort goes into maintaining direction."

Josie nodded.

"The two people paddle on opposite sides of the canoe, and they can switch off."

"So if I'm paddling on the right side," Samantha said, "Mama paddles on the left side. And sometimes we change sides."

"Right. Also, both people paddle at the same time and rate. The bow paddler chooses the pace, and the stern paddler matches. If both paddles go into the water at the same time, the canoe will stay steady and not tip."

"These boats tip over?" Samantha said, trying to sound calm.

"They can, yeah," Bill said as if it were an unlikely occurrence. "Steering is done by a J-stroke as well as simply using the paddle as a rudder. The J-stroke is just like it sounds. You pull the paddle back through the water and at the end of your stroke, you make the paddle curve and go away from the canoe. It's work, and you will get sore."

"Why the J?" Josie asked.

"Because there's a funny aspect to canoe geometry. The canoe wants to turn toward the side the bow person is paddling on. So if Josie is in the stern and paddling on the left side, and Samantha is paddling on the right, the canoe will want to turn toward the right. So you compensate by using a J-stroke that counteracts that tendency."

Bill showed them how. After a few minutes of practice, he had them move to the other side of the dock so they could get a feel for paddling on the other side.

"One more thing," Bill said. "When you lift your paddle out to bring it forward for the next stroke, twist it a bit like this, so the blade is horizontal. That way it is more aerodynamic and won't catch the wind. We call it feathering your paddle."

Josie thought the idea was excessive, as if Bill were talking about something that only Olympic athletes would care about.

Bill must have seen the doubt on her face. "Seriously," he said. "If you're paddling into a headwind, a feathered paddle can make it much easier."

Bill briefly went over the draw stroke and the push stroke. "But you won't use those very much. Although, as the stern paddler, Josie, you will use your paddle as a rudder quite a bit. Here's how that works." He showed her. "It will be self-evident when you are out on the water."

"I'm already sore," Samantha said.

Josie was thinking that very thing.

"The way to minimize muscle fatigue is to paddle very easily. You'll go slower, but it won't stress your muscles so much. Slow and easy is the rule in the beginning. Also, the easier you go, the less you'll get blisters on your hands. Nevertheless, by the time you get out to the island, you'll feel you've gotten quite a workout. You'll be glad to stay on the island for a week to recuperate."

Bill stood up. "You should load your clothes into one of these packs."

Bill picked up the Duluth packs and handed them to Josie and Samantha, and they headed to their car to get their things out of their roller bags. Josie made a show of leaving her phone in her roller bag. But Samantha wanted her phone with her even if there was no reception. It was an indication, Josie thought, that Samantha had an unhealthy connection to the device. Samantha packed both her phone and the separate battery that gave her backup power. Nevermind that there would be no cell signal.

When they returned, Bill helped them carry their few items to the dock. He lifted two canoes out of the huge rack that held twelve, two rows high and six across.

"There's a lot of dents in those boats," Samantha said.

"These are aluminum," he said. "Not pretty, but very tough. You'd have to really hit a rock hard to punch a hole in it. But we still lose several per year, so we ask that you try to be gentle and step out of the canoe before it hits the rocky shore. We have lighter weight Kevlar canoes, but they are easier to puncture. All things considered, I think aluminum is best."

Bill had them put their flotation vests on, then showed them how to set the canoe in the water. He put the packs in the center section of the canoe. He had Josie hold the stern while Samantha carefully climbed over the packs and got into the front seat. Then he talked Josie through the process of holding the stern of the canoe with one hand on each side of the canoe as she stepped in and sat on the rear seat.

Bill walked over to a post where a beach towel hung. He folded the towel in half, tossed it into the center section of his canoe, and stepped in. His canoe rocked dramatically in the water for a moment, then stopped. Bill put thumb and forefinger into his mouth, made a short whistle, then called out, "Unknown!"

The dog came trotting, not with excitement or wagging tail, but with purpose. The dog jumped from the dock into the canoe and sat down on the folded towel.

Bill paddled alongside of Josie and Samantha's canoe, and talked them through their initial paddle strokes.

"Whoa, this thing is tippy!" Samantha said.

"You'll get used to it," Bill said. "A standard canoe like these is actually much more stable than most kayaks. And they are the best way to haul lots of gear, whether furs like the early French explorers, or camping gear. You'll also notice that once you get some forward speed, the canoe becomes more stable. Even so, you need to actively maintain your balance. Don't lean over."

Bill paddled close to them and coached them as they piloted their way across the lake toward the first portage.

Josie was afraid they'd swamp the canoe. It was ridiculously tippy. The process of steering was awkward. She couldn't even make the canoe go in a straight line. With every stroke of the paddle, the water splashed on her hands, and it was ice cold. She immediately began to think they were going to freeze in the cabin. Even if the wood stove got hot, the fire would go out once they went to sleep. Bill had said that it got very cold this time of year. Josie started to think she'd made a terrible mistake. They should have gone someplace else. Someplace warm. Mexico. Someplace with restaurants. Even her idea of taking Samantha someplace where there was no cell reception seemed foolish. What if they had an accident? What if one of them got sick?

It was a big relief when they approached land. Bill showed them how to slow the canoe near the rocks. He got out and grabbed the bow of their canoe as it came to the rocks. Unknown trotted off down a trail, which must have been the portage toward the next lake.

Samantha jumped out of the canoe. Her leap made the canoe tip very far to the side.

"Sam, you almost sank our canoe!" Josie said.

"Yes, you should be careful when you step in or out of a canoe," Bill said. "But you can relax a little, Josie. It takes much more than that to tip a canoe over."

"Have you ever tipped a canoe over?"

Bill smiled. "I think every canoeist has done it, either on purpose for fun, or while goofing off. And of course, some of us have attempted to negotiate whitewater rapids that are beyond our skills. The price for that is ending up in the drink."

"In the drink," Josie said. "There's a phrase."

Samantha asked, "Does Unknown swim?"

Bill's grin got bigger. "After I first got Unknown, I managed to dump us in a simple Class Three rapids. I spun around in the current for some time, trying to direct my submerged canoe to shore. When I finally crawled out some distance downstream, Unknown was waiting for me on the rocks. She'd already mostly dried off. So yes, she's an excellent swimmer."

Josie got out of the canoe, uncomfortable with the idea that even a canoeing expert like Bill could tip over in a canoe. To be back on firm land was a huge comfort.

"Now we take our first portage," Bill said.

Josie paused and wondered if she should reconsider. She looked back at the water they'd paddled across. The waves sparkled. It seemed very far. They were already well into the wilderness. But it wasn't too late to turn back. She'd be humiliated, of course. But once they got to the cabin and Bill left them there, it would be too late. They would be trapped on an island in the wilderness. At that point, Josie knew she might well wish she had suffered the humiliation of quitting in return for staying in a motel with electricity, and heat that was controlled by a thermostat, and food that didn't come from powder, and no mice or bears.

As if Bill could read her thoughts, he said, "This kind of trip reveals character, don't you think? People start to sense just how much inner strength they possess as they head off on their first portage. Some cave and turn back. Others forge on. I often notice that the people who are most successful in life are the ones who stay the course."

Maybe Josie narrowed her eyes just a bit.

"Like Einstein said," Bill continued, "perseverance is more important than genius. But, of course, it took both genius and perseverance to become a professor, right? You probably have a Ph.D., and I suspect that took more than filling out a form and mailing in a quarter."

Josie gave him a long hard stare. "You don't just sink your logic weapon deep, you twist it, don't you?"

Bill grinned.

Samantha had walked a ways down the trail. She reappeared.

"The guillotine is still down," she said. She pointed behind her. "I went a ways up that hill, and still no reception."

Bill frowned and glanced at Josie.

Josie said, "My daughter communicates more with texting than speaking. Take away her phone reception, you nearly render her mute."

"Not true!" Samantha said. "And I can do amazing things with my phone."

"I agree," Josie said. "It's like an all-purpose tool for her."

"Like a Leatherman," Bill said.

Both women looked puzzled.

Bill pulled a compact tool from his pocket. It had swing-out components, and a wide range of tools like a Swiss Army knife. But it was larger and of heavier construction. "This is a Leatherman. For guys like me, a Leatherman is like the phone is to Samantha."

Samantha gave Josie a smug grin.

Bill pointed north. You can probably go about three thousand miles from here all the way to the North Pole and never get a cell signal. So the phone won't be of much use out here."

Samantha shook her head. "Phones are always of use."

Bill made a single knowing nod, turned back to the canoes, and showed them how to stow two paddles between the thwarts and the bow seat. Next, he showed them how to lift the canoe up and out of the water.

"Once you develop the technique, you can lift a canoe out of the water and swing it up onto your shoulders so that the bottom of the canoe faces the sky and your head is inside the canoe. I don't expect you to do that. Instead, two people can lift the bow off the ground and up into the air, bottom up." He had them do it. "Now, Samantha, you hold the canoe's bow while I bend a bit and get under the center. See these yoke pads here? They go on my shoulders." He positioned his shoulders and then stood up, lifting the canoe off the ground.

"Notice the rim of the canoe. That's called the gunnel. When I carry a canoe, I grip the gunnel with each hand so I can pull down on it or lift up on it. That helps me balance the canoe. Kind of like a teeter totter."

"What's a teeter totter?" Samantha asked.

Bill acted as if he didn't understand the question.

Josie said, "Bill, do you have kids?"

"No."

"Then consider this a valuable insight into the modern day generation gap. Kids these days play video games. They don't play on playground equipment. In fact, I'm pretty sure there is no such thing as playground equipment anymore. Just the colored plastic slides in the McDonald's Playland."

"Ah," Bill said. "Anyway, once I get the canoe into this position, I can easily carry the canoe over the portage. Would either of you like to try it?"

Samantha nodded.

They reversed the process, she got under the center of the canoe, and stood up. Then Bill showed her how to reach forward and grip the gunnels to hold the canoe and adjust how it balanced on her shoulders.

The canoe tipped forward then backward, banging its tip on the ground. Samantha wobbled. Bill steadied the canoe.

"Let's walk forward," he said.

Samantha giggled. "This is heavy!"

"Seventy pounds," Bill said.

"I only weigh one hundred five," Samantha said.

Bill walked alongside of her, his hand on the canoe to steady it. "Then you're obviously very strong."

"I better be, it's my name. Okay, that's enough. Otherwise, I'm going to fall over and drop it."

Bill helped her lower the stern to the ground and got under the bow to hold it up. "Okay, Josie. Ready to try?"

Josie frowned. "Are you sure that's a good idea?"

"Yes," Bill said. "You don't have to carry it far. But I want you to go home knowing you learned how to carry a canoe."

She didn't move.

"I doubt your fellow professors know how to carry a canoe."

Josie immediately recognized that Bill was a clever guy to use those words. She went over and stood below the yoke pads. She felt very tentative.

Bill lowered the bow until the yoke pads settled down on her shoulders. "Reach your arms forward and hold the gunnels. That position makes the yoke pads much more comfortable on your shoulder muscles."

"I don't have shoulder muscles."

"Yes, you do. Now walk forward."

Bill helped balance the canoe as Josie carried it.

"The trail goes straight and then curves to the left. Having a canoe over your head blocks much of your vision, but you can still see the trail."

Josie carried the canoe about 25 yards. She had no idea how many rods that equaled. "Enough," she called out, a bit of panic in her voice.

Bill took it from her and carried it the rest of the portage and set it down by the shore of the next lake. He came back to the beginning of the portage and helped Samantha and Josie get their packs on their backs.

"What's this extra strap?" Samantha asked once she had her arms through the shoulder straps.

"That's a tumpline. The French voyageurs used them. It goes over your head and wraps across the upper part of your forehead." He positioned it for Samantha. "Now lean your head forward into it. See how it takes some of the weight off your shoulders?"

She giggled. "Yeah. It takes the weight off your shoulders and squeezes your head down into your body."

"Don't overdo it. But you'll see that a tumpline can make a heavy pack easier to carry."

Bill got the packs on both Josie and Samantha and then picked up his own canoe. "Follow me, and we'll cross this portage in no time."

Josie didn't think she'd make it. The pack was ridiculously heavy. But Samantha trudged forward with her own heavy pack, following behind Bill, who was carrying his canoe. Maybe Josie could make it, too. She marched with something approaching a Herculean effort. They all made it to the next lake without stopping.

Bill coordinated their moves as they reloaded the packs into their canoe, and they once again paddled, with sore shoulders and arms and hands. Bill went along in his canoe, which was empty except for Unknown. Another 15 minutes of paddling brought them to the customs station.

It was a one-room log cabin on a rocky point of land. It was surrounded by conifers and looked like something in a picture book about the beauty of the north woods.

They pulled up to a small dock, got out of their canoes, and went up to the cabin door. There was a sign on the door. 'Please fill out the declaration form and put it in the box.'

Samantha said, "The border of Southern California is mostly a fence, but here there is not only no fence, but no customs officer?!" Samantha sounded appalled. "How do they know we're not smuggling anything? The coyotes could be bringing illegal aliens through!"

Bill said, "They figure anyone who's willing to paddle and portage through here in the fall when it's cold is probably not a coyote bringing in illegal aliens." He watched as Josie filled out their names and address, destination lake, dates of stay.

Once back in the canoes, they paddled to the second portage. Josie felt a little less awkward carrying her pack over the trail. But she was more sore. She'd need a long recuperation period before she would want to attempt it again. Once they were back in their canoe, it was a short paddle across to their island.

Unknown jumped from Bill's canoe onto the island. She didn't run with any energy the way most dogs would. She displayed no typical canine excitement. But she trotted as if her job was to check out various locations.

Bill helped Josie and Samantha unload, then carried their canoe up from the shore. He laid it on the ground, bottom side up, and slightly wedged between two trees. The smooth wet bottom looked like a long, shiny, wet table, pointed on both ends.

"The canoe will be secure, here. Even a strong wind won't blow it away."

The women nodded as they both rubbed their shoulders and arms.

Bill took them on a tour of the grounds, the campfire ring near the picnic table, the outhouse, which turned out not to be an enclosed closet but a large box made of heavy timbers. There were steps up to the box and a toilet lid at the top.

"There's no privacy!" Samantha said. "You're just sitting up here in plain view for all the world to see!"

"But no one in the world is here," Josie said. "So your privacy is only invaded by birds and other critters."

Samantha looked around. "After this trip, I'm never staying anywhere rustic again." She struck a dramatic pose, one hand on a cocked hip, her head held high, chin jutting forward. "Now I know what my friend Petra meant when she said she was a Marriott girl. Me, too."

"You've got your food in the bear canisters," Bill said, changing the subject. "Because they smell of food, don't leave them in the cabin. Put them outdoors. If you don't want the bears to bat the canisters around and maybe toss them into the lake, you really should put them in this bearproof food locker." He showed them where it was and how to work the latch.

"I read there are kerosene lanterns in the cabin. Will you show us how they work before you leave us here?"

"Of course. Come and look at the cabin."

He took them into a one-room log building, primitive and solid as a military fort and very spare. Samantha frowned as she looked at the bunkbeds and ran her finger along the single counter that served as a general purpose food prep.

Bill showed them how to use the wood stove, load wood splits and sticks, and adjust the draft so the stove didn't burn too hot.

There were two lanterns on the counter.

He showed them how to raise and lower the wick, reach a match up inside, lift off the glass for cleaning, and how to blow out the flames.

"Each of these lanterns holds enough fuel to burn for six hours. They are quite safe, but of course don't go to bed until you've put the lanterns out. And never set a lantern on the wood stove. If the stove is hot, it could cause a fire. Outside in the metal bear-proof locker is a red fuel can labeled kerosene. For safety, please store the kerosene can outside. Although, I should point out that we actually use a type of lamp oil that is highly refined and burns cleaner, with less smoke, fewer pollutants, more complete combustion. Even so, you should open two windows an inch whenever you light a lantern so you get cross ventilation. The windows have screens, so bugs won't be much of a problem."

"Not 'no problem,' just 'not much of a problem,'" Josie said.

"Any bug is a problem," Samantha said.

Bill raised his eyebrows. "I always remind myself that the bugs were here first. The main pest is mosquitos. But they are slow moving and easy to slap. When you smash them on your skin, think of it as a protein salve that will help your skin stay soft."

Samantha put her hands on her hips and let her mouth hang open. "Did you hear that, Mama? When we die of some deadly mosquito disease, at least our skin will be soft."

Bill grinned.

Josie thought that Bill could probably predict the success of a backwoods mission by the campers' attitude toward bugs. Campers from Southern California, despite being psychologically prepared for wildfires and earthquakes, probably didn't rate high in Bill's eyes.

Nevertheless, the man was charming, and having his company would probably be very welcome after a day or two in the wilderness. But she wanted to stay true to her mission: Time with Samantha, just the two of them. Bugs or not.

When he was done, he looked at Josie and Samantha, assessing their condition. "Our schedule has you down to be out a week.

What do you think? Should I come by every day and administer gin-and-tonics and cook you popcorn over the campfire?"

Samantha grinned.

Josie was serious. "Well, I don't think we should paddle back alone."

"I agree."

"Meaning you don't think we're especially competent in a canoe."

Bill paused. "This is your first time. All neophytes should do an entire canoe trip with experienced companions before they do a trip themselves. And you never know when a serious wind will come up."

Josie said, "But as for checking on us, I'm thinking you might hold off. I'm trying to be more firm in committing to my plans. It would be good for us to be forced to fend for ourselves. So maybe just come by halfway through the week and look from a distance."

"Mama's mid-life crisis," Samantha said. "Eliminating backup plans. She's been researching medieval warriors. Once they went into battle, they lost the option to decide they no longer wanted to fight. They were committed, and they had to charge ahead whether they lived or died."

"And this is like going into battle?" Bill asked, smiling, but only just a little.

Josie made a big sigh. "It's not that big a deal. A mid-life adjustment, maybe."

"Works for me," Bill said.

"If you secretly think we're hopeless," Josie said, "then yes, come by to make sure we're still alive. But maybe just observe with binoculars from a distance. The whole point of this trip is to attempt to take a few more risks and be a little braver in a strange new land."

Bill nodded. "We see it all the time. We call it the Heinlein Experience. Stranger In A Strange Land."

"Now who's the professor," Josie said.

"High school English teacher before I succumbed to the pull of the wilderness."

Samantha looked back and forth between them, unaware of what they were referring to.

"If I leave you now, you'll have most of the afternoon to explore and get used to your surroundings before you venture into the Heart of Darkness." Bill grinned.

Josie looked alarmed. "I wanted this wilderness trip to be sunny in spirit and flavor. No dark metaphors."

"Sorry. Forget I said it."

"At the end of the week," Josie said, "will you escort us back across the lake?"

"You bet," Bill said.

"And carry our canoe across the portages," Samantha said.

"Will do." Bill made a little salute with his hand. He climbed into his canoe and whistled. Unknown trotted out from a patch of shade under the trees and stepped into Bill's canoe. She sat up, her front legs spread a little for stability as Bill paddled away.

"One more question," Josie called after him.

"Yeah?"

"Does anyone live on this lake?"

"No," Bill called back. "The lake isn't on the regular canoe trip routes, either. So you'll enjoy a marvelous solitude. Perfect for a reset from your work life."

He and Unknown headed off into the distance.

FIVE

Josie walked out on a point and sat down on the rocks. Samantha joined her.

"We've already gotten more exercise than we usually get in a month," Josie said.

Samantha nodded. She pulled out her phone and looked at it. "Still nothing."

After they rested, Josie said, "Let's explore the island and see what it's like."

"Just a bunch of trees and rocks," Samantha said. "Same as what we've been looking at for miles."

"But exploring is fun. It's part of human DNA, the urge to find out what's over the next hill."

"To learn the territory," Samantha said.

Josie smiled.

"I explore in my phone. That's how I learn to do stuff when there's no cell reception."

"True," Josie said.

They stood up and began to hike along the shore, going around the island clockwise. In places, the rocks were smooth and easy to walk on. Other places, the rocks rose up high, preventing passage. Samantha would head inland and find a way through the forest and over the rocks, eventually heading back to the shore when possible. Josie followed, very glad to see Samantha exploring outside of her phone.

The island was beautiful, a rocky woods as magical as Merlin's forest with the occasional sun-dappled open area and some deeply-shaded places under the forest canopy where the ground was covered with a layer of green moss as spongy and thick as a mattress. Not far from that verdant splendor was a dry bed of uniform cobbles, all smooth oblong shapes no more than three inches in diameter. Samantha and Josie had to walk over them carefully to avoid twisting their ankles. Samantha picked up a few and moistened them in the shallow water at the edge of the shore. The colors became intense, deep grays and light grays with curious bands of white and navy blue.

The only place on the island that wasn't storybook perfect was a stand of skinny dead trees, eight feet tall and no more than an inch or two in diameter, like bamboo shoots, so crowded that they'd probably died from lack of sunlight and too much competition for moisture. They'd long since lost their needles. As Samantha tried to push them out of her way, one of the little trees broke off from its long dead roots and toppled to the ground.

As they came back around the far shore and approached the cabin, the ground rose up to a group of rocks. Samantha scrambled to the top. "This is like one of those places in a Western! You could hide up here and have perfect cover as you picked off the bad guys down below." She ducked down, and Josie could no longer see her. Josie was climbing up the slope to join her when something out on the water caught her eye.

She turned to look out at the lake. There was nothing. She raised her hand to shade her eyeglasses and held still for a bit.

There it was. Movement. As Josie focused, it appeared to be a canoe. But it was a long way away, and Josie's vision wasn't great.

She continued up to the rocks where Samantha had disappeared.

"See, Mama, it's a fortress! Like one of those castles you study." Samantha lounged on a group of rocks that very loosely approximated a recliner chair.

"Very cool," Josie said. "Hey, Sam, you've got good eyes. Look out at that boat on the water." She pointed. "Is that a canoe?"

"Yeah. A metal canoe like ours."

"Aluminum," Josie said.

"That's what I said."

"Can you see how many people are in it?"

"Just one guy at the rear. Probably Bill. No, it couldn't be Bill. There's no dog. And this guy seems a lot bigger. Not that Bill is small or anything. But this guy is huge. Not fat. Muscular. Kind of like that guy we saw at the airport."

"Nothing wrong with a man being small," Josie said. She didn't want Samantha to fall into the common prejudice that bigger was better.

"Can you tell which way he's going?" Josie asked.

"To the right. Sideways to us. It almost looks like he's looking at us." Samantha raised her arm and waved.

"Don't do that," Josie said.

"Why? I'm just being friendly."

"Yes. But we don't… We came out here for the quiet seclusion. If we seem really friendly, people might stop by, and we'd get stuck chatting."

"Mama, you are such a downer! What's wrong with being friendly? What's wrong with chatting? Oh, that's right. You couldn't be productive if you were making small talk. But, hey, if you got stuck chatting, you could move into professor mode. Teach them important stuff."

Josie felt her face flushing. Samantha was right. Josie was such an incurable introvert that she couldn't shake it. She'd always preferred to be alone rather than socialize. It was the big irony of her life, being an introvert yet also a professor and dealing with hundreds of students.

"Anyway," Josie said. "If you did more than a casual wave, someone might think it's a distress signal. You wouldn't want them to change course and lose time only to find out everything's okay."

Samantha looked at her hard. Josie sensed that it was one of those moments when both mother and daughter probably realized that, in some basic ways, they were completely different personalities. They'd never be similar in their social outlook despite any intentions otherwise. For the rest of their lives, their choices would always diverge because of their differences. And yet, Josie wondered if the goth girls at Samantha's school weren't mostly introverts. Was there a bit of introvert hidden in Samantha as well?

"What's the canoe doing now?" Josie asked.

Samantha turned to look out at the water. "He's going toward the portage. He's probably heading toward the lake where we came from. No, wait. He's angling a different way. I think he's going to the left of the portage. It looks like there's a bay over there. I can't tell, but the bay might go way back. What's that called? An inlet?"

"Right," Josie said. In a way, it was reassuring to have a fellow canoeist nearby. In another way, it was reassuring to have that paddler going away. But Josie couldn't help feeling uneasy at the idea that the guy could be the big muscular guy they saw that morning. What if the canoeist was in fact the man at the airport? The guy who looked like the sniper in the Navy SEALs movie? The guy who made the remark to Samantha about her earrings, and then, his "equipment?"

Josie went to the cabin and brought one of the packs outside. She dug around in the pack, pulled out the map, and spread it out on the picnic table. Then she started looking for the compass.

"Whatcha looking for, Mama?"

"The compass. But I feel I must point out that the occasional gonna or wanna or shoulda is acceptable in casual conversation. But you'll never get into college if you say 'whacha' in your admission interview."

"Mama! Will you stop being the professor for just once? We're on a camping trip. I'm just a kid. Give me a break!" Samantha walked away.

The girl's reaction was so immediate and strong, Josie realized she'd made a big mistake. She walked after Samantha.

"I'm sorry, Sam. I'm so sorry. I know I'm not the best at this parenting stuff. Please forgive me."

Samantha pulled out her phone, tapped a few times, and handed it to Josie. "Anyway, here's a compass." She walked off down toward the shore.

"Your phone has a compass?" Josie said. "That's amazing."

"Just a taste of my skill set," Samantha said.

"Thank you very much."

Josie carried the phone over to the table and set it down on the map. She'd never known that a phone had a compass in it. She rotated the map. The phone compass had a virtual "needle" that rotated just like a traditional compass. It also displayed the numerical compass reading to the nearest degree. It was impressive. Josie wondered if her own phone had a compass. But then, Samantha had told her that her phone could do practically anything. The only limitation with it was the user, not the phone.

Josie found their location on the map. She could see that Samantha was right, there was a bay across the lake, a long, curving finger of water that went well back from the main lake.

Maybe the other canoeist was camping back there. Or fishing. Josie reminded herself to apply common sense to the situation. Even if the other canoeist was the man from the airport, it wouldn't be an unusual coincidence to see him in the Boundary Waters. There were probably hundreds of thousands of Boundary Waters visitors who began their trips by flying into the Minneapolis-St. Paul airport. To imagine that he was a Navy SEAL sniper on some mission was what a thriller novelist would do. It made no sense. The man couldn't possibly have anything to do with Josie and Samantha. Except for Samantha's goth experimenting, they led the most unexciting life a mother and daughter could have. One taught school. The other went to school. The beach was two blocks away, so they went for beach walks and rented Netflix movies and ate too much Chinese takeout. Nothing exciting. Nothing dramatic. No enemies. No disagreements with anyone.

Josie did a little exploring.

She walked over to the cabin's woodpile, a nice supply of

small logs that had been stacked between two trees. Hanging on the lower limb of a nearby tree was an old rusty ax. It looked too dull to be of any use. Then she saw that the wood pile had the remnants of an old wooden chair. The dowels that made up the legs and cross braces had been recently chopped and stacked. When Josie looked more closely at the ax, she could see that the rust had been worn off of the cutting edge. It was still sharp enough for chopping firewood.

On one end of the woodpile was a small lean-to that provided some rain shelter for two folding lawn chairs. Josie opened the latch of the bear-proof locker and looked inside. There was a red fuel container that had the word Kerosene written on it. She picked it up. It was about half full. How nice of the hosts to provide it for their guests.

Josie went back inside the cabin and unpacked the cook pots. She took the largest pot and walked out onto the point. She scanned the lake. Nothing moved. When she approached the water, she stepped one foot out onto a rock a couple of feet from the shore and, straddling the water between her two feet, dipped the pan into the water.

Back at the cabin, she set the water pan on the outdoor picnic table along with a dry pan and the filter and a towel. Working carefully, she managed to filter the water into the dry pan without contaminating it with any unfiltered water.

As the sun lowered in the sky and the temperature dropped, Josie got a fire going in the wood stove, and she put a pan of water on to boil for dinner preparation.

Samantha came in from the rocks where she'd been sitting.

Samantha found a gossip magazine in the cabin, and she carried it out to read while sitting in one of the folding lawn chairs. In a minute, she was back.

"There are mosquitoes everywhere," she said. "It's like a cloud of them."

Josie found the repellant Bill had given them. "Let's put this on. They'll still buzz us, but they won't bite."

They both smeared the liquid over their exposed skin. Josie thought it smelled bad and felt worse.

When the dried dinner concoction was hydrated and cooked, Josie served it in bowls she'd found in the kitchen cabinets and they carried their dinner outside. They ate staring across the water toward a sunset that featured orange and pink clouds. They waved their hands at the clouds of mosquitos.

"It's so quiet here," Josie said. "No car or truck sounds. Nothing but the breeze in the pine needles."

"And the chainsaw buzz of mosquitoes," Samantha said, slapping at her neck.

"True. But I still think I've never been to such a quiet place."

Samantha nodded.

"It gives my brain a chance to clear," Josie said.

Just then came a cackling, staccato sound from across the lake. It sounded like a cartoon crazy woman laughing.

Josie jerked, and Samantha was also startled.

"What is that?!" Samantha said.

"I'm not sure, but I read about how there are lots of loons in the Boundary Waters. They make a wild laughing sound."

"What's a loon?"

"A big water bird. About twice the size of a duck. It swims underwater for long distances."

"It doesn't fly?"

"Actually, it flies very fast. The article made a joke. It said the loon's maximum flight speed is sixty miles per hour. And its stall speed is fifty-nine."

"Meaning it never goes relaxed and leisurely?"

"Right."

"Like a professor," Samantha said.

"You're mean," Josie said.

"Just describing what I see."

They ate in silence.

"Dinner's pretty good," Josie said.

Samantha didn't respond.

"The water tastes good, too." Josie said. "Who woulda thunk that water out of a lake could taste good."

"Woulda thunk?" Samantha said. "How'd you ever get into college? Or was that back when you just mailed in a check and they sent you a graduation certificate?"

"I do like the way you're funny," Josie said. "You've always been funny."

"Lotta good it does me," Samantha said. She paused, then rapped,

"I coulda been a contenda,

I woulda tried but then the,

Professa tol' me to mend the

rap, or I'd jus' be a college pretenda."

Josie laughed long and hard. "Like I said."

An hour later, they were in the cabin. They let the fire in the wood stove die down so they wouldn't worry about it when they went to sleep. Josie had washed their dishes according to the regulations and poured the water in the woods a long way back from the lake. Now she was sitting by the window, drying the dishes, stacking the kettles and bowls, and putting the utensils in one of the pans. She'd lit the kerosene lamp on the counter. It made the softest of sounds, a low hiss combined with the flow of air.

Josie dried the last fork, reached to set it in the drawer when it slipped out of her fingers. She was just beginning to bend down to retrieve it, when the window blew out.

The bullet missed her head and struck one of the other pans hanging on the wall, making it jump and ring like a bell.

When Josie realized that it was a rifle shot, she shouted in a whisper.

"Sam! Get down on the floor! Someone is shooting at us!"

SIX

Samantha and Josie both dropped to the floor.

"I don't understand!" Samantha said, her voice suddenly choked with fear and tears. "What do we do?!"

"Stay down." Josie was so shaky she could barely talk. She was on her hands and knees. Her right arm shook with a severe tremor. She crawled over and put her arm around Samantha's shoulder.

Josie spoke in a whisper. "The shot came in the window and hit that pan," Josie said. "So it came from that direction. That means it was fired from down by the lake."

Josie looked up toward the window. Six small window panes. One missing most of its glass. "Did you hear the shot?"

Samantha was crying. "I don't know! I... Maybe I did. It was a crack sound. Like slapping a belt on a table."

"Was the crack sound at the same time as the shot hitting the pan? Or did it come later?"

Samantha said, "I think it was later. But that doesn't make sense. So was there a second shot? What's happening?! I'm scared!"

"No, Sam, I think there was just one shot. I'm pretty sure a bullet goes faster than the speed of sound. So the shooter might be a long distance from here. The bullet came fast. Then the rifle crack came later. Like when you yell and hear your echo later because it takes time for sound to travel. The shooter could even be out on the lake. Or maybe across the lake. I don't know if bullets can go that far. Although I think they can."

"What should we do?" Samantha was crying.

Josie hugged her daughter. "I don't know, honey. I don't know. I'm thinking."

Josie had trouble breathing.

"Why would someone shoot at us?" Samantha whispered.

"I can't imagine why. Maybe it was accidental. It could be someone was goofing off, firing a gun, and a stray bullet came our way."

"What are the chances of that?" Samantha sounded desperate.

"Probably about zero," Josie said.

"So what does that mean?" Samantha's voice wavered. Terror mixed with focus.

Josie was trying to concentrate, trying to be productive. "We should consider the possibility that it was intentional. If it wasn't, then we'll be okay. But if for some reason, someone is trying to shoot us, then we should do whatever it takes to not get shot."

"What would that be?"

"I don't know! I don't know how to think about this."

"Then do the professor thing! Analysis or whatever you do."

"Professors don't live in the real world," Josie said. "Everything is—you know—academic. Hypothetical."

"Then make it hypothetical."

Josie was breathing so hard she couldn't think. She couldn't get enough air. But what Samantha said made sense. "You're right. We have to analyze. And test." She forced herself to take a deep breath. "Okay. First question. Is someone really shooting at us, or was it a stray shot? If we knew the answer, that would tell us what to do next."

"So that's a test," Samantha said.

"Yeah. I don't know how to test it. Wait, yes, I do. If I stand up and move around in front of the window, the shooter would probably shoot again, right?"

"Mama, you can't stand in front of the window!"

"Right. But I can make him think I am. I could put my clothes on a hanger and dangle the hanger in front of the window."

"How?" Samantha said. "I don't see any hanger."

"Okay, what about a pole of some kind?"

"There's a broom leaning in the corner by the door. I can crawl and get it."

Josie spoke in a harsh whisper. "Stay very low, Sam! Next to the floor."

Samantha scrambled over, got the broom, and slid it across the floor toward Josie.

Josie took off her windbreaker jacket and draped it over the bristles of the broom. Then she raised the broom up toward the window. The jacket hung. It didn't look realistic. But it might appear as if she was wounded and was slowly trying to push herself up.

The leverage of the broom was too much to manage from the side. So she crawled under the window, then used both hands to lift the broom up. The jacket wavered. Its fabric was maroon and hard to see. But the kerosene lantern threw a strong light. Josie slowly moved the broom and jacket. Even if the shooter couldn't easily see a dark jacket in dim light, he could probably see the movement. It was hard to hold the broom. The jacket wavered. But Josie realized the wavering made it look more realistic.

The broom fell back with a thud and a jerk. A moment later came the crack of a rifle.

"Another shot!" Samantha cried.

"Yes. Someone is definitely trying to kill us!"

SEVEN

"What do we do?!" Samantha could barely form the words through her sobs.

"We get out of here and run, fast as possible."

"Won't he shoot us as we run out the door?"

Josie struggled to think. "Then we'll go out the back window."

"That will be hard. You'll have to wiggle through it. It'll take time."

"Yes. But the delayed sound of the rifle means he's a good distance away. Even if he is paddling fast toward us, it's going to take him a minute or two. Let's hurry. Put on your hoodie. Grab your things. And let's whisper. Sound carries across water."

"What things should I take?" Samantha whispered.

"I don't know. The knife is already on your belt. That waterproof match container. Your flashlight. Your windbreaker. Put it on. It's going to be cold out there."

"Then we should take a sleeping bag, right?"

"Good idea."

Josie put her windbreaker back on, then reached up to the Duluth pack on the counter and pulled it down onto the floor. She fished around, and found the leather sheath that contained the hunting knife Bill had given her. She stuffed the sheath down into her front pocket.

Josie crawled to the back window. Her breath was so short, she was gasping for air. "With luck, this window is out of the sight line from the front window. Hopefully, the shooter can't see it from his position."

"We could turn off the kerosene lantern. Then he can't see

us." Samantha started crawling toward the lantern.

"No, don't!" Josie said it too loud. She lowered her voice. "Turning off the lantern will tell him that at least one of us is alive and thinking. He probably doesn't think there's any chance he got lucky and hit us both with his two shots. But we want him to think it might be possible. That might make him feel less inclined to rush."

The cabin's rear window had small panes like the front one. It was a double hung design. It wasn't latched. Josie pushed up on it. It didn't budge. "Sam, can you help me with the window?"

Sam crawled over. She was panting with panic. But she got next to Josie, and the two of them pushed up. The window slid up about a foot and then jammed. They could not make it go any farther.

"I think we can still get out," Samantha said, her voice more in control now that she was focused on a task.

"You can fit, but I don't think I can."

"We have no choice, Mama. Hurry."

Josie dragged a chair over under the window. "This will help. You first."

Samantha stuck her head and shoulders through the window. She wriggled forward and then fell out, head first onto the ground.

She got up in a moment. "Okay, Mama. I'll help pull you through."

"First, take the sleeping bag." Josie stuffed it out the window.

Josie stuck her arms and head through the opening. As she leaned forward, she filled the opening top to bottom. There was very little room left side to side, either. She felt stuck in position. She felt around with her feet and got one on the chair. She pushed down with her foot and pulled with her arms. Samantha pulled on her shoulders.

"Hurry, Mama!"

"Shhh!" she said. Then, "I'm stuck."

"No, you're not. Try harder!" Samantha's whisper was still almost a shout. "This is your new motto, remember? Forward into battle like a warrior. There's no retreat."

Josie pushed harder, got farther into the window opening.

The chair tipped over behind her. She was trapped, unable to breathe, all of her body weight on the windowsill. She jerked and wriggled. Samantha pulled.

"You can do it, Mama!"

Samantha put her foot up against the outer wall of the cabin. She tugged on Josie's arms.

Josie felt fabric ripping. She started wriggling like a worm. Left, right, left. Each motion moved her forward a tiny bit.

"It's working, Mama! Keep doing it. Harder. Faster!"

Josie got her chest through the opening. She hung from her waist. The windowsill gouged her and tore her clothes, scraped her skin.

"Don't stop!" Samantha said. "I'm going to pull hard. We'll get you out enough to fall to the ground. I'll help you down. I'll cushion your fall."

They got Josie out enough that she flopped to the ground.

It felt like she'd torn the skin off the fronts of her thighs and shin bones.

Samantha pulled her up to her feet. "You made it, Mama. Now where do we go?"

"We run into the woods. We hide."

"My flashlight's in my pocket."

"No. Your flashlight is too bright. It will make it easy for him to see where we're going through the woods. My penlight is the old style. Dim. If we shield it with our hands, it will be much harder to see."

Josie pulled the light out of her pocket. "You take it, Sam. Cup your hand around its rim before you turn it on. You can see better than I can. My eyes are worthless in the dark. You can lead us into the forest. I'll follow. Let's try to keep the cabin between him and us. So he can't see us. Once we're in the woods, we can move more freely."

Samantha picked up the sleeping bag. "Where to?"

"Remember the loop we made around the island? Let's do that again. Only, this time let's go the opposite direction. Counter-clockwise. That will take us away from where the shooter is. You'll probably recognize some of the places where we went. Take us to that secret bed of moss."

"Good idea." Samantha turned on the pen light. Her hand covered most of the light. She started to move into the forest.

"Wait," Josie whispered. "I saw an old ax by the woodpile. Let me get it."

"But he could already be at the shore, running toward us!"

"I'll hurry."

Josie took the light from Sam. But she realized that the moment she stepped out from behind the cabin, she'd be visible, no matter how much she covered the light. She handed the light back to Samantha, then moved toward the dark woodpile, going by feel and memory. It went okay until she stepped on a stick and it broke with a loud snap. Josie could feel her heart beating as if to set a speed record. She wanted to run back toward Samantha. But she kept going forward, her arms out in front of her, feeling for something, anything other than air.

Something brushed Josie's shoulder. She gasped. It felt like a bat had flown into her. But she knew bats didn't do that. She reached up to touch it. Pine needles. A branch. She followed it to another, thicker branch. That indicated the direction of a tree. She moved toward it, arms out. There was nothing. Then her fingers hit bark.

Josie heard Samantha whispering behind her. Calling for her. Josie didn't dare call back. What if the shooter was approaching the front door of the cabin?

The ground began to glow. Josie was startled. Was it a light from the shooter?

No, it was a glow from the kerosene lantern inside the cabin, light spilling out the window the shooter had broken.

Josie paused, studying the glow, watching for movement.

She saw nothing. Which probably meant nothing. The shooter could be ten feet from her in the dark.

There was a vague shape of darkness between two trees. The woodpile.

Josie remembered where the ax had hung. She slowly walked over in the darkness. Felt the tree. It wasn't there. She inhaled. Tried to stay calm. Moved her hands up and down. Shifted to the side. Moved them again. Hit something that wobbled.

The ax.

Josie lifted it from where it hung and started back toward Samantha.

"I got it," she whispered as she got closer.

"Hurry!" Samantha whispered back, her voice making clear her state of terror.

Josie got to Samantha and, still holding the ax, gave her a one-arm hug with her other arm. "Okay, lead the way."

Samantha turned on the dim light, her cupped hand absorbing most of it. She walked off into the forest. Josie stayed close behind, both of her hands gripping the ax handle.

When they had moved maybe 100 yards into the forest, Samantha spoke, her voice a little less panicked than before. "Do you think he will come after us? Will he try to follow us into the forest?"

"I think so, yes."

"Why?"

"I don't know why he wants to kill us, or me, Sam. But after tracking us to this island, I don't think he's going to give up easily. He knows we're stuck here unless we can get to our canoe. He'll want to finish the job."

"Then we should take the canoe."

"We can't. It's wedged between those trees. It would take both of us to get it out. That would take a long time and would make a lot of noise. And where would we go? There's no moon. The lake is as dark as it can get."

At that moment, there was a booming sound like hitting a bass drum. Samantha stopped walking. She turned off the penlight. Josie stood close behind her.

"What was that?" Samantha whispered, the terror back in her voice.

"I don't know. Maybe he paddled to the island and hit the shore without slowing down. It sounded like I imagine it would if you banged a canoe on the rocks. Keep going."

Samantha continued.

In another minute, Josie whispered, "Remember that area where all the super skinny pine trees had died and all the needles had fallen off?"

"Yeah. I bumped one and it fell over."

"Do you think you can find that place in the dark?"

"Maybe. Why?"

"Those trees would make decent spears if we could get them out of the ground and break off the branches. They are very straight, and the tops are hard and pointed."

"Are you saying we could spear this guy?" Samantha's voice was louder.

"Shhh. Maybe. Any guy who tries to hurt us—kill us—I'd stick him with a spear."

"I thought spears were for throwing. I saw that in a movie."

"Yes, they can be thrown. They're good thrusting weapons, too. Spears, lances, pikes."

"I never heard of a pike," Samantha said. Her dim light shined on a tall tree. The lower part of the trunk was free of branches. Samantha put her hand on it as she approached then walked part way around it as if the tree sent her off in a new direction.

Josie followed, keeping her arms in front of her face to protect from unseen branches. "Pikes were important medieval weapons. Pike men would plant the rear end of a pike in the dirt and hold the pointed end up so the charging army would run into it."

"Ohhh, that's gross!" Samantha said.

"Yes. But very effective."

"Could you actually do that?" Samantha asked. "Stick a person with a spear?" It sounded like fear had crept into Samantha's voice.

"I don't know. I'm just an out-of-shape teacher."

"Who's been thinking about medieval warriors in battle."

"Right," Josie said. "I know this much for sure. If I saw him hurt you, I'd definitely spear him." Josie was so afraid, she was almost unable to talk. But she wanted to keep Samantha distracted. If she could keep up some kind of patter, especially some positive talk about defending themselves, Samantha might not be consumed by her fear.

Samantha pushed around an outcropping of rock, then ducked through a group of trees. "How would a person do it?"she asked, her voice very soft. "Would it be like stabbing someone with a really long knife?"

"I suppose so. Maybe it would be more difficult. But most spears would weigh enough that if you threw one, it would have enough inertia to stab someone pretty seriously."

Samantha kept walking, pointing her shielded light, choosing her steps carefully. "Would a spear kill him?"

"I think it depends on where it hit him and how fast it was moving. The problem with those dead trees is that they have a hundred little dead branches coming off the main trunk. So even if we could break them off, the branch nubs would probably prevent the spear from penetrating very far."

"This is nastier than ever."

"I know," Josie said.

"Do you think you could do it? Stab someone?"

"I don't know. But I'm going to try to visualize stabbing a spear, over and over until it begins to feel familiar. Same for swinging this ax."

"Do you think that works? Visualizing?"

"According to defense experts, it does. When women take self-defense classes, they are much more likely to fight their attackers, and they have lower rates of rape and injury than women who don't take classes."

"Like sports," Samantha said. "Practice is the key."

"Yes. And practice is as much mental as physical. So we can start mentally practicing."

"How to stick a guy with a spear."

"That's correct."

"I can't believe this," Samantha said, her voice cracking. "The whole idea is so violent. It makes me think about Clarice. She died in such a violent way…" Samantha stopped walking and slumped against a tree.

Josie could only imagine how hard it was to have a friend be murdered. She hugged Samantha and rubbed her back. Samantha was taller than she was by several inches, but she was so skinny that she felt like a waif.

Samantha wiped her sleeve across her eyes. She took several deep breaths. Eventually, she separated herself from Josie, straightened, and walked on.

Josie followed.

Five minutes later, Samantha said, "This is it. The spear forest." She raised the light just a bit to shine on the dead trees.

"There's the one that fell over before." Josie picked it up. "It has got a sharp point. And the branches are brittle." She snapped one off and it made a loud noise.

"Mama!" Her whisper was nearly shouted.

"Sorry, I didn't realize it would be so loud. We can cut the branches off instead."

They each grabbed a skinny dead tree. They rocked them back and forth and around in a circle. The roots were tough. They weren't going to give way without using the ax on the roots or base of the trunk.

"Okay, let's forget this for now," Josie said. "Better to find the hiding place and practice with the weapons we have."

"The place with all the moss," Samantha said.

"Yes."

Samantha hiked on, carrying the broken tree. Josie stayed

close behind, trying to see by the light of the flashlight that Samantha had largely covered. The flashlight was getting dimmer as the battery discharged.

"Okay, here it is," Samantha said. She set her skinny dead tree down, bent under some tree branches, and stepped into what was a room of sorts with a spongy green floor. "Look, Mama, if we pull down some of these branches, it gives the room walls almost. See? It's a perfect hiding place."

"Yes, let's do that." Josie leaned on several nearby boughs, bending them to add to the sense of perimeter of the room.

Samantha did the same. In a couple of minutes, they'd created a private hideaway.

"Now that the hiding place is complete, we'll hide nearby."

"I don't get it," Samantha said.

"When the guy finds out we're not in the cabin, he'll see we haven't left in our canoe. So he'll begin looking for us on the island. He's probably skillful at tracking. He'll be looking for someplace that would make a good hideaway. If he comes this far and sees this place, he'll plan to surprise us by diving into the moss room and then attack us. But we'll be hiding nearby in a less perfect hiding place that he'll overlook."

Samantha didn't say anything. Josie knew she'd be disappointed. But she'd see the logic.

After a moment, Samantha said, "What other place do you think we should hide in?"

Josie took her flashlight, shielded it with her hand, and moved around the nearby area. "Here," she said. "This stand of trees has a group of large trunks close together. When the time comes that he approaches, you will stand in here like you are just another tree trunk. You're thin, and you have a dark hoodie. You'll blend in. It won't be perfect, but it will be very good."

Samantha stepped in between the tree trunks. "And you?"

Josie found some shrubs that together formed a low, dark mass of foliage. "As soon as I sense him coming, I'll sit down under these branches. I'll look like a shrub. He'll be so focused on this perfect hiding place, he won't see us."

"Okay, say he comes here like you're thinking. Tell me how you think this will work."

"I think he'll come in the first glow of dawn. When it's still dark, but beginning to get light enough that he won't have to use a flashlight. That way, he can sneak up on us without giving away his presence."

"Then how will we see him?"

"We'll be like the eyes and ears of the forest. If we are perfectly silent, and mostly still, we'll sense him before he senses us."

Samantha didn't immediately talk. "Let's say that happens. We see him as he approaches. What do we do?"

Josie had to think. This wasn't just new territory. This was a new planet in a new solar system. "Wait until I move. At the right time—probably as he aims his weapon into the mossy hiding place—I'm going to cleave him with my ax."

"Cleave? What does that mean?"

"Cut him. Cut him badly."

"And what do I do?"

"If he falls dead, nothing. But if he's still fighting, give him your best shot with your spear."

Samantha was silent. In time, she whispered. "This dead tree's still got all these little branches on it. You said we should cut them off so... you know."

Josie pulled her knife out of her pocket and removed the knife from the sheath. "Let me try this."

Josie started at the top of the tree and sliced off the branches, careful to cut away from herself. Some came off cleanly. Some felt like she was cutting wire. Josie could tell that the knife was very sharp. But it was still significant work.

In ten minutes, she'd gotten the branches off. Some left rounded stubs. But they wouldn't stop the small tree from being a dangerous weapon. The tree was now very much like a spear. She handed it back to Samantha. "Hold it in different positions. Get a feel for it."

Samantha lifted the spear, held it with two hands, and jabbed it forward. Then she raised it above one shoulder and made the motions of someone throwing it.

"I don't think I can do it, Mama. I'm not brave enough."

"You will. When the time comes, you'll find the strength."

"What do we do now?"

"We wait. Probably until dawn. The man wants to find us. But it's night and there's no moon. If he searches with a light, we'll see him coming. It makes sense that he'll start searching when he can begin to see without a flashlight."

"Dawn's a very long time away."

Josie reached for the sleeping bag and pulled it out of the stuff sack. "We can put this over us."

"If he's not coming until dawn, then maybe we could try sleeping on the moss mattress. I could set my phone alarm."

"Okay. But what about your battery?"

"I put it in low power mode when we left the motel. It'll last for another day. Then I'll plug in my backup battery. But that's back in the pack at the cabin."

"Your screen brightness is way down?" Josie said.

"Yeah. What time should I set the alarm?"

"I'd say ninety minutes before dawn."

"I can't Google that, 'cause I don't have a cell signal."

"We can figure out when dawn comes. We're just a few days from September twenty-first, the autumnal equinox."

"What's that?"

"The first day of fall," Josie said. "When the days and nights are about equal, meaning the day would start about six a.m. with standard time. But Ontario and Minnesota are still on Daylight Savings time, so that would make dawn closer to seven a.m."

"So I should set the alarm for five?"

"Yes, that would be good."

Samantha set the alarm. They crawled into the hideaway room and lay down on the moss. Josie spread the sleeping bag over them, and they huddled together in the dark.

EIGHT

They were silent for some time, but neither slept.

"Mama?"

"Yeah?"

"Do you think the guy shooting at us is the same guy we saw in the airport?"

"It seems highly unlikely that someone who was after us would be so careless as to let us see him in the airport. Unless he only decided to kill us after he saw us in the airport. But I've wondered that."

"Did you do something real bad that would make someone want to kill you?"

"No. Please don't worry about something like that. I haven't done anything different than my norm. Everything is as it's always been. And I've never seen that man before."

"Then why is this happening?" Samantha sounded on the verge of tears.

"I have no idea. It makes no sense. I'm so sorry you—we— are having to go through this."

"Did you make someone angry?"

Josie thought about it. "Not that I know of."

"Do you think I did something bad? Something I didn't realize?"

"No. This couldn't possibly be connected to you."

"Then you have to do the professor thing."

"Analyze and test?" Josie said. "Do you have any ideas?"

Samantha shook her head. "No. I'm just trying to do like you say. You always say, 'Move away from the emotion.' And 'Separate the question from feelings. Be...' I forget the word you use."

"Objective?"

"Yeah. So let's look at what you do. You teach. You grade papers and other teaching stuff. Conferences. Seminars. You... Wait. Maybe you gave a student a bad grade and they are so upset they're trying to kill you."

Josie shook her head in the dark. "I can't imagine someone having such an overreaction. And if it is the man we saw in the airport, I know he was never one of my students."

As Josie thought about these ideas, they seemed ridiculous. But there had to be some reason someone was shooting at them.

"Maybe the student hired the killer. Or the student's parents hired the killer because your bad grade hurt the student. Grades can do that, right?"

"Yes. Bad grades can make the student lose a scholarship or not get into graduate school."

"Can you think of any student who could be mad at you?"

"One or two."

"Then their parent could be angry, too?"

"I suppose. But hiring a killer to follow me to the Canadian wilderness... That's so extreme. I can't conceive of it."

"Maybe it's a case of mistaken identity. Maybe he's confusing us for someone else."

"I don't think so," Josie said. "This part of the country is very white. Even from a distance, even at night, looking into a cabin lit with a kerosene lantern, he could see we're black. In this wilderness, two black women are about as unusual as it gets. So, while there's a lot we don't know about this situation, mistaking us for someone else isn't one of them. I think we can assume he's after us."

Samantha was quiet for a minute. "What's that logic thing you talk about?"

"I don't know."

"The most logical explanation."

"Oh. Occam's Razor. William of Ockham was a Franciscan friar and philosopher in the fourteenth century. He observed that the simplest explanation for any conundrum is usually the correct one."

"Okay," Samantha said. "You're pretty sure you've never met this person who's after us."

"If it's the man from the airport, then that's true. I haven't ever seen him before. But if it's someone else, then I don't really know if I have ever met them."

"And you can't think of anyone who really hates you. Is that right?"

"Yes. Maybe I've angered a student with a grade or been rude to a TA."

"You mean a teaching assistant?"

"Right," Josie said. "Like Mira."

"The woman in your office," Samantha said.

They were quiet awhile. Josie felt that the tension of hiding in the dark wilderness forest was an unbearable pressure. It pressed in on them, made it impossible to sleep or find any comfort.

"Where do TAs come from?" Samantha asked. "Do you hire them?"

"Not in the common sense. TAs are usually graduate students working on advanced degrees. They help you teach, which is also good training for them in the event they become professors. Mira is working on her Master's. We're not especially chummy. But I've never had the sense that Mira doesn't like me. But even if I considered people who might not like me, I can't see any of them following us into the wilderness to shoot us."

"Then, the simplest explanation is that this man was hired to kill you. He's working for some other person who wants you dead. Someone who you can't think of."

"Meaning, he's an assassin," Josie said. "That's incredible. But I agree. That would be the simplest explanation."

"Then all we have to do is imagine the simplest reason why someone would want you dead."

Josie found herself nodding in the dark. "Okay, I'm still with you."

"That implies there is a reason." Samantha said it with finality.

"I understand," Josie said. "You're a good critical thinker. There is no point in me saying or thinking that there couldn't possibly be any reason for someone to want me dead, when we have obvious evidence that someone wants me dead."

"Or us dead," Samantha said. "This could all be about something I did. So now, we use Occam to find the simplest reason why someone wants one of us dead."

"All right," Josie said. "What are your ideas?"

"Well, if I don't think about the sweet Josie who's my Mama and instead just think about a stranger, it's easier."

Josie immediately felt joy at Samantha's use of the word sweet to describe her. Samantha never talked like that.

"The obvious stuff would be if you did something that caused a person's death," Samantha said. "Something that would make the person's spouse or child or closest friend boiling mad."

"Yes. But I can't think of any connection between me and anyone's death."

"Or let's say you destroyed something that person had worked on building for years and years. That would make the builder person totally furious, right?"

"Yes, I would think so. Keep going."

Samantha thought for a moment. "Let's say you did something that made someone lose their job or lose a lot of money. Or you stole a person's most valuable possession. Or you made their closest love not like them anymore."

"This is good," Josie said.

"Did you have an affair with some married guy? That might make his wife hire someone to kill you."

"Sam, it's kind of you to even consider that some married guy might be interested in me that way. But no, I didn't. I've never had an affair with a married guy. My sex life is about as non-existent as you can imagine. There hasn't..." Josie trailed off. She didn't want to start thinking about how her devotion to her job had pushed nearly all other activities out of her life.

"Maybe you saw someone murder a person and you could testify and put them in jail."

"Sam, you know that's not possible. You'd know about it if I saw a murder."

"But what if you witnessed a murder but didn't realize it was a murder?"

"How could that be?" Josie paused, then said, "Oh, wait. Maybe you have something there. Let me think... What if you see a nurse giving a shot to a patient? You think it's medicine. Later, you find out the patient died."

Samantha exclaimed, "It could have been poison!"

"Shh!" Josie whispered as she held her finger to her lips even though it was too dark for them to see anything.

They were both quiet for a time, listening to the night sounds of the forest.

Josie spoke first. "You're right. A person could witness a murder and not realize it at the time. But if you realized it later, you might remember what the nurse looked like. There could be a hundred things that would cause a death and the witness would never think twice about it because the thing is insignificant in every way. It only becomes significant and notable after the death occurs."

"Or what if a person got run over by a bus and died. But if the person was pushed, and you were nearby, the killer might think you saw them push the victim. So they come after you. Maybe you didn't even see a person get run over, and you didn't know someone died. But the killer thinks you did see it."

"I think you're onto something, Sam. Because I haven't witnessed anyone die, ever, I don't realize I've witnessed anything significant. But the concept fits Occam's Razor, so it's worth pursuing. The simplest explanation for why someone wants me dead is that I'm a witness to something major. But I don't know what I witnessed because it seemed to me like an unremarkable thing."

Samantha said, "And if the murderer thinks you know he did it, well, he's already committed murder. So what's one more murder if it keeps him out of prison?"

Josie was quiet, considering the possibilities.

"Think back over the last month or year or whatever," Samantha said. "What did you see? What is there that didn't stand out to you but could be real serious? Maybe you saw some kind of—I don't know—a payoff. Someone handed another person a bag of groceries. Except it was really a bag of money."

"You should write screenplays for thrillers," Josie said. "You're really imaginative."

"Think about it, Mama. The whole Occam thing needs you to process."

"I'm trying. All I can think of is just our regular routine. Going to school. Giving my lectures. Lunch by myself or, rarely, with one of the other professors. Even more rarely, a student. Having dinner with you. Walking on the beach. Picking you up on Saturday after your volleyball game. I've done nothing unusual other than going to a stupid endowment celebration party. I think I told you about it. I wish I hadn't gone. A bunch of drunk academics is worse than drunk college kids. Professors slurring their words while trying to sound brilliant and educated is hideous."

"Then why did you go? You always said you hate parties."

"I felt I had to. There's a professor named Roger Lopez, who teaches the history of the ancient Greeks. He put on a fete for a bigwig who gave a great deal of money to the European History department. He got another wealthy patron to provide the use of his Bel Air mansion. So Roger invited all of the faculty and made it clear that our attendance was practically required if we cared at all about funding for the department."

"What's a fete?"

"It's just a fancy party with a master of ceremonies who makes announcements. This one was a comedian. He roasted UCLA and the professors. Then he gave the donor a framed certificate honoring his financial contribution. The party was catered and there was a band."

"And booze," Samantha said.

"Yeah, no kidding," Josie said, remembering how dreary the party was.

"Who was the money guy?"

"I never met him. But I remember his name. Lawrence Winston Underwood."

"Whoa, that's a name, like, some rich dude on a soap opera."

"Yes. It turned out that he is the chairman of some big investment group. The comedian joked that it was easy for Underwood to hand out money because he owned the printing press that printed it."

"How much money did he give?"

Josie was surprised at Samantha's interest. "I heard someone say it was a twenty-million-dollar endowment. That's a good thing, of course, to get huge funding for a history department when it seems like all anyone ever cares about is technology and entertainment and sports. But they made the party so tacky. When Underwood arrived in his limo, the band played 'We're In The Money.' Underwood acted like he was some kind of god. He wore a shiny grey pinstripe suit. And there were dancers. It was like something you'd see in a movie about Las Vegas. And drunk people do stupid things at parties."

Samantha said. "I've seen boys do crazy things trying to show off. Girls, too. I bet that party is connected to why the killer is after us. You probably saw professors shooting up China White or something."

That was a surprise to Josie. "What is China White?"

"Heroin, of course. Smack. Dope. There's lots of names."

Josie was appalled. "How do you know about that?"

"Don't get so stern, Mama. Kids talk."

"Have you been to a party with heroin?"

"No. You know I don't go to parties 'cause you won't let me.

Anyway, the kids at school, they have older brothers and sisters. College age. They talk about what goes on. The younger kids pay attention. You're probably the only person at UCLA that doesn't realize what really goes on."

Josie didn't like hearing it. But it was true. Her only knowledge of drugs came from seeing the movies that Samantha wanted to stream. Josie also heard comments she didn't understand, comments that could refer to drugs. She could have gone back to her office and Googled the words, learned the slang. She could have spent time reading what people write in revealing Facebook posts or blogs. But Josie preferred to be in the dark. She didn't want to spend time staying informed about the mindless things that people do. There was so much to learn that was interesting and valuable. It was all about making good choices.

And now someone wanted them dead.

Obviously, she could have made better choices and stayed better informed.

"Keep thinking, Mama. Was there anything at that party that someone wouldn't want you to see?"

"The only thing that comes to mind was when I went out into the garden. I walked along, looking at the flowers. I went by a little private area surrounded by plantings, and I saw people snorting cocaine. At least, I think it was cocaine. White powder that they snorted using little straws."

"Did you know the people?"

"One of them was a professor. I don't know him, but I've seen him. I'm not even sure what he teaches. The other two people were celebrities. I only know them from..." Josie paused. "Movies."

"Who, Mama? That could be it!"

"I don't want to say who. Even celebrities should be able to have some privacy."

"What if they hired the killer?"

"I doubt it," Josie said. "Celebrities are always doing drugs, right? It's no big deal."

They were silent for a long time.

Josie wondered if Samantha's idea could be right. Was it possible that Josie had seen something at the party that made her so threatening that someone would want her dead? Was it possible one of those celebrities hired a killer?

It might make sense if she had been the sole witness to something outrageously bad... Someone like the mayor or a church cardinal or the L.A. Police Chief snorting cocaine with kids. But even that was a serious stretch. Even faced with ruin, most people would not see murder as a way out. There didn't seem to be anything about the party for Underwood that could connect to Josie and Samantha becoming murder targets.

Josie thought about the nickname China White. It reminded her of something else she saw at the party for the investor. She revisited it in her mind, recollecting the details that had meant nothing at the time. She'd gone to find a bathroom. As she went up the big staircase and down a hallway, a door at the end opened and a young man came out. He looked to be in his early twenties. But unlike the majority of the college students that Josie saw every day, this man telegraphed a different focus. He had a mesomorph build, thick with muscles, and short hair. He stood very straight and had a demeanor of reverence and possibly a touch of fear, as if he were a military officer who'd been addressing a five-star general. When he saw Josie, he looked embarrassed as if he'd been caught doing something wrong. As Josie recalled the incident, she remembered that she had briefly seen past the young man, through the open doorway into an elegant study, the kind of room with cherry wood paneling and bookshelves with first edition books and maroon leather furniture.

In the study was another person. But instead of a general with an intimidating uniform heavy with ribbons and medals, there was a slim, willowy Asian woman wearing a white silk blouse and a black silk skirt. She stood at a large multi-paned window behind a huge desk. Josie could only glimpse her from an angle as the woman looked out and down toward the drive. The woman was perhaps 50 years old. Her black hair was pulled up in a tight bun. She was beautiful like a movie star and had a regal bearing.

As the young man had made his exit, he made a little bow and gave the door a gentle pull to close it. The door swung slowly. Right before it shut, the beautiful Asian woman saw Josie. She immediately looked both angry and worried at the same time. Her eyes seemed to flash a controlled fury. Then the latch touched the strike plate. Because the door was large and thick, it had enough inertia to click shut.

As Josie thought back about it, she believed the incident was nothing. She was searching for something that wasn't there.

The cool breeze through the trees picked up and got colder. Josie reached across the dark and held Samantha's hand. The poor girl's hand was cold.

"Snuggle close," Josie said. "We have to stay warm."

They leaned against each other.

After a long silence, Samantha asked, "What do you think about when you're scared?"

"I like to think about Bibi," Josie said. "She was always so reassuring. She made me feel safe."

"Bibi was my great grandmother, right? Your grandmother. I just barely remember her. She gave me the lion ring."

"Yes."

"She died when I was really little."

"Yes. You were three, almost four."

"Wasn't Bibi really old?"

"Ninety-four. She was still mostly healthy. But she died from a brain aneurysm no one knew about."

"And Nana Strong?"

"My mother—your grandmother—died in a car accident before you were born. She was hit by a drunk driver who ran a red light."

Josie was worried that Samantha's questions would lead to her asking about her father. Josie dreaded the subject. She knew that one day she would tell Samantha the truth. She would have to tell her the truth. But she hoped to put it off a while longer.

Samantha said, "I remember Bibi's hair."

Josie felt a big sense of relief that Samantha went back to thinking about Bibi. Josie smiled in the darkness. "Thick and curly and white."

"It was like putting my fingers into deep carpet." Samantha paused. "She lived with lions, right?"

"Not with them. But not too far away. She grew up in Dar es Salaam, a big city on the coast of Tanzania, a country in Africa. The lions were out on the Serengeti."

"I forget the name of the lion."

"The image on your ring is a female lion. The Swahili name that Bibi used was Simba Wa Kike."

"I remember part of the story. Tell me again?"

"The story was about a girl who was named after the female lion. Simba Wa Kike was very strong and not very feminine. So the boys rejected her. She found that hard. But the queen prized her for her intelligence and her skills and gave her the best teachers. Simba Wa Kike grew up to be a great warrior. When the big war came, Simba Wa Kike led the main charge, and the queen's army won the war. Later, when the queen was dying, she named Simba Wa Kike as her replacement. So the warrior who was rejected as a child became queen and was embraced and loved by all."

"But it's not a real story, right?" Samantha said.

"That depends on what you get out of a story. It's not like journalism reporting something that actually happened. It's an African folk story. But when a story has characters who you care about and valuable lessons, in some ways it's as real as any other story."

Samantha's voice was small but firm. "It's about how a girl can grow up to be anything."

"Yes," Josie said. Josie could feel in the dark that Samantha used her other hand to rotate the Simba Wa Kike ring.

A few minutes later, Samantha fell into a deep sleep, her

breaths long and slow. Josie was grateful that Samantha could get some rest. Samantha had come with her to the wilderness against her desire. Josie had wanted them to take the trip for all the right reasons. Now it was a nightmare. If they survived, Josie thought she'd never be able to make it up to Samantha.

The air was cold and humid. A slight breeze rustled the conifer branches above their hiding place. The sky was absolutely dark with no moon. And because the nearest city was 150 miles away, there was no light pollution from civilization. Had the circumstances been different, they could have enjoyed fantastic stargazing.

In time, Josie started, aware that she'd been dozing. She had no idea what time it was. She tried to go back to sleep, but had no success. After what seemed like a couple of hours, she heard a vibration. Samantha stirred, and Josie realized her phone alarm was going off. Samantha got her phone out, tapped the button to turn off the alarm, then put it back in her pocket.

"Now what?" Samantha whispered.

"We have some time before the sky starts to lighten. We can do some stretches. But then we should ready our weapons and get into our real hiding places. Stretch well because we'll be hiding in close quarters for some time. Maybe a few hours."

"You still think he's searching for us," Samantha said.

"Yes. Anyone who travels to the Boundary Waters and Quetico and paddles out into the wilderness to kill me or us is very motivated. He'll certainly search the island to try to find us and finish the job."

"I can't believe we're doing this, that we're going to try to attack someone. I don't think I can do it."

"Just remember that he will kill us if we don't. This is Jack London's law of the wilderness. Kill or be killed. It applies to Simba Wa Kike as much as anyone."

"You think we have to kill him?" Samantha stopped. Then spoke in a frantic whisper, "Mama! I hear noise! Someone's coming!"

NINE

Josie whispered back. "Hiding place. Quick!"

They both stepped out from the mossy room. Josie watched to make sure that Samantha got in among the stands of trees. It was still cave dark. Although maybe there was a tiny bit of light from the approaching dawn, out beyond the tree canopy. Josie couldn't see Samantha's spear, but she assumed that her daughter was holding it close to her body.

Josie grabbed her ax, got down on the ground, and slithered under the low fir trees, trying to stay as motionless as a bush.

They waited. The silence was total. The darkness seemed overwhelming as if to choke off everything that light represented. As an assault, and their potential death drew near, Josie felt in shock. She hadn't fully grasped what they were doing. She was astonished to think that less than 48 hours after landing at the airport, she was about to do battle with a killer in the wilderness.

Josie heard a sound, like the scuffing of a boot in the dark. She sensed, but could not see, a large man lifting the pine boughs to peer into the perfect hiding place. A dim light came on. It was blocked by his hulking size. The man swore. He took a step back. Turned. The dim light he carried glinted off a large pistol in his left hand.

In a moment faster than Josie could understand came a roar that sounded like that of a bear, as if its mouth were open, teeth bared. The sound was so scary, Josie froze in position. Then, incredibly, a strobe light came on. Super fast flashes, illuminating the man's face. As Josie leaped from her hiding place, she saw the shock in his eyes.

She realized that Samantha had somehow made her phone play the roar of the bear. Then Samantha had turned her phone camera flash into a strobe. In the staccato flash of light, the man looked momentarily startled and night blind. He seemed to freeze for a brief moment. Then he raised the pistol.

Josie was already swinging her ax toward the man's hand and his pistol as the strobe stopped and the night became blacker than ever.

Her ax hit his arm and also made a clink as it hit his gun. A shot exploded with another flash of light, this one coming from the gun. Something thudded to the ground as the man yelled in pain.

Josie sensed motion from where Samantha had been. The brilliant light came on again, this time without flashing. It showed the whites of the man's eyes. It also showed him using his right hand to feel his left, exploring the extent of the gash that poured blood. His gun had fallen to the duff of the forest floor and was not visible.

Samantha's brilliant light shook with movement as Samantha rotated. The homemade spear shot forward toward the man. It looked like it would make a glancing blow at best. But it came to an immediate stop, and the man yelled again, this time a scream as if to shake the Earth.

The blinding phone light revealed that the spear had pierced the left side of the man's waist. It was a surface blow that would have missed any organs. But it went through enough skin and perhaps a little muscle that it hung, suspended. The spear's heavier rear end was pulled down by gravity and rested on the ground. The pointed end protruded from the back of the man's waist, pointing up at an angle.

"Sam, let's go!" Josie whispered.

Samantha was paralyzed, unable or unwilling to move, no doubt astonished at what she'd done.

Sam's light turned off. The man flicked a switch on his flashlight. He put it in his teeth and bent his head. The light shone down. The man must have immediately realized that it would be impossible to pull the spear out with all of the little branch nubs acting as barbs. In a surreal sequence of motion, he reached his good right hand down to his thigh, unsnapped a leather sheath and pulled out a knife as large and shiny as a Hollywood movie prop. He reached the knife across his body to the embedded spear and, with a single muscular swipe, cut through his flesh all the way down to the spear, releasing it to fall to the ground as blood gushed forth from his side and mingled with the blood pouring from his left hand.

"Sam!" Josie said again. "Run!"

TEN

Josie watched from behind as Samantha once again turned on the dim penlight, cupping the rim so the fading yellow beam was blocked from most angles. She couldn't run well in the near darkness. But she went quickly. Josie struggled to keep up. Her foot falls went down onto dark ground that she couldn't see.

"A little slower!" Josie whispered. "My glasses are fogged up. I can't see! I'll sprain my ankle."

Samantha didn't speak. But Josie could hear her whimpering.

"We'll be okay, Sam. We hurt him. We got away."

"He'll chase us!"

"Maybe. But I don't think so. At least not right away. He'll have to stop his bleeding or he could die. Where he cut himself free from your spear is a severe wound."

"That was awful! He cut himself! It was worse than throwing the spear at him."

"There aren't major arteries there. But it will bleed a lot. He has to get some kind of bandage on the wound. He has to close it up. And his hand is just as bad. It looked like an artery got cut. There was a lot of blood. He'll need a tourniquet and stitching. Lots of stitching. Otherwise, he'll die."

Josie's talking had made her even more out of breath. She gasped for air as she ran after Samantha.

"But he's a psycho! He might still try to kill us before he dies." Samantha charged through the forest.

"You have to slow down," Josie said. "I can't go that fast."

"I did slow down."

"Then stop running. Just walk. I have to breathe!"

Samantha slowed to a walk. She kept looking behind, panic in her eyes as she looked at the dark forest.

"That was a great trick with your phone," Josie said.

"When I learned about bears, I downloaded the roar, and the strobe light was a free app I got a long time ago."

"It saved our lives."

"No big deal."

They came to an open area. The path ahead was sparsely forested. The approaching dawn made it easier to see. Samantha turned off the penlight. Five minutes later, the roof of the cabin became visible in the distance.

"I don't want to take the time to get our stuff," Samantha said. "I just want to get to the canoe and leave."

"I agree. I'm trying to remember where we put the paddles."

"I think we slid them between the thwart and the front seat. Like Bill showed us at the portage."

"I hope so. I can't remember carrying them into the cabin."

Samantha started to speed up her pace again in anticipation of escape.

They came over a rise. The area around the cabin came into view.

Samantha came to a sudden stop. "Mama!"

"What, Sam? What's wrong?" Josie put her arm around Samantha to comfort her.

"The canoe is gone."

ELEVEN

Samantha ran to the trees where the canoe had been wedged. "This is where we left it, right?"

"Yes. At least I think so." Josie walked toward the lake. She turned around and came back, visualizing their movements when they arrived. "Yes, that has to be where we put it."

"The man took it!" Samantha started crying. "We're trapped, Mama! Trapped on this island!"

"Let's look around. Maybe he hid it in some trees."

"Why would he do that? He'd know we might find it. He wants us dead. So he'd get rid of it."

Josie stopped, thinking. "Last night we heard that loud bang like his canoe hitting the rocks."

"But it was our canoe," Samantha said.

"I think so."

"He probably threw it into the water so it would drift out into the wind and blow away. It could be miles from here by now."

"But he'd still have his own canoe here someplace."

"Then where is it?" Samantha asked.

"Let's think. He'd know that if we somehow escaped him and discovered our canoe was gone, we'd have these very thoughts. So he must have hid it in bushes or under trees so we couldn't take it."

"He probably didn't land on the island where we did, right?" Samantha said. "He might've come ashore way down to the right or left. A long way from the cabin. Then he would have hidden his canoe. We could hunt for days and not find it."

"True," Josie said. "Even so, we should look for it. If it happens to be close and we could find it, we could escape with his canoe."

"And then he'd be the one trapped on the island," Samantha said. She sounded a little less depressed as she said it. She looked out at the lake. "The portage we came over was off to the right on that far shore. So it would've been shorter for him to paddle that way."

"You think we should look that way, first?"

Samantha nodded. "Yeah. We could go the way we first explored yesterday. But he could be coming that way." Samantha sounded shaky. "We need a weapon. Where's the ax?"

"I dropped it when I hit him with it."

"Then he has it now."

"Maybe. And he has his gun. He wouldn't want to carry the ax with his wounded hand."

Samantha stared down the path they'd taken the day before. "So he could be in those trees. He could be coming for us."

Josie shook her head. She pointed out at the lake. "I think that's him."

Samantha turned to see what she was pointing at. There was a canoe out on the water, a single occupant paddling away from them.

"Does it look like him?" Josie asked.

"I can't tell. But he's paddling slow."

"Which side is he paddling on?" Josie asked.

"The right side."

"When you did your strobe trick, I saw that he held a gun in his left hand, so I aimed for that. I think my ax hit his left hand, and it made a clinking sound, so I think I hit his gun. And then your spear hit him on his left side. So he's pretty much a one-sided guy now. He's probably taped his wounded left hand to the top of the paddle. He can do most of the paddling work with his right hand."

"So we're definitely trapped here," Samantha said.

"Safe from him for the time being," Josie said.

"You think he's going to come back?"

Josie thought about it. "Yes. He knows we've seen his face in the strobe light. So he's got extra motivation to come back. One, to complete his mission. Two, to eliminate two witnesses who can testify that he attacked them."

Samantha frowned. "But we have no evidence he attacked us. We don't have a bullet from his gun. And he didn't hurt us out in the woods. He could probably say he saw us from his canoe and was worried that we were lost and he was coming to save us."

"You're right." Josie felt overwhelmed. "The evidence makes it look like we attacked an innocent man. But we'll still tell our story, and there's a chance he's got a criminal record. The sheriff will look into his background and maybe find out that there's something to our story. I don't think he would want to take that chance."

"Okay," Samantha said, trying, Josie thought, to push back the fear and keep it out of her voice. "Let's assume he's coming back. When would that be?"

"Good question. He's got to find a doctor and get himself patched up. His injuries could look like a really bad accident, so a doctor wouldn't be suspicious and report anything to the sheriff. But he'd probably have to go to Grand Marais to find a doctor. Let's say he gets there today and gets stitched up this afternoon. He gets some pain killers and comes back up the Gunflint Trail tonight. He could be back out here first thing tomorrow morning."

Samantha was shaking her head. "He could do like in the Navy SEAL movie. The Black guy got hit by shrapnel, and he was behind enemy lines. So he drank a bunch of vodka to numb the pain and got this huge needle for stitching fishing nets. He found some fishing line and used it for thread. Then he poured vodka into the wound to sterilize it and stitched himself up."

"That would be very difficult," Josie said. "The pain would be extreme."

"But it would be possible, right? Our assassin could come back out here today. This evening."

"I agree," Josie said. "It would be possible."

Samantha looked off across the lake. The surface was smooth in the windless morning, a calm that belied the tension of being hunted by a professional killer.

"We need to eat something," Josie said.

Samantha nodded. "I'm starving."

"We don't have much time, so we'll eat those crackers and cheese."

"And chocolate," Samantha said.

"You once told me something about Medieval war," Samantha said as she wolfed down food.

Josie frowned. "I don't remember what you're referring to."

"It was some kind of principle. Maybe the word is strategy. What a war planner does."

Josie shook her head. "Nothing comes to mind. Oh, wait. I do remember. You're right. One war strategy principle is that in war, you don't plan for what you think your enemy will do. You plan for what your enemy can do. You're smart to bring that up. I might think this assassin won't come back until tomorrow morning. But we should plan for his return at the earliest possible time. Tonight. Or this evening. Or late afternoon."

Samantha stood up from the picnic table, took a few steps then stopped. Her eyes streamed sudden tears. "I can't believe this is happening, Mama! What do we do?"

Josie hugged her. Then she turned Samantha and walked her back to the picnic table. They sat down.

"Here's what we do," Josie said. "Like you pointed out, it's possible he's going to bring his war to us much sooner rather than later. So we'll prepare to meet him head-on."

"What does that mean?"

"We bring war to him," Josie said.

"But we're trapped on this island."

"So we make this our castle. We make it so he has to storm our territory. Because it is our territory, that gives us a big advantage."

"He has guns." Samantha's voice was meek.

"We make it hard for him to shoot us with guns by setting up in the fort you already found. The high territory. He won't be able to shoot us without coming up to our castle and literally looking over the rocks at us."

"We have no weapons at all."

"We will by the time he gets here."

"What do you mean?"

Josie said, "Remember what I have in my office at UCLA?"

Samantha shook her head. "Your desk and books and file cabinets and... Oh, yes. That model. The model of the medieval shooting thing or whatever it is."

"It's called a crossbow. I built it as part of my dissertation research. It's based on a design the Ancient Romans developed."

"So it's a kind of bow and arrow?"

"Similar."

"Does the crossbow work? Does it actually shoot arrows?"

"Yes, it works. But crossbows are different than longbows. Most of them don't shoot arrows. They shoot bolts, which are shorter and don't usually have fletching."

"Fletching?"

"Sorry," Josie said. "Those feathers on the tail end of arrows. They keep the arrow flying straight. Bolts are usually heavier like a spike. They're often made of metal. Even back in the Middle Ages, the bow and arrow was popular just like today. It's faster to load and shoot and easier to make. But the crossbow can produce a much higher drawing power and then hold it cocked until you pull the trigger."

"What's drawing power?"

"Instead of pulling back the string or cord with your arm muscles like you've seen on longbows, you draw the cord with a mechanical device. Mine uses a windlass, which is basically a crank gear with a ratchet."

"It sounds complicated."

"Compared to a longbow, yes. But it's still something a person can make. Although, we probably don't have time for that. But the reason I bring it up is to say that we're not helpless. We can make weapons like I did with the crossbow. We just need to scout out the various materials available to us. Based on that, we'll decide what to build. A crossbow takes quite a bit of time to make, so it probably wouldn't suit us here." As Josie said it, she felt overwhelmed. Creating a weapon for academic purposes, especially when one has all the resources of civilization, was one thing. But building a weapon out in the wilderness was hugely more difficult.

Samantha interrupted her thoughts. "You built that crossbow? I didn't know that," Samantha said. "Or maybe I did but I forgot."

"One of the classes I teach is called Medieval Weapons."

"I remember hearing that. It's real popular, right? I wonder why."

"Partly, students have a morbid fascination with medieval weapons. But partly, it's because of the marketing."

Samantha frowned. "I don't understand."

"A catchy phrase can sell anything. The class description says, 'What you don't know can vivisect you.' It's supposed to be a joke, but it's actually true. It's the most popular class in the department. Tom Silver, the dean of students, loves it because it gets kids interested in history. Kids who otherwise just think that history is boring."

"So you teach college students how to make medieval weapons?"

"Well, that's not the purpose. Talking about historical weapons gives me an opening to teach the history of the time. But in the process, yes, I give kids the basics about how to construct some medieval weapons."

"What kind of medieval weapons can we build on this island?" Samantha asked.

"I don't know. I've never felt under pressure like this. But we can scout the territory, looking at the trees and rocks and consider if any of them can be used to build a weapon. I'll think about the possibilities as I look around." Josie realized she didn't sound inclusive. "We'll think about it. We're severely limited by not having any tools."

"We have the ax," Samantha said, her voice a bit brighter. "Will that help?"

"That's right! But I stupidly left the ax where I hit the assassin."

"I can go get it."

"I'll come with you. We'll each take a Duluth pack in case we find useful material to carry back."

They got the two packs, emptied them, and headed off.

Josie knew that her presence made Samantha go more slowly. She tried to move as fast as possible.

Samantha shuddered as they revisited the scene. Both the ax and the spear were on the ground. There were lots of blood stains on the weapons and on the ground.

"Let's take the spear, too," Josie said. "For that matter, let's go see if we can get some more of those skinny dead trees out of the ground."

Samantha led them to the dead-tree area. They tested each of the trees, looking for the ones that could be moved most easily. Some wobbled back and forth easily. But none just flopped over like the one they had turned into the spear. Josie tried chopping at one with the ax. But the tree was so flexible that the ax just bounced off. She dropped the ax on the ground.

After five minutes of wrestling with the trees, Samantha had freed two, Josie had freed one. They each had found one more close to coming free. Josie used the ax to chop at the roots. She was careful to spread her legs wide, aware that she had no ax skills and the blade, though dull, was sharp enough to cause a severe injury to her feet.

Eventually, they had five small trees broken free.

"Before we carry them back, I want to load our packs," Josie said.

"With what?"

"Remember when we walked across that area that had all those large pebbles?"

Samantha nodded. "The smooth rocks we walked over, yeah."

"I want to bring a bunch of them back."

"What for?"

"Sling bullets."

"What's that?"

"I'll explain how they work when we get back and are working on these spears."

Samantha led them to the area of rocks. They looked for rocks that were approximately the size of a golf ball and loaded a few dozen in each pack.

The packs were very heavy, but they were able to carry them back along with their dead trees, the ax, and the bloodied spear they'd retrieved from where the man had dropped it when he cut it out of his side.

They worked at the picnic table. They began on the trees, sharpening the points and trimming the little branches with their camping knives. Josie showed Samantha how to always cut away from herself and keep the hand holding the tree back from the hand with the knife.

"I've been thinking about the amount of time it takes to make a weapon and get proficient with it," Josie said. "I think our priority is to shape these spears first. Second, I'll make a sling for our sling bullets. If we have time, we'll build a booby trap."

"You think this will work on an assassin with guns?"

"Guns are certainly the deadliest of weapons. But despite not having guns, we can still go on the offensive and wage war. A medieval war. He won't believe what hits him."

"How do sling bullets shoot?"

"It's actually one of the deadliest weapons ever, and it far predates the Middle Ages even though it was used a lot in medieval times. Did I ever tell you the story of David and Goliath?"

"No." Samantha was focused on the small tree in front of her, sawing with her knife, cutting all the little nubs of branches off the tree.

"It was originally a Biblical story that is now used more commonly as a secular story about the potential for an underdog to triumph against great odds. David was an ordinary Jew. Goliath was a giant Philistine. In a war between the Israelites and the Philistines, Goliath challenged his opponents to send any man out to fight him. He said they would decide the entire war based on this single combat if only the Jews had a man brave enough to fight the giant.

"Goliath wore massive armor, and everyone knew that he could not be defeated. But David was very brave, and he went out to represent a common man. He had no armor, and he was small. But he carried a sling and four rocks known as sling bullets. While Goliath postured and roared and taunted his adversary to attack, David used his sling to hurl a single rock. The rock went past Goliath's shield and armor, hit Goliath on the head, and killed him."

"The underdog won," Samantha said.

"Yes. The great part of the story is that it shows that smarts and guile and strategy can triumph over brawn and overwhelming odds."

"Are you saying that this assassin hunting us has the advantage of overwhelming odds?"

"By most measures, yes. He's huge and strong. He has a rifle and other guns. He's trained. He knows the territory. Two small women are hardly any contest against that."

"But we're like David," Samantha said.

"I hope so," Josie said.

"How do we make a sling?"

"We have the cord that Bill gave us. I think I can make one. I learned how to do some macrame back in college."

"How does it work?"

"It's actually very simple and yet super effective. Imagine having a rope with a little bag at the end. You put a rock into the bag. Think how fast you could swing that rope and bag around. If you hit someone with it, it would be devastating, right?"

"Totally," Samantha said.

"Now imagine that, at just the right moment, you could let the rock fly out of the sling. The stone would rocket through the air at high speed. If it hit someone, it would be much more powerful than a rock that someone threw like a baseball."

"Yeah. But how do you release it from the rope and bag?"

"It turns out to be easy. Instead of a rope with a bag at the end, you have a longer rope with a wide spot in the middle. If you fold the rope in half, you can put a rock in the wide spot, and you can swing it in a big arc."

"Sure," Samantha said. "It would be just like the rope with a bag at the end."

"Right. And if you let go of just one end of the folded rope, the end you let go would fly out, the pouch would open up, and the rock would fly free."

Samantha nodded understanding. "How do you control releasing one end of the rope?"

"It's pretty simple. One end of the rope has a loop. The loop goes over your middle finger so you don't let go of it. The other end has a tab that you grip between your thumb and index finger.

You swing your rope and sling bullet. At the right moment, you let go of your thumb-and-finger grip on the tab. That end flies out. The other end is held by the loop around your middle finger. The sling bullet flies away at high speed."

"How do you aim the rock?"

"Practice. There's no other way. You learn to do it by feel."

"Do you think you'll have time to practice before the killer comes back?"

"You will."

"Me?"

"You're good at volleyball, Samantha. You're athletic. You would be much better at this than me. I'll make a sling, and you can practice with it. Maybe I'll have time to make two slings. At first, I'm pretty sure you'll think the sling bullet goes anywhere and there's no way to control it. But with practice, it will start to make sense. I'm pretty sure that after an hour of practice, you'll be much better than you expect. Another aspect to the sling and sling bullets is that it doesn't even have to be very accurate to be effective."

"Why not? That doesn't make sense."

"Once the assassin sees good-sized rocks flying toward him at very high speed, it will make him cautious. He won't be as eager to run out into the open because he'll realize there's a decent chance that his head is going to be caved in by a sling bullet."

Samantha finished trimming the little branches on one of the trees. She set it next to the bloodied spear that had already penetrated the killer. "Spear two done."

Josie finished hers and added it to the group. "Spear three done."

While Samantha kept trimming branches, Josie took the coil of cord Bill had given her and cut several six-foot pieces off. She experimented with several knots in different places. She tried braiding pieces. Eventually, she used ten lengths of cord and developed a combination of knots and braided lines that resembled something closer to a strap than a rope.

"Spear four done," Samantha said. She added it to the pile.

Josie thought the focus on the task helped Samantha. Despite their dangerous predicament, Samantha seemed less stressed because of her focus on making weapons.

While Samantha began trimming branches off the next tree, Josie continued with her sling creation. In the middle of the strap, she widened it so that, when folded, it would act like a pouch that could hold a rock. At one end was a loop and at the other a large knot that would be easy to grip and just as easy to release.

She stood up. "Time to test." She folded her sling in half, slipping the loop over her middle finger. She picked up a rock and set it in the makeshift sling pouch. "I'll go over here and do an overhand throw so that no matter what happens, the sling bullet won't fly toward you."

Samantha stopped trimming branches and turned to watch.

Josie did some practice loops, swinging the sling and rock around in a slow circle. Then, moving even more slowly, she let go of the release end. The sling opened up, and the rock fell to the ground. Perfect. Function was established.

Josie heard Samantha make a noise. "If you laugh, girl," Josie said, "I'm going to ground you."

"You already grounded me for a week, forcing me into the wilderness that cut off my connection to everything I care about. How could you ground me even more?"

Josie had picked up the rock, put it back in the sling, and was swinging it again. This time, she swung it gently forward then let it stop and swing back down. She added power to the motion and brought the sling and bullet down and around and back up in a forceful loop as if swinging a tennis racquet in a serve. She tried to let go of the release end at the top of the arc. The rock flew out. But instead of arcing forward, it seemed to disappear. When Josie realized it had gone up and could possibly come down on top of her, she did a little quick-step dance of anxiety. Then she collected her thoughts and lifted her arms up over her head for protection.

The rock thudded onto the ground just ten feet from where she stood.

Samantha shrieked with laughter.

"Girl, didn't I ever teach you respect for your elders?"

Samantha was doubled over with giggles and couldn't respond.

"Okay, you're so smart, you try it," Josie said. She was grateful that her awkwardness with the sling had made Samantha laugh.

Samantha eventually stopped laughing. She stood up and walked over.

Josie handed her the sling and the rock. Josie said, "I'm going far away so I don't get killed by my wild daughter firing a deadly weapon." She walked over to the trees on the other side of the picnic table and stood behind them, peeking out.

Samantha put her middle finger in the sling loop and pinched the release end of the macrame strap with her thumb and index finger. Without putting the rock in the pouch, she swung the strap around in a vertical circle and then in a horizontal circle.

"Note my style, Mama," she said.

"Like the propeller on a plane."

Samantha put the rock in the sling. She focused on a boulder about ten yards away and made a few more practice loops. Then, with the strap swinging at a modest revolution speed, she let go of the release strap. The rock flew out and hit the boulder hard enough to send a chip flying into the air.

"Hey!" Josie said. "That was fantastic!"

TWELVE

"Beginner's luck," Samantha said. She put another rock in the sling and shot it out at a much higher speed. The rock flew directly over the boulder just inches above it.

"No luck at all," Josie said. "Obvious skill. It's like when you spike the volleyball. The projectile is a different size and type. But you know how to make that rock fly."

"Thanks, Mama. I think you're using professor speak to say I'm good at throwing stuff."

"Yes. I guess so. You keep practicing while I trim this last tree."

Samantha fired her sling bullets at multiple targets. Trees and rocks. Objects above her and objects below. Her accuracy was as hopscotch as that of a promising new ball player. She couldn't hit a small target with any reliability. But she could hit it some of the time and get close nearly every time. She used lots of rocks in practice. But there were still many left.

"You are amazing," Josie said.

"What next?" Samantha asked.

"I'm going to see if I can find materials to construct a ballista."

Samantha waited for the explanation.

"It's like a type of catapult. It requires the right pieces of wood. But if I can find them, it could be very effective. You could keep practicing with the sling. Or switch to the spears."

Samantha rubbed her shoulder. "This uses different muscles than in volleyball. I'm already sore. If I practice any more, I'll go backward, and I won't be able to throw again for a week. So put me to work helping you."

"Let's first carry the spears and sling bullets up to the castle. We'll stand our ground up there."

They carried their supplies and arrayed them so they could hide behind the tallest rocks and have everything within arm's distance.

"Now we'll look for a young sapling that is about twelve or fifteen feet long."

"What's a sapling?"

Josie shut her eyes for a moment as if to contemplate how she could raise a child who was a phone expert yet didn't know what a sapling was.

"A young tree," Josie said. "The nature of a sapling is that it is still somewhat bendy. Hence, people will describe a sapling as something that is flexible enough to survive a major storm."

"This would be something alive instead of dead like the spear trees."

"Yes. Exactly."

"So you'd use the ax to chop it down. We're going to kill a perfectly good tree."

"Right. To save our lives. A reasonable tradeoff, I think."

Samantha didn't give her opinion.

Josie picked up the ax, and they walked off.

"What kind of tree would this be?" Samantha asked.

"I don't think the kind is critical. What's critical is that when you bend it, it wants to snap back. It's that snap tension that we could exploit to make a ballista weapon."

There was a low-lying area near the shore that had a stand of aspen trees, their leaves golden with fall colors. Samantha walked over to them.

"Here's a bunch of small trees. I don't know if you'd call them saplings or not."

Josie looked at them. She grabbed at a few of them and pulled. "I think these are too stiff." Josie walked toward some smaller trees, reached among them, and wiggled one. "This one is close, but still too stiff. Too long, too."

"You could cut it shorter with the ax."

"I think it would take me an hour just to chop it. I might not be able to get through it."

"I could try," Samantha said. "Maybe I'd be as good with the ax as I am with the sling."

"Wait," Josie said. She'd moved over to the edge of a group of fir trees, looking under their branches. She bent lower and pushed into the trees and kicked at an old dead branch that was leaning against one of the tree trunks. "Sam, can you come help me, please?"

Samantha appeared.

"See this old branch with the bend in it? Help me pull it out."

"That doesn't look like a sapling."

"No. But it gives me another idea. If it works, we won't have to chop a sapling."

They both grabbed onto the piece of wood and dragged it out into the open. The wood was weathered and had no bark and no small branches. It had worn smooth a decade or two ago. It was about 8 feet long and had a 30-degree bend near the center.

"This chunk of wood grew totally crooked," Samantha said. "It must have had a tree fall on it when it was young and it stayed that way as it kept growing. It's nothing like the bendy sapling you were looking for. How could this work for what you wanted? What did you call it?"

"A ballista. This piece of wood wouldn't work for that at all."

"I don't get it," Samantha said.

"But this would work for an onager."

"What's that?"

"It's one of the siege weapons. The onager was powered by

torsion and was perfected by the Romans around the fourth or fifth century."

"But this is just a bent piece of old dried wood. How would it work?"

Josie was staring at the piece of wood, visualizing. "Help me haul this to the cabin and I'll show you."

"Why the cabin?"

"We can set up a booby trap. The guy walks into the cabin and bam, the onager hits him. Let's drag this wood to the cabin and figure out how to set it up."

They each took one end of the heavy branch.

"If we booby trap the cabin, we'd have to get the guy to go inside. How would we do that?" Samantha asked as they carried the wood.

"One way would be for us to stay hidden outside and watch. When we see him appear, you could call out something like, "Mama! The man is coming! You have to get out of the cabin! Hurry!"

Samantha looked at Josie. Her eyes were wide with surprise. "Mama, that is so sneaky! I never knew that about you!"

"It's just standard misdirection."

"No, it's not standard. It's like, we had the perfect hiding place out there in the woods last night. But you kept us from hiding in it because you knew he would see it and go there. This is devious!"

They hauled the bent wood into the cabin. Once inside, they set it down. Josie looked up at the rafters, studying the layout.

"You called it a siege weapon. What's that mean?" Samantha asked.

"You've heard the terms 'under siege' or 'laying siege.' Much of the time in the Middle Ages, when an army laid siege to a castle, they would simply surround it like a blockade and hold that position so that the men inside the castle would run out of food and water. But when medieval soldiers wanted to physically attack a fort or castle, they developed special machines, usually made of wood. There were lots of kinds. Catapults and ballistas and such. But they all used the principle of building up tension in a machine that would then suddenly release a projectile or a battering ram."

Josie realized that Samantha's face had become blank. "Okay, here's a better way to explain. You know how a mousetrap works."

"Of course," Samantha said.

"That's a miniature siege machine. The little spring is a torsion device. It has a trigger that is very sensitive. When the trigger is activated, the spring tension is released all at once."

Samantha eyes went wide. "We're going to make a giant mousetrap to catch a man!"

"Kind of. Better yet, we're going to make it throw fire."

"Really?" Samantha sounded doubtful.

"Yes." Josie walked around the cabin, looking at objects.

"What if Bill comes back when we're throwing fire?" Samantha asked.

"I hope he does. Then he can help save us from the killer."

Josie took the wooden chair that was over at the window where they'd climbed out the night before and dragged it over next to the second chair that was at the table. She turned both of them around so the chair backs were next to the table. The tops of the chair backs projected about ten inches above the tabletop. Over at the corner of the kitchen area was a counter and on it a pad of paper and a pencil. Josie picked up the pencil and brought it to the chair. She held the pencil across the top wooden bar of one of the chair backs, perpendicular to it as if to balance the pencil.

"This pencil will be what's called the lever for our weapon. Sam, could you take a length of your line and wrap it around the pencil and this wood bar?"

"Sure."

Josie held the pencil while Samantha wrapped line around it and the top rail of wood in both directions.

"This is just a demonstration, so you don't have to cut the line off your coil. You can just tie the line off with a bow for the time being."

When they were done, the pencil was held in place at the top of the chair rail.

Samantha wiggled the pencil. "It's kind of floppy, Mama. Not secure at all."

"Right. Just what we want. This line you used to tie the pencil to the chair is the torsion device. Now, we can twist the pencil so it's under tension. The twisting will stretch your wrapping line until it is very tight."

Samantha was watching very closely. It reminded Josie of her college students when she demonstrated medieval siege machines in class. It was one of the few times that they were so intrigued by what was about to happen that they looked away from their phones.

"We twist the pencil so that it's nearly vertical. It's under significant tension from the stretching of your line."

"The torsion wrapping line is like the spring on the mousetrap!" Samantha said.

"Exactly. Now we need a trigger to hold the lever in place."

"Is that like the little paddle on a mousetrap?"

"Yes, it is."

Samantha pointed to the pencil as Josie held it under tension. "If we propped a little stick between the table and this end of the pencil, you could let go and the pencil would stay in place. It would be our trigger, ready to explode anytime it was touched."

Josie nodded. "I'll hold this while you find a stick."

Samantha ran outside. She came back in a minute. "Here's a thin little stick that I can break to whatever length we need." While Josie still held the pencil in position, Samantha held the stick next to the chair so she could make a crude measurement.

Then she broke off a portion of the stick. She went to position it, but it was too long. She broke off another half inch, and moved it to position again. "I think this is the right length to be a trigger stick."

"Okay. Before you put it in position, take another piece of line and tie a loop in one end. Then put the loop over the trigger stick."

Samantha did that. "Now I put the trigger stick in position, right?"

Josie nodded.

Samantha held the little stick in place.

"Perfect," Josie said. "Hold it right there, and I'll gradually release my grip on the pencil.

Their movements were well coordinated, and as they removed their hands, the pieces all stayed in place.

"A pencil-type mousetrap!" Samantha said.

"Yes. An onager."

"So how does it work?"

Josie tore a small rectangle of paper off a pad and set it on the table near the vertical pencil. "This paper represents the cabin door." She picked up a paper pepper shaker, and set it on the table. "This is the man coming through the door. Now imagine that this trigger line runs to the door. As soon as the door opens a certain extent, the trigger line pulls the trigger stick away, and the pencil snaps back to its original position."

Samantha's attention was as focused as Josie had ever seen it.

"Another possibility is that we run the trigger line through the window to that group of bushes where we are hiding. We're holding the end of the trigger line. When we see the man walk into the cabin, we pull on the trigger line. The loop will slip off the end of the pencil, and the pencil will snap back to horizontal." Josie gestured toward the line. "You do it."

Samantha tugged on the trigger line. The trigger stick fell

away, and the pencil made a pronounced snapping motion. It
swung and hit the pepper shaker so hard, the shaker flew off the
table onto the floor.

"Whoa!" Sam said. "That was faster than you could see!" She
beamed, then frowned. "But how do we make this work on the
killer?"

"Come look." Josie walked over to the door of the cabin.
She pointed up to the cabin roof, which was made with big log
trusses, horizontal logs that spanned the width of the cabin, and
verticals that went up to the angled roof.

"See that horizontal beam?"

Samantha nodded.

"That's the top rail of the chair."

Samantha immediately understood and got excited. "Oh,
man, this is going to be so cool! That's where the pencil goes.
What did you call it?"

"The lever of the onager weapon. Ours is the big bent wood.
We'll hang it so the bend is over the log beam. Then we'll angle
the lever so one end points straight down and tie it in place. The
end that points straight down will be the impact end. After it's
secured, we'll tension it by pulling down on the other end of the
wood. We'll call that end the tension end."

"We pull on the tension end of the bent wood," Samantha
said.

"Yes. The farther we can pull the tension end of the wood
down and raise the impact end up, the more torsion there will
be, and the more powerful the lever end will be."

"Setting a mantrap is like setting a mousetrap."

"Right."

Samantha was looking up, visualizing. "Then we prop the
tensioned wood in place with a trigger stick. Only this time
we would need a big, strong trigger stick. I think it could go
from the tension end of the lever over to the next rafter. And the
trigger line could easily go from the trigger stick down to the

door or out the window."

"When we pull the trigger," Josie said, "the lever will flip back to the position where the impact end goes straight down."

"And that's where the man will be as he walks in the door!" Samantha was doing a little bounce on her toes.

Josie said, "First, we need some way to get up to that rafter beam. Let's pull one of the beds over near the door."

Josie pulled the thin little mattress pad off one of the top bunk beds and added it to the bottom bunk. They each grabbed an end of one of the bunk beds and dragged it beneath the big log beam.

"Now we'll put one of the chairs on the top bunk."

Samantha picked up one of the chairs and set it on the top bunk. Josie was amazed that Samantha could lift the chair up head high without a struggle.

Josie set the other chair next to the bed. She stood back to assess the situation.

"You will be in charge of this project," Josie said. "You'll be the captain, and I'll be your first mate."

Samantha grinned. "Okay, mate. Help me get the lever up to the beam."

The two of them set the bent wood on the top bunk. Samantha climbed up to stand next to it. Josie climbed up to stand on the chair. As Samantha lifted one end of the wood up to a vertical position, Josie tried to help boost it from below.

"Sorry, Mama, but that doesn't help me. You'll have to come up on the bunk bed next to me."

"I don't think I can do that. It's high, and the bed frame is rickety."

"A few hours ago, you attacked a killer with an ax, and now you're afraid of a bunk bed?"

Josie took several deep breaths. She let go of the wood, put her hands on the top bunk next to where Samantha stood. She lifted her knee up onto the bed, pushed down, then got her other knee up, so she was on all fours.

"You're shaking, Mama. This is no big deal. You can relax."

"Don't tell me to relax, Sam. This bed quivers. It could collapse with both of us on it."

"I don't think so, Mama. It probably can hold a really big guy on each bunk bed. I think you'll be okay. But you have to stand up to help me."

"I don't think I can do that. I'll fall."

"No you won't. I'll hold onto you. Here, take my hand."

Josie grabbed onto Samantha's hand. Her arm shook violently. She raised one knee, got her foot on the bed, then pushed up until both feet were on the bed.

"You're trembling, Mama. It's okay. You don't have to be afraid."

"I'm a professor, not a gymnast."

"And I'm the captain. So I need my first mate to stand up tall and help me get this siege weapon into place."

Josie straightened. Her tremors made the entire bed shake. Samantha was still holding the bent wood. Josie held onto it. It was like a support cane for a giant, and it helped stabilize her. After a minute she calmed.

"Okay, let's lift this into place," Josie said.

The two of them lifted the wood, got one end over the roof beam, then slid the bent wood until the bend was over the beam and the wood angled down on both sides.

Samantha said, "Now you have to hold this in place while I tie the wood to the beam."

"Yes, Cap'n," Josie said in a shaky voice.

Samantha got up on the upper chair. Her head was now above the rafter beam. She pulled her bundle of cord out of her pocket and started wrapping it around the intersection of bent wood and roof beam. "It should be tight, right?"

"Yes. The tight cord provides the torsion when we go to rotate the wood."

Samantha passed her cord round and round, pulling it at each revolution to make it snug.

Josie stood as still as possible, her arms above her head, hands holding the big bent wood. But she kept her head turned to the floor to help her keep her balance.

"I like being captain," Samantha said.

"Don't push it. Mother pulls rank on captain any day."

"That's all my cord," Samantha said as she came to the end of her line. "How should I tie it off?"

"I'm not sure. There must be some kind of knot that won't slip and loosen when we rotate the wood to tension it." Josie was tempted to look up as if that might give her an idea. But her fear kept her looking at the floor.

"I thought you knew about ancient knots."

"Actually, I know about several. The square knot, the half hitch, the thief knot, and the bowline go back over a thousand years. But I'm not a Girl Scout. I don't know how to tie them. I just know about them."

"There's a big sliver of wood that is partially split off from the roof beam. I could tie my cord around that. Do you think that would be good?"

"You're the captain. I'll go by your recommendation."

Josie still didn't look up. But she could feel the vibration of Samantha's movements.

"What's a thief knot?" Samantha asked as she worked.

"It's like a square knot but with one little difference. It's something very few people would notice. Legend has it that sailors would tie their duffel bags with a thief knot. They knew that any thief who poked around in their bag would be unlikely to notice that the knot wasn't exactly a square knot. So when they retied the sailor's bag, they'd likely use a square knot. If a sailor ever found their bag knotted with a square knot, they'd know that someone had gone through their belongings."

"Wow, you professors really do know some strange stuff."

"It's our job."

"Okay, this is tied off. But I don't think my cord wrapping is strong enough for this big piece of wood. When we pull on it, the cord might snap. It would be great if we had some stronger rope."

"I haven't seen any," Josie said. "Maybe you could add my cord to it."

"Okay." Samantha held out her hand.

"I think it's in the Duluth pack," Josie said. "Maybe you could get it."

"Because," Samantha said, "even though you're scared up here, you'd be more scared to climb down and back up."

"Something like that."

Samantha got down off her chair, sat on the edge of the bunk bed, and jumped to the floor. She rummaged around in their gear and found the other bundle of line.

"Hey," she said. "What if I cut the tumpline off the pack? That would be just about the right length to go around the beam."

"How long is it?" Josie asked.

"I think about thirty inches."

"It would have to be longer."

"How do you know?" Samantha asked. "I was the one wrapping the beam and wood lever together."

"The beam is about twelve inches in diameter. Probably fifteen if you add the thickness of the wood lever. Circumference is Pi times diameter. Pi is three point one four. So, rounding to three, we'd have fifteen times three, or forty-five inches."

Samantha seemed to think about it. "No wonder I couldn't do many wraps with my cord. What if I cut the tumpline off both of the packs? I could tie them together. And I could add your cord. That should be enough, eh, mate?"

"Perfect, Cap'n."

Samantha used her camping knife to cut the tumplines. She

tied the tumplines together, then carried them and the other bundle of cord back up onto the bunk.

"My arms are falling off," Josie said.

"You're not holding up the lever wood. You're just stabilizing it. It shouldn't be that much work."

"Just holding up my arms is that much work. You're a volleyball player. You have muscles."

"Yeah, well, they're sore from sling practice."

Samantha got Josie's cord and the tumpline wrapped around the lever-and-beam intersection and tied it off.

"There, I think you can let go. This onage… what?"

"Onager."

"It ain't goin' nowhere. And no, Mama, I ain't gonna talk like that for college."

Josie climbed down. She studied their contraption as Samantha applied more cord to the wrapping.

When Samantha climbed down from the upper bunk bed, she stood next to Josie.

"What do you think, mate?"

"I think the onager looks very capable. There's no doubt in my mind that the line you lashed around it will provide much resistance when we tension the wood by twisting it. Once released, that resistance will snap the impact end back down to its current vertical position. And once we tension the wood, your idea of where to put the trigger stick is good. The problem is how to tension the wood."

They both stared up at it.

"We'll have to pull down very hard on the tension end," Samantha said, "so the impact end rises up. Then the trigger stick will hold it in place. Why don't I go find a trigger stick while you figure it out?"

"Do you have an idea of the length it needs to be?"

"I'll measure with my arm." Samantha jumped up onto the lower chair, vaulted up onto the top bunk, then stepped up on the upper chair. She reached her arm out toward several points and seemed to use it like a yardstick.

As always, Josie was amazed to see Samantha's comfort with heights. She had no fear.

Samantha jumped back down and went outside.

Josie leaned back against the kitchen counter and studied their homemade onager. The large, bent wooden lever looked like a clock set to 11:30. They needed to pull down on the hour hand to get the minute hand to rise up.

Josie looked around at the cabin. When she noticed the Duluth packs that were now missing their tumplines, she got an idea about how to tension the onager.

Samantha came back in carrying four sticks.

"Four sticks, four different lengths. Once we get our badass weapon locked and loaded, I'll pick the stick that fits best."

"Locked and loaded?" Josie said. "Where do you get this lingo?"

"Basic captain speak," Samantha said with a little grin as if pleased to be terse and mysterious. "Any first-mate inspiration on how to load our weapon?"

"First, we need a lot of weight to pull down on the tension end of the wood. That will lower the tension end so you can fit your trigger stick in between the tension end and the rafter or ceiling boards, whichever you use."

"Right," Samantha said. "So how do we attach weight to the tension end, and what do we use for weight?"

"Look at these Duluth packs. Even though you cut off the tumplines, they still have the straps and buckles they use for closure. So we take one pack, turn it upside down, and hook the body of the pack over the tension end of the lever. Then we take the straps of that pack and thread them into the buckles of the other pack. That way the packs will be attached to each other. The lower pack will hang like a big scoop. We'll put weight in that. A Duluth pack can probably hold a lot of weight."

"What do we use for weight?"

"Me."

Samantha stared at Josie. Then she started laughing. "Mama, you don't weigh that much."

"I weigh one forty."

Samantha stared at her. "I thought professors were all about the truth."

"Maybe it's one fifty."

Samantha was still staring.

"Or one fifty-five."

"Hard to remember, huh?"

Josie ignored the comment. "Add in some rocks and logs or whatever, it could probably add up to two hundred pounds. I bet that would apply some decent tension."

"But the upper pack would be way up there. You'd be like a flying trapeze artist."

"No. We'll just shift the bunk bed a bit. The pack will be above the bed."

"But you were afraid to just stand on the bed. Sitting in a hammock swinging in the air would be a lot scarier."

"I've thought about it. I think I can do it. I have to do it."

"Okay."

They got the packs connected as Josie had described, and they hooked one over the tension end of the lever. They collected rocks that were light enough to carry into the cabin and up onto the chair and the upper bunk. Josie did her best to help. But Samantha was much stronger. She could pick up and carry rocks that Josie couldn't even lift.

In twenty minutes, they had the rocks loaded into the lower pack. The weight pulled down on the tension end of the lever, moving it from eleven o'clock on an imaginary clock to the ten o'clock position. As the lever rocked, the impact end raised up from six o'clock to five o'clock. With more rocks, the tension end of the lever had dropped to nine o'clock, and the impact end had raised to four o'clock.

"Okay, time for me to sit on that pack."

"Are you sure?" Samantha asked. "If the tension end of the lever drops much more, like, past eight o'clock, the pack will slip off. You'll fall, and the impact end will smack down and crush anything in its way."

"Some psycho is trying to kill us. I'll do whatever I can. I think the onager can be tensioned until the impact end is raised to three o'clock."

Samantha helped guide Josie as she climbed up yet again to the upper bunk. With much trepidation, Josie lowered herself, shaking, down into the open pack. In time, she was sitting on multiple rocks.

The pack lowered farther, and the tension end of the lever went down to eight o'clock, while the impact end rose to three o'clock.

"Okay, fit in the trigger," Josie said. "Make sure it's as well-placed as you can make it, because the weapon is aimed right at us."

THIRTEEN

Samantha took her four sticks and climbed up on the upper chair. Josie leaned her head back and watched as Samantha started with her shortest stick and tried placing it in different positions. Then she switched to a longer stick. Then longer still. That one spanned the required distance.

"Okay, Mama. I think our weapon is locked and loaded. The only problem is that when you stand up from the Duluth pack, you need to be real smooth and not make any sudden moves that would shake the trigger stick loose."

"I understand, and you should step to the side so you're out of the path of the impact end of the lever. If it should release, it will take our heads off."

"It could, Mama. It really could! I didn't realize how dangerous this could be!"

"Scholars think Hippocrates was the first to say, 'Desperate times call for desperate measures.'" Josie eased out of her sitting position on the Duluth pack and stood on the upper bunk bed. She stepped away from the path of their weapon.

"If you can, step over here and help me ease the Duluth packs off the tension end of the lever. But stay away from the impact end of the lever."

Together, they carefully lifted up on the packs, slipped them off the wood, and let them drop to the floor.

"The last thing we need is a trigger cord," Josie said.

"To tie to the trigger stick."

Josie nodded.

"We used all our cord."

"Oh, right. And it's too late to remove any of it." Josie climbed down from the bunk and looked around. "There must be something around here that we can use." She picked up one of the Duluth packs. There were a few errant threads at the seams. Several of the threads looked very strong. The ones that had been used to stitch the leather buckle straps were especially thick. But Josie couldn't tease them loose. She walked over to their clothes that they'd taken out of the packs before they collected the rocks. She went through them, shirts, underwear, pants, socks. The sock fabric had the loosest weave. But as she pulled at the threads, it was obvious that it would be very time-consuming to extract thread from them.

"Your sweater, Mama," Samantha said from up on the bunk where she still stood.

Josie glanced up at her, then back down at their piled clothing.

"It's not with the clothes. You're wearing it."

Josie looked down at herself. Of course. Her dark gray sweater, handknit by a colleague's mother. The knitting was very loose, which made for a floppy—and very comfortable—sweater. Josie took her knife and cut into the sweater hem. Then she pulled at some of the yarn. It came apart more easily than the sock fabric, but was still very difficult to unravel.

Josie pulled the sweater off. She turned it over, looking at the various patterns. The sweater was constructed of multiple kinds of knitting, and then the broader areas had been stitched together. Once again, Josie used her knife on the sweater, this time cutting the yarn that bound together the areas of different knitting styles.

That yarn unraveled well. It was still tedious work, but it was doable.

"Should I come down, Mama?" Samantha called from up on the bunk bed.

"This is going fast. Give me another two minutes." Josie found that the yarn unzipped the length of the seam, then stopped. If she cut another section, another piece would unzip. Once she understood the pattern, it went fast. Soon, she had several short pieces. She tied them together to make a long piece. Josie knew that yarn wasn't very strong, so she doubled her piece twice to make a cord comprised of four strings of yarn.

"I'm going to bring you this piece. You should be able to tie it around the trigger switch without knocking it free. The yarn is so light, it will hang down from the trigger stick. Then we'll tie more yarn to it after I unravel more of this sweater." Josie stepped up on the first chair. She leaned to the side so she was out of the line of fire from the impact end of the lever arm, then she handed it up to Samantha.

Josie got down off the chair, stepped back, and watched.

Samantha moved with surgical precision. Josie thought she was remarkably calm for a young kid. She was the opposite of Josie, who felt like she stressed about everything. It seemed as if the girl had trained to handle tense situations. Was that something that came from volleyball competition?

Samantha attached the yarn to a point near the end of the trigger stick. Then she carefully lowered the tail end. It hung down and dangled in the air about five feet above the cabin floor.

"Now let's get you down off the bunk bed without making any sudden movements. No jumping like before. I'm worried that even a slight vibration might set off this mantrap."

When Samantha reached the floor, Josie pointed to an area near the bunk bed. "This area is the path of the onager. So we should never step into this area because that weapon could go off when we don't expect it."

"Like a mousetrap," Samantha said. "Onager danger."

Josie nodded. "Exactly. Help me unravel some more yarn."

The two of them worked at the table. Cutting, unraveling, and tying short pieces of yarn together. When they had assembled a piece about thirty feet long, Josie said, "You can tie this to the other piece that's hanging from the trigger stick. Then we'll thread the yarn out the back window."

Samantha did as Josie said. She moved slowly, careful to not tug on the trigger yarn. Samantha was feeding it out the back window when she said, "You mentioned Hippocrates. Who was he?"

Josie was a little startled. It was the first time Samantha had ever asked her a question about a historical figure. "He was a Greek dude two thousand five hundred years ago," Josie said. "He's considered the father of Western Medicine. Even today, new doctors take the Hippocratic Oath, which outlines the obligations of physicians, such as 'First, do no harm.'"

"Greek dude?" Samantha said. "Ain't you a hip first mate."

"If you're just figuring that out now, Cap'n, you should pay more attention to whom you let onboard your ship."

"You mentioned fire. How would that work?"

"Like so many things, using fire as a weapon also comes from the Greeks. In the very old days, it was called Greek Fire, because the Greeks figured out how to focus fire with metal tubes on the prows of their ships. We won't do that. But we can still use fire." She turned toward the bunk beds. "Help me slide this bunk bed a little toward the door."

They both grabbed it and slid it about a foot and a half.

"This is our fire platform. Straight in the path of our weapon."

Samantha frowned.

"Remember how Bill showed us where he stores the kerosene can?"

Sam nodded.

"Let's go get it."

They walked outside. Samantha pulled the big red can from out of the locker where it was stored.

"We need to punch some holes in it," Josie said. "Have you

seen any nails anywhere?"

Sam shook her head. "No. But what about the ax? Could that cut a little hole in the kerosene can?"

"Even if we could swing the ax with a lot of control, it would probably cut a big hole."

"Then what about a spear. We could use the back of the ax to pound on a spear."

"Perfect!" Josie said. "You're a medieval weapon genius."

Samantha picked up one of the spears. "This one doesn't have the sharpest point." She switched it with a different one. "This one is better. Much better."

"Badass better?" Josie said.

"Yeah, Mama. Totally. I'll hold it, while you use the ax like a hammer. Where should we make the holes?"

"Let's put them on the side near the top. That way kerosene won't run out of the can if it isn't bumped. But if it is hit hard, the kerosene should spray out of the holes."

They set the kerosene can on a large flat rock and lay it on its side. Samantha held the can between her feet and set the spear on it. "Here?"

"Yes. Try to hold it so the back end of the spear doesn't wobble."

Josie raised the ax and gently lowered the back side of it and set it on the rear end of the spear, getting a sense of its position.

"Ready?"

"Yup," Samantha said.

Josie raised the ax and then let it drop. It contacted the spear with little force. The spear seemed to bounce off the metal can.

"Harder, Mama. This metal can is tough."

Josie hit the spear harder. Then harder still. The spear still bounced.

"You gotta whack it like you're trying to hit a home run, Mama!"

Josie hit the spear much harder.

The spear point jabbed through the metal an inch or more.

"Way to go, Mama!" Samantha lifted the spear. The can came with it, flopping to the side, kerosene dribbling out around the wooden point.

"The spear's stuck in the can," Samantha said.

"I'll hold the can," Josie said, "while you pull up on the spear."

Samantha jerked over and over. Finally, the spear pulled out of the can and more kerosene dribbled onto the rock.

"That's bad for the environment," Samantha said.

"I know. But hopefully, it will evaporate soon."

"Outfitter Bill would say that we sound like Californians, all bent out of shape about ecology or something."

"I think you're right, Sam. Bill would say that. But I'm guessing he agrees with us. He's just learned to be circumspect about his attitudes when he's around some people."

"Circumspect," Samantha muttered as she repositioned the spear on the can. "You want more holes, right?"

"Please. Eight or ten."

"Okay, hit it a little less hard."

Once again, it took Josie several tries to puncture the can. And, once again, the final blow resulted in the spear getting stuck in the can.

Eventually, they had perforated the can with several holes.

"Now what?" Samantha said.

"We set up our Greek Fire."

Josie carefully carried the can into the cabin and set it on the bunk bed, directly in the path of the onager weapon. She turned the can so the holes pointed toward the cabin door.

Samantha said, "When the mantrap fires, the impact end of the lever swings down and hits the kerosene can. Kerosene sprays out the holes. The guy gets soaked with kerosene. But where's the fire?"

Josie walked over to the kitchen counter where they'd left the kerosene lantern burning when they escaped from the cabin the night before. "We left this lantern burning, and it's now out of fuel. But this second lantern next to it is still full."

Josie found the matches and lit the second lantern. She turned the wick knob so that it was low. The lantern still burned well, but the low setting would provide the longest time before the fuel ran out.

Josie picked up that lantern and set it on the bunk in front of the perforated kerosene can. She backed up, looked at the impact lever poised in the rafters, stepped back to the lantern, and made a little adjustment.

Samantha was beaming. "When the mantrap goes off, the impact lever slams down, smashes the kerosene can and the lantern at the same time! That's what creates the fire!"

Josie nodded. "If that he gets hit by Greek Fire, he'll be fried."

Samantha said, "Fried?"

"I know. I better not talk like that at my tenure review."

"What do we do now?"

"We wait. Maybe a long time. If the kerosene lantern runs out, and we may have to replace it with the other one."

"Which is now empty," Samantha said.

"Oh," Josie said. "That was an error in judgment. It would be hard to pour fuel into it when the can is full of holes. Let's think about how to do that. In the meantime, I think we should grab some more clothes and bring them to the fort so we'll be warm. The other sleeping bag, too."

"I'll take the sleeping bag and the spears we used. The ax, too. I'll come back for clothes." Samantha left.

Josie was stuffing clothes into one of the Duluth packs when she heard a scream.

She dropped the pack and looked up to see the assassin in the doorway. He had a gun in one hand and he held Samantha over his other shoulder.

FOURTEEN

It was the huge man they'd seen in the airport. He looked just as hard and menacing as before but with his hand bandaged and an abdomen-wrapping bandage showing at the open zipper of his sweatshirt. Samantha thrashed up on his shoulder, but the man seemed unaware, except that her thrashing made it so he couldn't easily come through the cabin door.

"Please," Josie said, pleading. "Let my daughter go. You can take me. I'll give you whatever you want. Do you want money? I'll come with you to a bank."

The man spoke in a deep rough voice. "What I want is payback for how you hurt me out in the woods. So I'm gonna bring this little honey inside and shut the cabin door so the mess is contained and no one hears the gunshots and screams."

He pushed in through the opening. Samantha's legs and feet caught on the door frame as she kicked.

"OUCH!" he screamed. "You bit my neck you little bitch!" He gave Samantha a toss. She landed with a hard thump on the cabin floor by the kitchen table. The man walked in the door, turned to shut it behind him, and looked at the kerosene can and lantern on the bunk bed.

He frowned.

Josie pulled the trigger yarn.

FIFTEEN

The impact end of the onager weapon moved so fast it was a blur. The wood snapped down, smashing into the perforated kerosene can and breaking the lantern before it slammed into the man's face. The man's head bounced sideways as if he'd been hit by a heavyweight boxer. There was an explosion of fire. Greek Fire.

The man screamed as flames engulfed his upper body and head. He felt for the cabin door, moving his hands like he was blind. He found the handle, threw the door open, and ran out.

Josie ran to Samantha. "Sam, baby, are you okay?" Josie knelt down on the floor and hugged her daughter.

"I'm okay, Mama," Samantha said through her tears. She looked up and out the open door. "The onager worked. We kicked his ass."

"Yes we did," Josie said, crying, hugging Samantha's head. "Yes we did."

Flames were crawling across the cabin floor and up the wall. Josie grabbed their pot of water and threw it at the flames. Most went out. She picked up some clothes and started beating at the few remaining flames and rubbing the spilled water over the surfaces. In the process, she swept most of the broken lantern pieces to the side.

"Will the cabin burn up?" Samantha asked as she helped Josie put out the flames.

"No. It's not easy to light solid wood logs on fire. The man was a perfect fire target because most of the kerosene landed on his absorbent clothes. Now we have everything else put out."

Samantha pushed up, looked out the door. "Oh, my God, he's still burning. His hair is on fire. He must have fallen. Now he's running again. To the lake. He's diving into the water to put out the fire."

"Which means he's still alive," Josie said, her disappointment clear. She stood up next to Samantha and looked out at the man thrashing in the water. "He was going to kill us. Kill you. I want him dead."

"Maybe that will happen, Mama."

"Can you see if he still has his gun?'

"I don't see it. He's not holding it. But maybe it's in a pocket or a holster that we didn't see."

Josie looked around the cabin. "Here it is in the corner."

Sam bent toward it and reached out her arm.

"No, Sam, don't touch it. If you aren't a gun expert, you shouldn't even pick one up. Plus, you don't ever want your fingerprints on a gun."

"What if he comes back for it?"

"I'll use my foot to slide it under the other bunk bed. With his vision damaged, it will be hard for him to find it."

Samantha made a sudden inhalation. "We can escape now, Mama! We can find his canoe and get away!"

"Do you see his canoe?"

"No."

"Which way did he come from when he grabbed you?"

"I don't know. He grabbed me from behind."

"Where were you when it happened?"

Samantha walked out of the cabin. "About here. No… Here. I remember because I was about to pick up the ax as he lifted me off my feet. There's the ax."

Josie looked around. "There's no major obstructions in the landscape. So the man might have run from anyplace, trying to quickly grab you. Think about that moment. Did you have a sense of someone breathing from behind you? Or footsteps?

That could indicate where he ran from."

Samantha shook her head. "I don't know!" She was frantic. "We just have to run!"

Josie looked down toward the man. He kept putting his head underwater, then lifting out to breathe, then putting it under again. As if he couldn't get enough cold on his burns.

"Okay, let's imagine what he would have done as he paddled toward this island," Josie said.

"I don't care, Mama! We have to get out of here! Maybe we'll find the canoe when we run. Maybe we can beat him to it."

"We have to take some of our weapons."

Samantha sounded panicked. "You think he can still catch us? Even though he's burned and maybe blind?"

"You never know. You run and collect our spears and the sling. I'll bring one of the packs up to the fort and load up some of the sling bullets."

Samantha glanced again at the man down by the water. "Mama, he's walking along the shore."

Josie turned to look. "Is he holding his arms out?"

"Yeah. Zombie style. Like he's blind. Or mostly blind."

"I bet he's walking toward where he left his canoe."

"So we're going to be trapped all over again?" Samantha sounded devastated.

"Maybe not. We can find his canoe by following him. Then we take it away from him."

"What?! How will we do that?"

"He's severely wounded," Josie said. "We aren't. And we have weapons."

"You're right! Let's hurry!"

Josie grabbed a pack and trotted at her fastest speed up to the castle fort. She kept turning to check on the man as she loaded sling bullets into the pack. She quit before the pack was too heavy to carry any distance.

When she got back to the cabin, Samantha had gathered the

spears, the sling, the knives, and the ax. "Your pack is too heavy," she said. "Let's transfer some of those sling bullets to this one."

When the packs were more even, they each put them on. Josie carried the ax over one shoulder and carried a spear in her other hand. Samantha carried a spear in each hand. She also had the sling in one pocket and a few rocks in her other pockets.

They hiked down toward the water. The man was just approaching the forest where it met the shore. He still had his arms out, clearly unable to see well. Periodically, he waded into the water and dipped his face under the surface.

Samantha whispered as they got close. "How are we going to take his canoe away from him?"

"We'll just tell him we're taking his canoe. If he resists, we attack him until he's completely disabled."

"How do we attack?"

"Spears and ax and sling bullets."

"Do you think we can attack a man like that?"

"We already did. Twice."

Samantha nodded. "Good point."

They followed the killer along the shore. As he entered an area thick with trees, they lost sight of him.

"We better have spears ready," Josie said in a whisper. "He could surprise us still."

"What about the sling?" Samantha spoke in a whisper that was louder than her normal voice.

Josie held her finger to her lips and spoke even more softly. "You can't use a sling in close quarters. If we grapple with him in the trees, the sling would not work at all."

Samantha used a quieter whisper. "What if I don't release the sling bullet? What if I just use it like rope with a rock at the end. I could swing that without much room."

"Yes, Sam! A rock on a rope is a terrific weapon up close."

Sam pulled out both the sling and a rock. She fitted the rock into the center part of the sling and folded the sling in half. Then she backed her hand along the sling and swung it in a circle to test it.

"When I choke up on the sling, it's kind of like a club. I can use it up close."

They walked on.

They heard a noise and stopped.

SIXTEEN

"Damn it!" the man shouted. It sounded like he was in the trees about 25 yards away. There was some thrashing noise like branches breaking.

Josie whispered. "Hurry! We can't let him put his canoe in the water. Even if he didn't get in it, it could float away."

They rushed through the trees, branches pulling at their clothes. They went through a dense thicket. Then the woods thinned. Through the trees they could see the man wrestling with an aluminum canoe just like the one they came in. He was trying to pull it through trees but it was caught and he apparently couldn't see how. His face and neck and arms were bright red with burns.

Josie and Samantha came into a clearing. The man was just ten yards away. Josie whispered very softly in Samantha's ear. "Get ready to use your sling as a sling."

When they were in the clearing, Josie called out. "Drop the canoe. We're taking it."

"Go to hell. I'm going to shoot you in a way that you'll stay alive while I cut you into pieces."

"Last chance," Josie said.

The man reached down into the canoe and pulled out a rifle.

Josie pushed at Samantha and whispered. "Run that way and hide where you can use your sling."

Josie ran the opposite direction. The man made a noise with his rifle. Josie couldn't identify it. Maybe he was cocking it or loading bullets. She didn't know how rifles worked. The man raised it and fired toward them. The noise was loud and terrifying. But it seemed that the man couldn't really see them and was going by sound. If they stayed quiet, they'd have a chance.

In Josie's peripheral vision, she saw Samantha stand up and swing her sling. A rock flew, too fast for Josie to track. It hit the aluminum canoe in an explosion of ringing sound.

The man jerked with surprise. He fired his rifle again. Clearly, he had no idea of where Samantha was or what had made such a loud noise on his canoe.

Another rock flew. It hit a tree next to the man's head.

The man spun, trying to understand. His motions made noise, and his body hit tree branches.

Josie used the cover of his sounds to run through the trees toward him.

A third rock flew past the man. It hit nothing. But the whistle of its passage through the air was loud enough that the man turned his head. He fired his rifle again. Turned. Fired a fourth time.

Samantha's next rock hit the man on his chest. The blow was so hard that the man blew out air. He put his hand to his chest as he doubled over and sank to the ground. He set his rifle on the ground, leaning on it.

Josie got within ten feet of him. She threw her spear. It was a weak throw. It arced toward the ground. But its point struck the side of the man's knee. It didn't penetrate very far. But he howled in pain. He jerked his leg to the side. The spear point came out of his leg, and the spear fell to the ground. The man reached for his knee, yelling in agony.

Josie stepped closer. The man's face was red, his skin covered in oozing blisters. His hair was singed, his nose was blackened, and his eyes looked very strange as if the heat had melted them into a brown goop.

"Tell me why you are trying to kill us," she said.

"To hell with you."

"Tell me, or I'll put the next spear through your heart."

He was breathing hard. He seemed about to talk when Samantha ran up.

"Good job, Sam!" Josie said, still whispering. "You are a one-woman army."

"You two are going to die," the man hissed.

Josie picked up a nearby chunk of wood that was old. Its bark had been weathered off, and it was very hard. Even though they were some distance from the water, it looked like driftwood. She swung it at the man's head. It struck the man on the left rear side of his head, just behind his ear.

He fell over unconscious.

SEVENTEEN

Josie reached to pick up the man's rifle. It was incredibly heavy. Because she was worried about prints—whether leaving hers or smudging his— she didn't let her palms or fingertips touch the metal, instead scooping up the rifle with the edges of both hands, keeping them away from the trigger, and carried it so the barrel pointed toward the ground. She went over to the lake, walked out on some rocks, and tried to throw the rifle into the water.

It only went three feet before splashing in. But it sunk to the bottom, which was maybe two feet deep. It would be easy for the man to find it if he regained his vision. Impossible if not.

She went back to Samantha and hugged her. "You did great. Just great."

Samantha looked from her sling to the man as if she couldn't believe what had happened. "I never thought I could aim a rock like that. But I also never thought of what you just did, simply picking up a branch and using it like a club."

"A club is great, but you can't always find one. But if you commit this one medieval trick to memory, it could possibly save your life some day."

"What's that?" Samantha was staring at the unconscious killer. He seemed to occupy all of her attention.

"It's like the rock on a rope. Only it's a rhyme," Josie said. "A rock in a sock. Anytime you need a deadly weapon and you think you don't have one, just pull off your sock and put some small, heavy item in it. When you swing a rock in a sock, it is the equal of any club."

Samantha was still focused on the man.

But Josie noticed her mouthing the words. 'Rock in a sock.'

Samantha pulled out her phone, leaned close to the unconscious man, and took his picture.

Josie bent down and, moving very gingerly, reached out to feel if the man had anything in his pockets. There was something hard in his right front pocket. Cringing, she reached inside it. She pulled out the small flashlight he'd used before and a large pocket knife. She put them in her pockets.

"Help me roll him over so we can check his back pockets."

Samantha kneeled on the ground next to the man. He was very heavy, but they got him rolled onto his stomach.

Josie checked his back pockets. "There's nothing here. He doesn't even have an ID."

"That's like in the movies," Samantha said. "The assassin never carries any identification, so he can't be traced."

"Where would he leave it?"

"Hidden with his car keys and spare gun and a burner phone."

Josie stared at her daughter.

"And in the movies," Samantha continued, "when the innocent victim wounds the bad guy, she never finishes the job."

"You mean she doesn't kill him?"

"Right. And the audience squirms because they know that if the bad guy isn't dead, eventually he's gonna come and hurt the victim even worse than before."

"You're saying we shouldn't leave this man alive," Josie said.

"Right. He'll find us, Mama. Just like when we already hurt him bad, and he came back to kill us."

Josie looked down at the prostrate man, all muscle and sinew and evil. "It's hard to kill a man. We would have to strike his head with a rock. Probably many times."

"Or we could spear him through his heart," Samantha said.

"Or use our camping knives."

"Maybe we should. But I couldn't bring myself to do that. And even if I could, it would change our situation from self defense to murder."

Samantha looked at the canoe. "If we paddle away, what will happen?"

"We'll get to the outfitter's, find Bill, and tell him everything that happened. He'll call the police, and we'll tell them, too. They'll come out here and bring this guy in. They'll charge him with attempted murder, and he'll go to jail."

"What if he's not here when they come?"

Josie looked around. "We could tie him to a tree."

"With what? We used up all our line. I don't think we should take the time to go back and take apart the onager weapon just to get the line."

"I agree," Josie said. "Let me ask you. Maybe it's a hypothetical question or maybe not. Could you kill an unconscious man? This man? Right now? Crush his head in with a rock or stab him until he's dead?"

Sam stared at the man, and her eyes filled with tears. "It's not right. He's, like, totally evil, right? He shouldn't be allowed to live. I don't care about laws and trials and innocent until proven guilty. He was going to kill us. He shot at us in the cabin last night. And just now out here. It was obvious he wanted to kill us when we hid in the woods. He should die."

Samantha stepped back and looked out at the lake. It broke Josie's heart to see her daughter in such a situation.

Samantha continued. "But no, I couldn't just kill him now. Not while he's lying there unconscious."

Josie hugged her again. "I'm sorry, Sam. I'm so sorry. Let's get in the canoe and get out of here."

They dragged the canoe to the water. They took off their packs with the sling bullets and set them in the center of the canoe. Samantha brought over two of the spears and the ax.

There was one paddle on the floor of the canoe. A second was inserted between the bow seat and the thwart behind it, just as Bill had shown them.

Once the bow was in the water, Sam climbed in, crawled to the bow seat, and sat down.

"Wait here," Josie said. "I just thought of something." She went back to the unconscious man and began untying his boots. He'd double-knotted them, so it took time to undo. They were very hard to pull off because the man's legs were heavy. Eventually, Josie got the boots off, carried them back, and tossed them in the canoe.

"Wow, Mama, that is so smart. He won't be able to run at all."

Josie pushed the canoe a bit farther so it was off the rocks, then she climbed in. She forgot how tippy it was. Samantha inhaled as the canoe rocked. When Josie sat down on the stern seat, the canoe steadied. They started paddling away from the island, leaving the burned killer where he lay in the trees.

They didn't speak. Samantha paddled hard. Josie matched her pace. Josie's arms ached.

As they approached the first portage, Samantha said, "Do you think he'll die from his burns?"

"I don't know, Sam. His burns were serious. His skin was blistered and peeling. His nose was black. The edges of the burn area were curled like the skin was peeling off. But I have no idea if the burns are deadly or not. It might depend on whether they get him to a hospital and give him skin grafts before he gets infected."

"What do you think will happen to his vision from the burn?"

"I don't know that, either. When something splashes in your eyes, even burning kerosene, your automatic reaction is to shut your eyes. That protects them. But he acted like he couldn't see. So obviously, there's some major damage. Maybe his eyelids were burning and couldn't protect his eyes enough. And your rock against his chest was major, too. It may have broken his sternum. My club easily knocked him out. Maybe the total combination of injuries will kill him."

"You say maybe," Samantha said. "Like you mean, maybe not, too."

"Right. I want him dead. But I'd guess that if he can get himself to a hospital, he'll live."

"He doesn't have a canoe even if he becomes conscious."

Josie looked down at the canoe they were paddling. "I'm pretty sure this isn't the one we came over in."

"No." Sam stopped paddling for a moment. She touched the place where her seat was riveted to the edge of the canoe. "There's some short hair stuck in this crack. I'm sure it wasn't there when we came here yesterday. This is a different canoe."

"Then that means our canoe is somewhere. Maybe he pushed it into the lake and it drifted for a mile. Or maybe he hid our canoe in the woods of the island."

"If so, he could find our canoe and paddle away. He could still come after us!"

Samantha stopped paddling and looked behind them.

"That could be, Sam. But his eyes would have to get a lot better for him to see us. Maybe that's possible with a burn. Like inflammation that gets less in a short time? I don't know."

"We should paddle fast, Mama. Fast as possible!"

"Do you remember where the portage is?"

"No!" Sam was shaking her head. "It was on the map. But I don't remember. We just went where Bill said." They paddled for a minute. "And no, we didn't learn the territory. I get that. Where's that map now?"

"I think it might be on the counter in the cabin. Let's study the landscape. You must remember something. Some landmark."

Samantha looked around at the lake and the surrounding forest. "I remember that the portage was in a kind of valley.

What's that called? A ravine. Like maybe a creek flows there in the spring. So that would mean the portage couldn't be at one of those higher hills."

"I agree," Josie said.

"So we should look for low places along the lakeshore. Look over there. That looks like a valley. A stream could flow into the lake. Or out."

Josie pointed even as she realized that Samantha, sitting in front, wouldn't see her. "I think we came from around that point. More to the right."

"You might be right. Let's head there!"

They paddled with urgency. Josie felt her palms developing blisters. She was using all the same muscles and wearing down all the same places on her skin as when they paddled the day before.

In ten minutes, they approached the shore where the land dipped down.

"That's the portage, Mama! I remember those rocks."

Josie steered over to the rocks. She used her paddle to slow the canoe.

As the bow touched the rocks, Samantha jumped out, turned around, and pulled the bow up onto the rocks. Bending over and holding onto the edges of the canoe, Josie walked her way forward. She stepped out at the bow.

"Now what, Mama?"

"We have to carry this canoe across the portage. Paddle across the next lake, then cross another portage."

"But neither of us could carry the canoe."

"We have no choice. Remember how Bill showed us. We both lift up on the bow."

Samantha looked at the baggage that was still in the canoe. "But we have the packs, too."

"They're heavy. Let's figure out how to lighten them. Sling bullets aren't as important as actually making it across this portage."

They pulled the packs out of the canoe.

"These are so heavy," Josie said. "If we want to have any chance of making it back to the outfitter's on Bear Trap Lake, we should just leave them here. Bill can pick them up when he next comes through."

Samantha looked at the sling bullets and the ax and the spears. "We can't be defenseless."

"Put your sling and a few sling bullets in your pocket. And we'll each carry a spear. But if we don't get rid of the packs, we might not even make it across this portage."

"Okay."

They set the packs off to the side of the trail where they'd be obvious to Bill.

"The assassin's boots are also really heavy," Josie said, glancing at the rear of the canoe where she'd put the boots. "We should throw them in the woods." She looked at Samantha. "But I'm no good at throwing."

Samantha picked them up one at a time and hurled them into the woods.

Samantha asked, "What about the paddles? They're heavy. Whichever person isn't carrying the canoe should carry the paddles."

"But Bill said the paddles have to go under the thwart. I'm not sure why. I think the canoe doesn't balance unless that weight is toward the front."

"Oh, yeah, now I remember. Plus, it gives you something to hang onto," Samantha said. "I remember how Bill pulled down on the paddles so the canoe would be level."

Josie did a little stretch, twisting left and right and leaning side-to-side like a dancer warming up. "Okay, help me get this boat up on my shoulders."

They each grabbed the bow of the canoe and lifted it up. The stern of the canoe was still on the ground.

"Now we turn it over so the bottom faces the sky," Josie said. They wrestled it into an upside-down position. "The stern point is supposed to stay on the ground. Lift higher. Okay, you hold it up. Careful. It wants to fall to one side or the other. I'll walk underneath and stand with my shoulders under the yoke pads." Josie hurried to the center of the canoe, her head up inside it.

"This is really heavy!" Samantha said.

"Okay, lower it down."

Samantha started to lower it, but lost control. The pads slammed onto Josie's shoulders.

Josie wavered.

"I'm sorry, Mama! Are you okay?"

"Yes. Help me pull down on the end to lower the bow and lift the stern off the ground."

The canoe leveled out, balanced with the yoke pads on Josie's shoulders.

"You're not kidding," Josie said as she began walking forward. "This thing is really heavy."

Josie placed her footsteps thoughtfully, careful not to twist an ankle. Although her head was up inside the overturned canoe, she could see the trail, and she followed it.

She'd only gone a short distance when her shoulders began to ache.

"Okay, time to switch," she called out.

"What do I do?" Samantha asked.

"I'll lower the stern end until it touches the ground. You stand underneath the bow and hold it up like before. I'll come and take your place. Then you get under the yoke pads and carry it."

Samantha did as told. They switched positions.

As Josie held up the bow of the canoe, she thought her arms would collapse.

"Hurry! I'm going to drop this!"

Samantha just got the yoke pads on her shoulders when Josie

let the canoe down.

"All yours, Cap'n. You're the canoe warrior now."

Samantha had moved barely farther than Josie had, when she too called for relief.

"But you're young and strong," Josie said.

"And I'm not much heavier than this thing. If you carried the same amount relative to your weight, you couldn't do it."

"That's not fair, girl. I'm your elder. You should respect me."

They made the switch, and Josie once again carried the canoe.

"I'll respect you if you take this ship to the next ocean."

Josie called. "It's about the weight of a ship, I'll give you that." Her voice boomed from having her head under the canoe.

"Okay, switch!" Josie sounded panicked.

Samantha held up the bow. "We have to rest, Mama."

Josie came out from under the canoe and held up the bow. "You only have to carry this a little farther until we can rest. I see a board on that tree down the trail. If you carry it to the tree, we can rest the bow of the canoe on the board."

Samantha got under the yoke pads, took the canoe, and carried it down the trail.

"Coming up," Josie said. "Okay, stop here."

Samantha stopped. She raised the bow, which lowered the stern. Josie stood underneath it and took hold of the thwart like before. Her arms shook.

"Come help me hold this up. See that board sticking out from the tree?"

"Yeah."

"Let's get the bow of the canoe on it. It should balance there while we rest."

They struggled, lifting and even dragging the canoe a couple of feet. They were just tall enough to get the bow up on the board that was attached to the tree.

"Now that it's balanced, don't bump this thing," Josie said as they stepped away. "If this boat falls to the ground, we may never get it up on our shoulders again."

They walked away and sat down on a fallen log to rest.

Samantha looked at the board they'd rested the canoe on. "Look, Mama. See how that board is braced? And there's no hook or anything for hanging something else. I think somebody built that just for resting canoes. What do you think?"

"I think you're right. Not everyone who comes through here is a macho Navy SEAL. Even out-of-shape women go canoeing. I bet there are canoe rests on lots of portages."

"Speak for yourself," Samantha said.

"About what?"

"I'm not out of shape. I'm just small."

"Taller than me, Cap'n. Most captains can handle their ship, no matter the headwinds they face."

"I don't know about headwinds. But the job of first mates is to do the heavy lifting. Anchors. And kegs of beer. Bags of brats to barbecue."

Josie turned and frowned at Samantha. "What do you know about kegs of beer?"

Samantha didn't immediately reply. "It's just something I heard about on TV."

"Sure. I knew that," Josie said. "I'm going to believe that."

"You should." Samantha looked back down the portage toward where they'd come from. "We should get going."

"You're worried."

"Of course. There's a psycho out there who's coming after us."

"He's burnt and wounded and unconscious."

Samantha shook her head. "He was unconscious. That probably just helped him rest. Like a nap. He's probably up now. Doing jumping jacks and push-ups. Revving himself up for, you know, the final hunt."

Josie knew that Samantha was joking, but she saw tears in

Samantha's eyes.

"That image doesn't help," Josie said. "Okay, let's go." Josie used her arms to help push herself to her feet.

They repeated their earlier routine. Josie carried the canoe as far as she could. Then they switched to Samantha. Over and over. Each time, the distance they could carry it got shorter.

Eventually, they got to the next lake.

"Am I wrong," Samantha said, "or was that portage three times as long as when we came over it yesterday?"

"Four times as long," Josie said.

"Yesterday it wasn't so bad because Bill did most of the carrying," Samantha said. She turned around and glanced at Josie. "What was the name of this lake?"

"I think it was called Lac Le Grande. The customs' station was on this lake."

They got into the canoe and began paddling.

Josie looked at her, proud of how her daughter had faced the worst that a person can face—imminent death by a deranged killer—and still maintained her attitude. But as Josie studied her daughter's face, Samantha turned her head farther, a sudden jerk. She stared at the shore where they'd just gotten into the canoe.

"What?" Josie said, fear in her voice.

"I just thought…" Samantha focused toward the distance behind Josie. "I just thought I saw movement in the trees."

"What kind of movement?"

"I don't know, Mama. Just movement."

"A bird flying? A deer browsing? A broken branch falling out of a tree?" Josie realized too late that she sounded very tense. It was the opposite of what she should do with a daughter who's just been stalked by a killer. She felt she should communicate a sense of calm, a feeling that things will work out okay. But maybe that was misguided. She remembered what Shakespeare wrote in Hamlet, that the best safety lies in fear.

Josie turned and looked back at where they'd gotten into

their canoe. She saw nothing.

"This is the lake with the customs station," Josie said. "Yesterday, it was unstaffed. But maybe someone is there today. They could help us."

Samantha made a small nod. She resumed paddling without saying anything.

They paddled for twenty minutes.

"Shouldn't we have come to the customs station by now?" Samantha asked.

"I didn't want to say anything, yet. But, yes, I thought that too."

"Do you think we went the wrong way?"

"I don't know, Sam. It seems like... Wait, look up ahead on the left."

"Oh, of course," Samantha said. "That's the log cabin. Safety at last."

They slowed as they approached the dock.

"I can't believe we were here just yesterday," Samantha said.

"It seems like we've been through a week of terror."

Josie used her paddle to steer alongside the dock. "Run up to the cabin and see if someone's there. I'll keep our position at the dock."

Samantha jumped out, ran up to the cabin door. She tried the handle. She looked at the notice that was still on the door from the previous day. Then she went over to the window, cupped her hands around her face, and peered inside.

She ran back to the dock. "Same as yesterday. No one is there. How can they protect our borders if no one is there?"

Josie looked around at the lake. "It doesn't seem like many people are trying to sneak across our borders in this area."

"Why?" Samantha asked. "Down by San Diego and El Paso and all the desert in between there's a lot of people coming across."

"Maybe it's because this is an ice-cold forest wilderness. The only people who have access to this place are Canadians who'd just as soon stay in their own country."

"And they want to stay away from psycho killers," Samantha said. "Should we leave a note for the customs' person?"

"I think that might be a good idea. But we don't have paper or pen or a way to attach it to the door where it will be seen. And the customs' agent might not be back until next spring. So you should get back in the canoe, and we'll paddle to the next portage."

"Do you remember where it is?"

"No," Josie said. "But it's marked on the map."

"Which is on the counter in the cabin."

"Oh, right."

Samantha got back in the bow. They backed away from the dock, turned, and began paddling forward. She scanned the horizon as she paddled. "Over there, a little to the left, is a kind of dip."

"Eleven o'clock?" Josie said.

Samantha paused. "Like we're at the center of a clock? So six o'clock would be directly behind us. Three o'clock is to our right. Nine to our left?"

"Yes. It's a good navigation aid."

"Then, yes, I'm looking at that dip in the land at eleven o'clock."

"Eleven, it is." Josie made an adjustment in her paddling and turned the bow.

Fifteen minutes later they approached the shore.

"This is it!" Samantha exclaimed. "This is the portage that will take us to Bear Trap Lake!"

"With no help from the GPS robot," Josie said.

"We're learning the territory."

"Better yet," Josie said, "we're learning to read the landscape."

They got out of the canoe.

"Do you remember, is this portage shorter or longer than the last?"

"I think it's a little bit shorter."

"Good! Let's go."

They repeated their routine, lifting the bow, and holding it so one of them could get under the yoke pads to carry the canoe. After a relatively short distance, they switched, and the next person carried the canoe. Four exchanges later, they came to Bear Trap Lake. Josie felt like she'd never again be able to carry anything on her shoulders.

When they got into the canoe and were pulling away, Samantha once again looked back at the forest they'd just come through.

"Do you hear something?" Josie asked.

"I don't know. One part of my brain is saying yes. The other part is saying that I should ignore it. That I'm hypersensitive."

Josie said, "Sam, I want you to be hypersensitive. I value any hypersensitive perception you have."

Samantha made a small nod, turned forward, and began paddling hard.

The wind came up, turning the water dark and angry. The waves splashed hard against the bow, coming in at an angle from the right. Josie tried to adjust her paddle strokes to keep the canoe from turning. It was hard work. It seemed at times like the canoe wasn't moving forward at all, that all their efforts succeeded at doing was to keep the canoe in place while the wind and waves battered them back. Or maybe the wind really was pushing them back toward the shore from which they'd come. It seemed a Sisyphean task, to paddle with no progress beyond slowing their retreat.

"What did Bill say about our paddles?" Samantha called out, her words nearly lost in the growing wind.

"When you pull them out of the water, you turn them so the blade is horizontal. That way, the wind doesn't push you back so much. He called it feathering the paddle."

They both tried the technique.

The far shore gradually came closer. A structure appeared that grew into the outfitter's building. Small bits of light and dark took shape, morphing into vehicles in the parking lot.

One of the vehicles flashed a red light. Then another. The red lights were interspersed with blue.

As Josie and Sam drew closer, the vehicles became county sheriff's vehicles.

"Mama, what's going on?"

"I don't know, Sam. Some kind of police business, I would assume. Lucky for us, no matter the reason they're here!"

"They can send someone to find the killer!"

"Yes," Josie said.

They kept paddling.

"Is it okay that we paddle in? Should we be going someplace else?"

"No, I don't think so. They know that people come here by canoe. We'll tell them who we are. They'll find Bill. Maybe he's already outside with the police."

"Look, Mama, there's Bill's dog! Unknown. Out on the dock."

They paddled closer, slowing. Josie eased their canoe up to the dock.

"Unknown!" Samantha called out. "Remember us from yesterday? Come over here," she said as the canoe bumped up against the dock.

Unknown didn't move. She was sitting on the dock, halfway out toward the end, looking back toward the men moving about near the sheriff's cars.

"Mama, something's wrong! Look at Unknown. She's shivering. Her front legs are shaking hard."

"I'll hold the canoe in place while you get out. You can go to Unknown. Then I'll paddle to the shore."

Samantha jumped out and ran to Unknown. She kneeled down and hugged the dog.

Josie paddled through the water, driving the canoe forward along the dock, toward the shore.

There was a small sand beach. The bow hit the sand and the canoe ground to a stop. Josie set down her paddle in the stern and stood up in a bent position, her hands on the canoe's edges. She worked herself forward until she was at the bow, then stepped out onto the sand. She pulled the bow up onto the sand so the canoe couldn't be rocked off the beach by waves and blow away.

Josie turned to look around. Samantha was still out on the dock, holding Unknown. There was a group of men over by the sheriff's vehicles. Josie walked toward them.

"Excuse me. I'm looking for Bill Masenrud. Is he around?"

The smallest man in the group said, "Who's asking?" He was the only man in the group who wasn't wearing a uniform.

"I'm Josephine Strong. Out there on the dock is my daughter Samantha Strong. Yesterday, Bill rented us a canoe and camping gear, and he took us out to Lac Falls, where we were to spend a week camping on an island. But we've had some real problems, so… We came back. We need to talk to him."

"I'm sorry, that won't be possible. Bill Masenrud was found dead this morning."

EIGHTEEN

Josie felt struck down by the man's statement. It took her a long moment to speak. A dizziness swept over her, forcing her to grab onto the fender of the nearest sheriff's vehicle.

"I'm sorry. I don't understand. He was healthy and fine yesterday."

"Healthy doesn't stop his kind of death," the man said.

Josie sagged as if she couldn't hold up her weight.

"He was murdered?"

"Tell me again, ma'am, how do you know Mr. Masenrud?"

"I don't, really. He rented us our gear. He gave us canoeing lessons. Then he took us out to Lac Falls and brought us to the cabin there. He was nice and helpful. But beyond that, we don't know him at all."

"Where are you from?"

"Los Angeles. We flew in the day before, stayed at a motel in Grand Marais, and then drove up the Gunflint Trail to the Bear Trap Lake outfitter's yesterday morning."

The man frowned and seemed to study Josie. "You say you had some real problems. What would those be?"

Josie steeled herself, thinking that there was no way to describe what happened that wouldn't seem ludicrous. "After Bill left us on the island, someone tried to kill us."

NINETEEN

They spoke in a room off the side of the outfitter's building. The man without a uniform turned out to be the county sheriff. He introduced himself as Sheriff Denser. He'd come out to personally investigate the crime because—Josie came to understand—murder was unheard of in this area.

Josie and Samantha sat on one side of a six-foot folding table. Josie was still rubbing Samantha, consoling her after the news of Bill's death made her nearly collapse.

Samantha held a leash that kept Unknown close to her. Unknown's front legs were still shaking with nerves or fear or some other trauma. Samantha tried to coax Unknown into lying down on the floor, but she wouldn't.

Sheriff Denser and one of his deputies sat on the other side of the table. Denser had turned on a recorder and had Josie and Samantha state their names and addresses and phone numbers. He had them explain their experience twice. He asked many questions to clarify the details of what had taken place.

Josie understood the law enforcement principle of asking witnesses and suspects to repeat their story in an effort to see if they remain consistent through retellings, consistency being a feature that often demonstrates truth and inconsistency often demonstrating falsification. The simple fact is that the details of the truth are much easier to remember than the details of a lie.

"Let me clarify some details," Sheriff Denser said. "How did you make the sling?"

"I constructed the sling out of line that Bill Masenrud had given us," Josie said.

"And the rocks?"

"We collected large pebbles to use as sling bullets from an area on the island."

"The spears?"

"We found an area with several small dead conifers. We were able to break them free from their roots. We used the camping knives that Bill gave us to carve off the small branches that would have inhibited the spears from penetrating flesh."

The sheriff frowned. "You think about stuff like that? How a spear penetrates flesh?"

"I've never thought of that until last night. But a killer was after us. And I'm a professor. Thinking analytically is what I do."

He nodded. "Then you built the onan weapon that makes fire. How does that work?"

"An onager is the name for a type of wild donkey in Asia. When the Romans developed a type of siege weapon that is powered by torsion, they gave it the onager name because the weapon's kicking motion is similar to the kind of kicking that wild donkeys use to defend themselves. The onager was first used around the fourth century AD and perfected over the next two hundred years. Eventually, it was discontinued in favor of the trebuchet, a more powerful weapon that came from the Chinese."

The sheriff looked impassively at her as if unable to comprehend why a woman would even know these things let alone teach them at UCLA.

Josie continued, "Greek Fire is simply a name given to a process that directs fire, something the Greeks were very sophisticated at. We created a version by punching holes in a kerosene can, positioning it in front of a lit kerosene lantern, and then setting the combination where the onager would strike both."

The sheriff didn't react.

Samantha spoke up. "The onager is like a man-sized mousetrap. Our trap included fire."

"You went to all this work because the man was after you."

"The man was trying to kill us," Josie clarified. "He shot at us twice with his rifle. And he had a pistol. He's huge. What were two small women supposed to do?"

The sheriff didn't answer the question.

Josie had seen cops who were brusque and dismissive. But she didn't sense that in this sheriff. She thought that perhaps the sheriff had simply never seen anyone go to such lengths. It could be that his experience taught him that victims scream and run or plead and bargain. They don't fight. And they certainly don't bring medieval warfare to their pursuers.

"You teach how to make these weapons at college," he said.

"Not exactly. I'm a professor of medieval history at UCLA. I teach an intro class that uses medieval weapons as a way to interest students in the Middle Ages. My goal isn't to teach weapon-making. My goal is to intrigue kids enough that they want to learn about the historical period. Because of the teaser about weapons, the class is very popular."

The man made a single slow nod. "Why do you think this man you describe is trying to kill you?"

"Neither of us has any idea," Josie said.

"You've never seen him before?"

"Not before we arrived at the Minneapolis airport. He was in the baggage claim, carrying an unusual suitcase. It looked like it was made of aluminum. A few minutes later, we saw him in the car rental area. He was at the counter next to us. He made a crack about Samantha's earrings."

The sheriff glanced at Samantha's ears and her dangling safety pins. "And the next time you saw him was…"

"Last night when he tried to kill us. We didn't get a good look at his face, but he seemed like the man from the airport. Then today, when we were setting up an ambush in case he came back, Sam went outside the cabin. The man was hiding outside. He grabbed her, picked her up, and carried her back inside the cabin. When I saw him in clear daylight, that was when I knew it was the same man from the airport."

"Because you saw him in the baggage claim, you think he came in on a plane." The sheriff phrased it like a statement, not a question.

"Yes. But I can't say he did for certain. I suppose it's possible that it just looked like that. It's also possible that he purposely arranged for it to look like he came on a plane."

"Could he have come in on the same plane as you did? From L.A.?"

"Yes. But I don't recall seeing him in the plane when I went to use the restroom. Did you, Sam?"

"No. I would have noticed."

"Were you in economy or first class?" the sheriff asked.

"Economy. So if he'd been in first class, we wouldn't have seen him except when we boarded."

The sheriff nodded. "But even though first class passengers get priority boarding, they sometimes arrive late, right?"

"Yes, of course."

"Did he pick up his suitcase from the same baggage carousel where you got your bags?"

Josie thought about it. "I believe so. What do you think, Sam?"

"Yes. His bag was on the same carousel as ours."

"Can you think of anyone in L.A. who would want to hurt you?"

"No. And I certainly can't imagine someone following us from L.A. to the Boundary Waters and Quetico wilderness."

"Oh, I forgot I took his photo!" Samantha said.

She pulled out her phone, brought up the picture, and handed the phone to the sheriff.

He looked at it and frowned. "His face is blackened. Is that from your fire?"

"Yes."

"So he was still alive when you left the island." Another statement.

"Yes. At least, I assume so. Sam had hit him with a sling bullet. He fell to the ground. When we went closer, he threatened us, and I hit him with a piece of wood. It knocked him unconscious."

The man looked at Samantha. "You got skillful at this sling thing because you've practiced it in California?"

Samantha shook her head. "I never tried it before until this morning when Mama made the sling out of macrame."

"So she taught you the skill."

"No," Josie said. "I'd never tried one before, either. But I knew it could be done. I knew about slings because many cultures around the world have used them. And of course, the David and Goliath legend is something everyone is aware of."

"Right," the sheriff said. He looked at Samantha again. "You got good at the sling after just a short practice?"

"It was easy."

"It wasn't easy for me," Josie said. "But Sam is a volleyball player. She's quite athletic."

"Speaking of being athletic, how did you get from Lac Falls to here in the canoe. Are you good at portaging canoes?"

"No, we're terrible. We kept trading off, a dozen times or more on those two portages. I thought we'd never make it."

Samantha said, "What made us keep going was thinking that psycho was probably coming after us in another canoe."

"He had his own canoe," the sheriff said. "Where is it now?"

"Our canoe was gone, so we took his. At least, I think it was his."

"Mama, remember the hair I told you about? That was probably Unknown's fur! That means the canoe we took from the psycho is one that Bill and Unknown used!"

"Where is it now?" the sheriff asked.

"I pulled it up on the beach right out there. Maybe you can find clues on it. You could probably get his fingerprints off of it. It could be that the assassin killed Bill, then took his canoe to come and find us."

"You call him an assassin. Why?"

"When Sam and I realized we'd never seen him before, we thought he must have been hired to follow us to the wilderness to kill one or both of us and leave our bodies there. So we just started referring to him as an assassin. There's no way he wants us dead for political reasons or because he thinks either of us is important and working at causes that run counter to his desire. So the use of the word assassin is not self-aggrandizing. It's just the simple, if inappropriate, adoption of a term."

The sheriff looked at Josie with a confused frown.

Josie realized she came off as unusual, maybe even strange. As with many professors, the sense of being unlike most people in society was a familiar feeling.

"We'll need to have both of your fingerprints to rule out when we're looking for his prints," the sheriff said.

Josie nodded. She didn't like the idea of having their prints entered into a law enforcement database in Canada or Minnesota. But it seemed necessary in this situation.

"You are both experienced canoers?"

"Not at all. But we did as Bill taught us. The bow paddler sets the pace, the rear paddler follows."

"Can you tell me where you left this man who was chasing you?"

"I can draw you a map," Josie said.

The sheriff looked at the deputy. "Do you have extra paper in your notebook?"

The man opened it to the last page and tore a sheet off the metal spiral.

The sheriff handed it and a pen to Josie.

She spoke as she drew. "Here's the island on Lac Falls. This is the approximate position of the cabin. After the assa… the killer shot at us, we took one of the sleeping bags, climbed out the rear window of the cabin, and spent the night over here. There is a nice bed of moss hidden under a group of trees."

"So you slept there."

"No, we realized that the killer could find the hiding place, so we hid nearby. When he came, Samantha used her phone to play a recording she'd downloaded of a bear's roar to startle the man just as he went into the hiding place. Then she used a strobe light on him to further destabilize him."

The sheriff turned to his deputy. "You should have this girl's skills with a phone."

Samantha grinned as she elbowed Josie.

Josie continued, "As the man brought up his gun, Sam threw a spear at him and hit him in the side. I swung the ax that we'd taken from the cabin. I hit his hand."

The sheriff picked up Samantha's phone and looked again at the photo of the man.

"Didn't the spear slow him down?"

"Yes, it went all the way through the side of his abdomen. It wasn't deep enough to puncture organs. But it was a severe wound. He took out his knife and cut it free."

"He cut into himself?" The sheriff sounded doubtful.

"Yes. It was horrifying. We ran away. When he came back several hours later. His hand and his abdomen were bandaged."

"Lac Falls is some distance away. How could he have gotten to a doctor so fast?"

"We think he may have performed his own suturing."

The man frowned.

"You explain, Sam."

"It's like in the movies," she said as if it were obvious. "The wounded killer finds a fish hook, cuts off the barb, sterilizes his wound with whiskey, then uses the fish hook like a curved needle.

He stitches up his wound using fish line or something."

The sheriff seemed to consider the idea. He pointed to the map. "Where did you leave him?"

"Oh, sorry," Josie said. She continued drawing. "If you go down to the lake from the cabin and walk along the shore of the island, you come to a thicket of trees here. That was where he had hidden his canoe. We left him just on the other side of the thicket. I was worried he'd come to. So I picked up his rifle, careful not to smudge any of his fingerprints. I dropped the gun in the lake right about here. It's only in a couple of feet of water, so it's easy to see. But the killer had substantial eye damage from the fire, so I don't think he'll be able to see it. Also, when the onager struck him, he dropped his pistol in the cabin. I kicked it under one of the bunk beds. And one more thing. We rolled him over and checked his pockets for ID. He had nothing on him."

Sheriff Denser took his time, then said, "You probably learned to check for ID from watching movies, too?"

Samantha nodded. "You can learn a lot from movies."

"Oh, one more thing," Josie said. She reached into her pockets, pulled out the killer's knife and flashlight, and set them on the table. "I took these from the man's pockets. And I took off his boots to hobble him. We threw the boots into the woods near where we left our packs on the portage."

"Hobble him by taking his boots," the sheriff muttered. "Smart."

The sheriff handed the drawing to his deputy. "Take Ian and paddle out there as fast as you can. See if you can find this guy and bring him in."

The deputy left.

The sheriff turned to another deputy. "The canoe these women left at the shore. Dust it for prints." The man nodded and left.

"Can I ask where you found Bill Masenrud's body?" Josie asked.

He pointed. "It was down the shore of the lake. About a hundred yards to the east of this outfitter's building. His dog was standing next to him, crying so loud we could hear it from the outfitter's building."

"How did he die?"

The sheriff looked at Samantha as if judging how she would respond. "The coroner thought his neck had been broken."

"It wasn't an accident?"

Sheriff Denser shook his head. "It appeared quite violent."

Josie swallowed and took a deep breath. "You might look for the killer's car nearby. Maybe the metallic suitcase is visible. If not, it's probably in the trunk."

"Do you know what model he drove?"

"No. But I think we can assume he had a rental, unless his appearance at the car rental counter was part of a ruse. At one point while we drove up from Minneapolis, I saw a small white car in the rearview mirror, and I wondered if it could be that man."

"Did you get a glimpse of him or something that made you think that?"

"No. But I did notice that most of the rental cars in the airport lot were white sedans."

"So there was something about seeing him in the airport that had you wondering about him, running possible scenarios through your head."

The sheriff was smart, Josie thought. "Yes," she said. "When we saw him at the rental counter, he made a suggestive remark to my daughter. It made me cringe. I worried about him after that."

"A worry that was borne out when he came shooting at you."

"Absolutely," Josie said. "What should we do next?"

"First, I want you to stay in the area." He pointed to his recorder. "We can have this typed up for your statement. But we'll probably have more questions. If you can tell me where you'll stay, then I can get hold of you."

Josie said, "I don't want to stay in the same motel in Grand Marais where we stayed on the way up the night before last, because the killer might know where that is."

"Smart," the sheriff said. He wrote down a name. "Try this place. Tell them I sent you."

Josie took the piece of paper.

The sheriff stood up and pushed his chair back from the table. "Let me get one of our evidence kits, and we'll get your fingerprints."

Sheriff Denser handed Samantha a card. "My email's on my card. Can you email me the photo of the man who attacked you?"

"Sure." Samantha held up her phone and showed it to Josie.

"I thought you didn't have reception," Josie said.

"The guillotine has risen."

At her statement, the sheriff turned back and looked at Samantha, a concerned frown on his face.

"The outfitter has wifi," Samantha added.

The sheriff apparently decided not to say anything. Perhaps, Josie thought, everything about Southern Californians was strange to a man who made his life in the northern wilderness.

Samantha tapped on her phone. "I just sent you the photo," she said to the sheriff.

Josie used Samantha's phone to find the number of the motel the sheriff had given her. They had a room available, and she booked it for one night.

Josie gave the phone back to Samantha, and they walked outside, Samantha still holding Unknown's leash.

The sheriff was talking to another man.

They walked up. Josie said, "We have a room tonight at the Northwoods Haven motel. If you have any more requests from us, could you please let us know by ten a.m. tomorrow so we can make plans?"

"Yes, will do," Sheriff Denser said.

Josie gave him her cell phone number.

Sheriff Denser said, "I should introduce you to Bill Masenrud's boss, Wally Jones. Wally owns the outfitter's business. Wally, this is Josephine Strong and her daughter Samantha. They had a scary experience out on the island on Lac Falls. They may have dealt with the man who killed Bill. I've got two deputies on their way out to the island now to see if they can find the man."

Wally shook Josie's hand. "You're the couple Bill brought out to the Lac Falls cabin, right?"

"Yes."

"I apologize on behalf of all of us in the north woods. We don't often have bad guys come this way. The rotten eggs seem to be a driving group, whether pickup or motorcycle. The people who paddle canoes are rarely bad eggs. But it happens. And I'm sorry about it."

"I should let you know that the cabin is a mess," Josie said. "It has charred burn scars and there's a broken kerosene lantern. The kerosene can has holes punched in it, and kerosene was spilled on the cabin floor. Also, there is a large bent branch hanging from one of the rafter beams. It will all take a cleaning crew some time to put it back in shape. So please contact me when you know how much the cleanup cost will be. My contact info is on the form Bill had. You can also get me by contacting the history department at UCLA. If you like, I can pay you a deposit now for the expense."

"That won't be necessary. I'll wait until we get the cabin cleaned up. Perhaps our insurance will cover the cost."

"Thank you. I'm also so very sorry about what happened to Bill. He went out of his way to be helpful to us."

"Thank you," Wally said. "He was a good guy all around."

"Does he have family? I should tell them how nice he was."

"Yes and no. I recall him saying he had an ex-wife and some

cousins back east. But he made it clear that he came to Northern Minnesota to get away from family and everything else. So as far as anyone around here knows, he was alone out here. He rented a cabin I own just outside of Grand Marais. He kept to himself. Worked here at the outfitter's in the summer and fall. Went cross-country skiing with his dog and read books in the winter." As Wally said it, he looked down at Unknown, who was at Samantha's feet, sitting quietly, her front legs still shaking hard. "Speaking of his dog, we don't have anyone else here who can take on that lifestyle or that responsibility. I don't suppose you two would like to take her?"

Josie was a bit taken aback. "Well she seems a sweet dog. But we live in a small condo, and we're gone most of every day."

Wally nodded. "Just thought I'd ask. We'll have to take her to the pound. Maybe they can find someone to adopt her. It won't be the first time for her. Bill himself found her wandering in the woods a couple of years ago."

"Mama, we can't let Unknown go to the pound! I saw a show on those places. Do you know what they do? Just a fraction of the dogs get adopted. It's mostly the little dogs and puppies and the most popular breeds like Golden Retrievers. The other dogs get killed! They call it euthanizing. But that's what it really is! They kill them, Mama! We can't let that happen to Unknown!"

Samantha stepped protectively in front of Unknown and stared at Josie with worry and panic on her face. Tears welled up in her eyes.

TWENTY

Even though Samantha hadn't spent more than a few minutes with Unknown, Josie realized how important the dog suddenly was.

"But where would she live?" Josie asked. "Where would she stay during the day? And how would we even get her home? We live over two thousand miles from here."

"We'll take her on the plane. Dogs travel on planes all the time. My friend Mikhaela and her family fly their dog to Tahoe when they go skiing and to Martha's Vineyard in the summer."

Wally Jones and Sheriff Denser had wisely stepped away to leave them alone.

"I don't know anything about dogs," Josie said.

"You can learn. That's what you do. You're a professor."

"But we have a small condo." Josie felt her control of the situation slipping away.

"She can stay in my room at night. And you can take her to your office during the day."

"Sam, I teach. I lecture. It would be unfair to keep a dog trapped in my office when I'm lecturing."

Samantha was quivering almost as much as Unknown. "More unfair than having a dog pound kill her?"

Samantha's comment was potent. There was nothing Josie could say after that. And any response that might push away the possibility of adopting Unknown would drive a wedge between Josie and Samantha, just like the hundred other disagreements that continuously tested their relationship. Just like all the problems that this trip to the wilderness was supposed to ameliorate.

"We'd have to get one of those cage things for the plane."

"They're called kennels, Mama. That's what Mikhaela's family has. Their dog even likes it."

"The airline probably has rules about vaccinations and such."

Samantha was already nodding, anticipating. "I'm sure there are veterinarians between here and Minneapolis."

"We'd need to buy a dog bed and other equipment."

Samantha practically jumped on Josie, giving her a bear hug, pushing her back. "That means we're taking her! Thank you, Mama! Thank you, thank you, thank you!" Samantha turned, bent down to Unknown, and hugged her so hard the dog almost fell over to her side. "Did you hear that, Unknown? You've been saved! You have to meet your saviour."

"I already met her, Sam."

"No, I mean you have to really meet her. You've never even pet her. Bend down and say hello to the new member of our family."

Josie realized she had to do it for Samantha if not for Unknown. She squatted down in front of Unknown, reached out and pet her. "I'm pleased to meet you, Unknown." Josie ran her hands along the side of the dog's head. "I'm so sorry about the circumstances. I'm so sorry about Bill. If we hadn't come up here, he'd still be alive."

As Josie said it, she gasped at the sudden realization. Tears flooded her eyes and ran down her cheeks. She couldn't breathe. She rocked forward on her feet until she was on her knees in the dirt. She wrapped her arms around the dog. Josie struggled to breathe, jerking as she tried to get air. Samantha kneeled next to her, and the three of them made a huddle, the women leaning on each other, crying, while Unknown tried to bear up under their weight even as her legs continued to shake and nearly buckle.

TWENTY-ONE

The sheriff had walked away. He returned with a plastic tool box. "I can get your prints now."

It took just a few minutes.

"When you find this killer, will you please call me so we can stop worrying?"

The sheriff nodded. "It will be a pleasure to make that call."

Josie thanked the sheriff for his efforts, and they left.

That evening as they drove into Grand Marais, they stopped and bought chow mein, then stopped at a grocery to pick up a small bag of dried dog food.

When they got to the motel, they left Unknown in the car and stepped into the office to check in. Josie explained that they had an unexpected addition to their group in the form of a dog that had been orphaned when its owner died.

The motel owner looked concerned but not about the dog being orphaned. "We are dog friendly. But our limit is forty pounds."

"We don't know how much this dog weighs."

"Let me see him. I can tell."

"Her," Samantha said. "Her name is Unknown. She's the sweetest dog ever. Trust me."

The office clerk didn't look impressed.

"Can you go get her, Sam?" Josie said.

Samantha went out to the car and came back with Unknown.

The clerk looked at Unknown and said, "Size is no problem. That dog is probably twenty pounds. Twenty-five pounds max.

Is he housebroken?"

"She," Samantha said again. "Yes, I'm sure she's housebroken."

"But you don't know."

"She's very obedient. She must be housebroken."

The clerk took a deep breath and looked at Josie. "If there is even the smallest accident, we add a two-hundred-dollar cleaning fee to your bill."

Josie nodded. "I understand."

They went to their room. Sam reached in and flipped on the light. Unknown hesitated at the door as if not sure she would go inside.

Samantha tugged on the leash. "It's okay, Unknown. You'll be safe in here. No psychos at this motel."

Unknown took two steps forward, looked left and right, then followed Samantha inside. Samantha unhooked the leash, and Unknown sat down in a corner.

"Don't dogs usually explore when they go to new places?"

"Maybe," Josie said. "But I've never had a dog. I don't know what to expect anymore than I know what to do."

"Mikhaela's dog explores all the time. She's always sniffing. It's like she's on smell patrol."

Samantha said, "We forgot to get a dog bowl. How will we feed Unknown?"

Josie looked around the room. "Maybe just open the top of the bag and let her eat out of the bag."

"Good idea," Samantha said. She got the string unraveled from the end of the bag, opened it up, and sniffed its contents. "This stuff smells weird."

"It's not people food. It's supposed to smell different."

Samantha set the bag in the corner of the room, leaning it against the walls for support. "C'mere, Unknown. Time for dinner!"

Unknown was sitting over by the door. She didn't move.

Samantha took her leash and pulled her over to the food. The dog came reluctantly. Samantha held the bag out so Unknown could sniff the food. "See, Unknown? You can just eat it out of the bag. Like the way people eat munchies."

Unknown turned away and sat down. Her front legs were still shaking, though not as much as before.

"I think she's depressed, Sam. Depressed people often don't have an appetite. It's probably the same with dogs. Let's just leave the bag open. She knows where it is if she gets hungry."

Samantha sat down on the carpet next to Unknown and pet the dog. "I'm so sorry, Unknown. You had a good life in the woods. And now we've ruined it."

Josie felt her own sadness grow deeper. But she took solace in the idea that she couldn't recall ever seeing Samantha show such empathy for another living being, human or not. The dog's presence was already having a positive effect on her daughter.

When she and Samantha ate their chow mein, Samantha said, "Could I feed a little of this to Unknown?"

"I don't know. In theory, dogs are carnivores, right? But I remember reading that dog food makers use grains and such in dog food. Maybe chow mein would be okay. But let's play it safe and give her just a little bit."

Samantha tore a couple of pieces of paper off the little notepad on the motel table. She spooned a little chow mein out onto the paper and held it in front of Unknown. "See, Unknown? People food. You'll love this." She set it on the floor in front of the dog.

Unknown looked indifferent. She turned away and lay down on the floor, her head facing the wall.

"She won't eat. What should we do?" Samantha was distraught.

"I don't think you need to worry, Sam. Maybe try giving her some water."

"We don't have a bowl."

"There must be an ice bucket in this room."

They looked around but couldn't find one.

Samantha said, "I bet there's an outdoor faucet at this motel. I've seen dogs drink from hoses. Let's go look."

Josie stood up. She didn't want to alarm Samantha, but she wasn't going to let her out of her sight until she heard that the sheriff had the killer locked away in jail.

Samantha hooked the leash on Unknown's collar and tugged. "C'mon, girl, let's get you some water."

Josie watched from the doorway as Samantha took Unknown outside and down the sidewalk past the other rooms. The early evening light was beginning to dim. At the end of the building was a grassy green yard that was lit by a whitish-blue yard light. There was a faucet with a hose attached. Samantha turned it on. When water flowed out the hose, she lowered the hose toward Unknown's mouth.

The dog turned away.

Samantha called out, "Oh, Mama! She won't drink, either. What will we do? She'll die of starvation!"

"Easy, Sam, let's stay calm. You can see that Unknown is smart. She's observant and, well, lucid, if that's a word you can use with dogs. She knows what's what. It's not like she's lying down with a terrible illness, unable to get up. She's mobile. She knows exactly what you're doing, trying to get her to eat and drink. But she doesn't want that. So let's be patient. As long as she's able to move around and be alert, she'll be fine."

Josie didn't know if it was true, but it made sense. And it might help Samantha to not overreact.

"I have an idea," Josie said. "Let's go for a walk. Unknown has been cooped up in our car and now in the motel room. It's still light out. If we stay right here on the main street of town, we'll be safe. Walking might stimulate Unknown's appetite."

They headed down the street. Samantha concentrated on Unknown, looking down at her continuously as they walked.

Unknown was a model of good behavior. She walked without pulling forward or sideways on the leash. She kept pace with Samantha's speed but not as rigorously as Josie had seen with some hyper-trained dogs that heel in lockstep.

Josie focused most of her attention on the street. It was twilight, with just enough light to see beyond the illumination from building lights. They'd only walked four blocks when Josie began to feel unsettled. It was getting too dark for her comfort.

"Let's turn around. We can walk again in the morning before we leave."

Samantha and Unknown about-faced.

Back at the motel, they once again tried to entice Unknown into drinking from the hose. She showed no interest.

Inside their room, Samantha repeated her efforts with both dog food and the previous helping of chow mein. She got the same result. Unknown lay down near the wall and didn't move.

"It didn't work, Mama. Exercise made no difference. If she won't eat or drink, she can't last long, right?"

"That's no doubt true. Just like with people, it's especially important to get liquids into her. We'll try again in the morning. In the meantime, why don't you research where we can find veterinarians between here and Duluth. You can copy their phone numbers, and we'll call them in the morning."

Samantha nodded. She looked dejected. She sat down next to Unknown, leaned against the wall, and started tapping on her phone.

They went to bed early. Samantha tried to entice Unknown into sleeping at the end of the bed. But Unknown didn't budge and stayed on the floor. Josie heard Samantha fall asleep, but Josie couldn't follow her example.

The next morning, Samantha tried to get Unknown to eat without success. Mother, daughter, and dog walked down the street to a dog-friendly breakfast cafe. They sat in a booth and had eggs and bacon. Unknown sat on the floor next to Samantha.

As they ate, Samantha said, "Mama! Look! Unknown isn't shaking! Maybe this means she'll eat!"

Josie, having always thought that humans and dogs should have some separation in lifestyle, tried hard not to react when Samantha reached down with a piece of bacon.

Unknown sniffed the meat. Then, with no apparent enthusiasm, took it from Samantha's hand.

"She ate it!" Samantha shouted. "She's going to be okay! We just need to give her the right food."

Against Josie's will, she imagined a future where they'd be buying large quantities of bacon, cooking it just so, and feeding their prima donna dog. "That's great, Sam," Josie said. "And salty bacon will certainly make her thirsty as well."

Josie watched the time, waiting for a phone call from the sheriff before the 10 a.m. time they'd agreed to.

They were walking back to the motel when her phone rang. "Hello?"

"Ms. Strong? Sheriff Denser here."

"Did you catch him?"

Josie heard the sheriff take a deep breath.

Josie felt devastated.

The sheriff said, "I'm sorry to report that when my deputies went out to the island on Lac Falls, they did not find him."

"What?! Didn't my map make sense?"

"No, it made sense. They found signs of him. And the cabin was as you described. They also found the Duluth packs you abandoned at the first portage."

"How would he get away?" As she said it, Josie was aware that Samantha had jerked her head to stare at Josie.

"We don't know. We can only assume he had another canoe hidden on the island. The one you initially paddled in, perhaps."

"Could he have gotten off the island by swimming?"

"I suppose. But his pistol was gone from the cabin. And his

rifle was not in the water where you said. I don't think he could have swum with two heavy weapons."

"I don't see how he could find either weapon! The fire in his face left him as good as blind! We watched him walk with his arms out in front of his face!" Josie had raised her voice. She was aware that anyone else near the sidewalk could hear her words.

"Yes, I saw the picture on your daughter's phone. I'm sorry, Ms. Strong. But you can know I'll be in touch when we find the man."

"What about the canoe we came back in? The one we took from the man on the island. Did you get his fingerprints?"

"No. Unfortunately we only found prints from you and your daughter. There were a few older prints that were smudged, but nothing useful."

"But we saw him dragging that canoe!"

"Maybe he was wearing gloves of some kind," the sheriff said.

"I don't think so. Look again at the photo my daughter emailed you. I think part of one hand is visible in the picture."

"Hold on." There was a pause. "Yes, you're right. He's not wearing gloves. Nevertheless, we couldn't find any prints. Maybe he's more sophisticated than he seemed. He could have obscured his prints by dipping his fingertips in some kind of coating. I've heard of polymer dips."

Josie felt distraught. "If only you could have searched all the cars in the area yesterday."

"We couldn't without a warrant, and we couldn't get that without clear evidence that pointed to a particular car. But we did an inventory last night. This morning, when we went through the lots, we found that two of the cars had gone missing in the night."

"Any idea what kind of cars they were?"

"One was a green Suburban. An old one. The other was a new Ford Focus. White."

"A common rental car," Josie said.

"Yes. I'm very sorry if he slipped through our fingers. We're currently trying to re-construct an inventory of canoes to see if we have more or less than the outfitter's rental numbers would suggest."

Josie was distracted by Samantha who was waving her hand in front of Josie's face. She turned toward Samantha.

"Tell him to put out a BOLO on the Focus," Samantha said.

"What?"

Samantha repeated herself.

"Sorry, sheriff. Can you hold on a moment?" Josie said.

Josie turned to Samantha. "What's a BOLO?"

"A 'Be On The Lookout' bulletin for law enforcement."

Josie repeated Samantha's comment into the phone.

"I can hear your daughter in the background. More advice from the movies, I suppose."

"Sorry, but yes."

"Tell her we already did it. Maybe some cop down the road will see the car. They can't pull just any car over without a reason. But if the man's vision is as bad as you say, maybe there will be a reason."

"Thank you very much, sir," Josie said.

They said goodbye and hung up.

"I knew it," Samantha said. "We should have killed him."

TWENTY-TWO

"I don't know what to say, Sam. I agree with you that he doesn't deserve to live. But that doesn't mean we had the right to kill him. That's a right only the state has."

"Is Minnesota like California that way?"

"Well, yes. But when I said 'state,' I meant it as a general term of government. Most ethicists agree that the only possible authorization for taking a life would come from government. Not from an individual."

"But we should have, anyway."

"Maybe. These are tough philosophical questions," Josie said.

"Tough for professor types who have to analyze everything. Easier for regular people who face the evil that bad guys do."

"You may be right. Let's get our things and get on the road. Then you can tell me what you found out about veterinarians."

"First, let's try to give Unknown some more water."

Josie agreed, and they turned on the faucet. Unknown seemed indifferent. Then she turned and lapped at it twice.

"She drank! Not much. But that's good, right?"

"Yes, indeed. Do you want to try giving her some of the dry dog food?"

"No. I can tell she won't touch it. Not yet, anyway."

"And you can tell, how?"

Samantha looked at Unknown and then at Josie. "I can just tell."

Samantha wanted to sit in the backseat with Unknown. They headed down the North Shore highway, crawling along the majestic coast of Lake Superior. The view was spectacular, but Josie missed most of it because of her concentration on the rearview mirror, watching for a small white sedan, similar to the rental car they were driving.

Samantha told Josie about the veterinary offices she'd found, several of which were in Duluth. Josie suggested that Samantha call the offices, and she gave her a few ideas of what to say. Samantha seemed a little intimidated but also proud to be given the assignment. An hour later, they had an appointment.

They found the vet office in a small commercial building on a steep street just outside of Duluth's downtown. The doctor saw them in a small exam room.

"Hello," she said as they came in. "I'm Doctor Sarah Coral." She reached out her hand.

"I'm Josie Strong, and this is my daughter Samantha."

They all shook hands.

"And who is this?" The vet bent down.

"This is Unknown. We just adopted her because her owner died," Josie said.

"Hi, sweetie, let's get a look at you." She pulled up a chair and sat down so she'd be at Unknown's level. She pet Unknown, ran her hands along the dog's ribs, felt her hips, her legs, lifted up one of her paws, spread her toe pads, fingered her claws. Then she pet Unknown again, rubbed her ears, and gently touched her mouth, lifting her lips and looking at her teeth.

"Let me scan her for a chip. If she has one, it would have useful information." She pulled a device out of a drawer. It looked vaguely like a gray remote for a TV. She passed it over Unknown, concentrating on the back of her neck.

"Unfortunately, there is no chip," she said.

Dr. Coral turned and picked up her clipboard, looking at the top sheet of paper.

"When you called, you said you're going to be taking her on a plane. Does that mean you need a health certificate?"

"Yes, we need to take her to Los Angeles," Josie said. "But we don't know what we need."

"I can get you a certificate. You'll also need a kennel because she's too big to go in the cabin. She'll have to be checked with baggage."

Samantha inhaled. "You mean they just stack her in with the suitcases?"

"No. Airlines do a good job. They put pets in a part of the cargo hold that has lights and space. It's pressurized and heated. Dogs usually do very well. Over five hundred thousand dogs fly every year, so this is quite routine."

Samantha looked worried. "Can you tell other stuff about dogs? Like, how old she is and what kind of dog she is?"

"I can make some educated guesses. Judging by her teeth and general condition, I think she's about five or six years old. In case you're wondering, that's a good age for adopting a dog. She's old enough to be knowledgeable about the world, but she's young enough to easily adapt to a new owner. She's still got most of her life in front of her. As for breed, she's clearly a mix. I'm thinking part Aussie, although she's small for an Aussie. Let's put her on the scale." The doctor led Unknown over to a large, rectangular scale. Unknown stepped onto it willingly.

"Nineteen pounds," the vet said. "So she's got some smaller breed in her as well."

"What's an Aussie?"

"An Australian Shepherd. It's a breed that, contrary to the name, was developed out in the American west during the nineteenth century. Aussies are ranch dogs. They are extremely smart, similar to the Border Collie, which was developed in England. But unlike Border Collies, Aussies are not so hyper, not so demanding. They're good workers."

"I don't get it," Samantha said. "How does a dog work?"

"Have you ever had a dog before?"

"No. Mama wouldn't let me have anything but a goldfish."

The vet glanced at Josie and then gave Josie a little smile. "Well, dogs were bred for work. Guarding the cave, helping people hunt, tracking game or other people. In the case of Aussies, they are natural herders. If you've got a bunch of sheep, an Aussie will keep them in a herd. If a sheep is a straggler, the Aussie will go get the sheep and drive it back to the group. Aussies don't even have to be taught how to do that. It comes naturally."

"Really?" Samantha said. "That's kinda cool."

"It's actually very cool," the doctor said. "Aussie's are also good watch dogs. If a stranger comes near your house, they will let you know."

"But Unknown doesn't even bark," Samantha said. "She watches stuff. But she's not like, you know, on guard."

"She's probably traumatized. You say her former owner died. Can you tell me about that?"

"We don't know much about it," Josie said. "Her owner worked at a canoe outfitter on Bear Trap Lake. We only just met him two days ago when he rented us gear to go canoeing. He introduced us to Unknown and said he'd found her lost and wandering a couple of years ago. That's why he called her Unknown. When we came back from our canoeing yesterday, the sheriff was there. He said that the dog was down the shore, crying. It turned out that her owner's body was next to her."

"Do they know how he died?"

"They thought it looked like his neck was broken. Not necessarily from a fall but possibly from a violent fight."

The doctor bent over Unknown, rubbing her again. "Oh, poor girl. Most dogs are very devoted to their owners. A death like that would be very difficult for her. People are like gods to a dog. You can't expect her to get back to normal for several months. And she will probably never forget that trauma. You say she doesn't bark?"

"Not yet, anyway. But we've only been with her for the last day and a half and for a few hours the day before. So maybe there hasn't been anything to bark at."

The doctor frowned. "Any Aussie mix would generally be a good barker." Dr. Coral ran her fingers along Unknown's neck. "Her larynx feels okay. I sense no other signs of physical trauma. You say she was crying when they found her owner?"

"Yes."

"So we know she can vocalize. Maybe she's got some Basenji in her."

"What's that?"

"It's a dog that was bred in Africa. It's a hunting dog that doesn't bark. But it cries and even makes a kind of howling noise. So it's plenty vocal. A Basenji also has a curled tail. Unknown's tail doesn't hang as straight down as that of a purebred Aussie. So a little Basenji in the mix could explain no barking and the not-so-straight tail. Also, Aussies have thicker, longer coats than Unknown has. Basenjis have short hair. It could be that Unknown has other genetic influences as well. But Aussie mixed with Basenji would be a good guess. Now, I should double check that you don't have a cat or other pet."

"No." Samantha said. "Why?"

"Because Basenjis and Aussies aren't a good mix with cats. These dogs have too much energy. And sometimes they look at cats as the perfect animal to chase."

"From what we've seen," Josie said, "Unknown doesn't have much energy. She doesn't race around. We've never seen her run. She sort of trots."

The vet felt Unknown's hips. "I don't feel anything unusual. It could be that running causes pain. That's common with hip dysplasia. But she likely wouldn't get that unless she was much older. It could just be the shock of having her owner die."

Josie said, "Even before he died, she just trotted. It's as though she's curious about the world, but she's not in a hurry to get there."

"Does she have any kind of limp?"

"I don't think so," Josie said. "What do you think, Sam?"

Samantha shook her head. "Not that I've seen. And her front legs were really shaking. But look, Mama, she's not shaking now."

"That's a good sign. Some dogs shake in any new environment. But some only shake when they go to the vet. We think it's the smells of other animals and chemicals in a strange environment. The fact that she's not shaking now tells me she's been to vets before and that she's comfortable in new environments. That shows she's well adjusted. Does she eat well?"

Samantha shook her head. "That's our other question. We haven't been able to get her to eat anything except a little piece of bacon this morning. Same for drinking except a couple of swallows from a hose."

"Have you seen any signs of sickness? Vomiting? Diarrhea? Pain when you move her that makes her cry out?"

"No."

"I'd like to take a blood sample. I can check for several things here in the office. Depending on what I find, I may need to send a sample out to a lab for additional work. Is that okay?"

Samantha looked at Josie. Josie nodded.

"Sure," Samantha said.

"I'll have you help me lift her up onto our exam table."

They gently raised Unknown to the exam table.

"Now you put your arm around her neck and hold her head. Be firm, but don't squeeze hard."

Unknown didn't protest.

"Ms. Strong, you can hold her chest. I'll draw a sample from her front leg."

They did as told. The doctor used a scissors to snip some fur just below Unknown's elbow. Then she took a disposable razor and shaved a small area. She dabbed some alcohol on the skin, then drew blood.

"Very good," she said, removing the syringe. "Unknown

didn't even know what I did. Now if you two could please stay here with her while I go run some tests. I'll be back in a few minutes." She took the blood sample and went into another room.

When the doctor returned ten minutes later, she said, "I did some basic blood work, and it looks like she's fine. That doesn't mean she can't have something wrong with her. But I'm guessing that she's just recovering from the trauma of her owner dying. I think your focused attention on her is helping. As for eating and drinking, let me try something."

She opened a refrigerator and pulled out a liter-sized, white plastic bottle. She unscrewed the top and poured some liquid into a bowl. She put the bowl into a microwave and ran it for ten seconds before taking it out.

"This is a chicken broth. It has a little salt. The combination generally appeals to dogs. Let's see what Unknown thinks." The vet set it on the floor. She looked at Samantha. "Maybe you can set her down and show her the bowl."

Samantha lowered Unknown to the floor. "C'mere, Unknown. We have a treat for you."

She pointed to the bowl and moved Unknown close. The dog took a sniff, lapped once as if judging the taste, then drank it all.

"She drank!" Samantha was excited. She rubbed Unknown and nuzzled her ears.

"Now, we'll try some food." The doctor removed a glass jar from the fridge, unscrewed the top, and spooned out some food into the bowl. She warmed it as well.

Unknown ate it in gulps.

"There, I think we just answered the question. Your dog will eat once she's relaxed and when she's given the right food."

"What is that food?" Josie asked.

"It's basically shredded chicken." The doctor handed Josie a piece of paper with printing on it. "Here are some brands of similar food that come in cans. You can get them at some groceries and many pet stores."

"How much should we give her?"

"Dogs love this stuff so much that they'll overeat it if given a chance. So just give her half a cup twice a day for the first few days. Then begin mixing it with dry dog food. Those names are also on the list. Once she's eating well, you can reduce the proportion of canned food, using it to flavor the dry food. And always let her have access to as much water as she wants."

"What about flying on a plane?"

"Don't give her any food for six hours before the flight. When you are back home, ease back into the food routine. The rule is to reduce food whenever your dog goes through changes of environment or other potential stress. I'll give you some food to take with you." She pulled four cans out of a cupboard.

"Now for some caveats." The doctor looked at Samantha. "Warnings," she added.

"I know what caveats are. Mama's a professor. So I know way more words than I need."

"The key to a happy dog is socializing. That means that, as much as possible, you have your dog mixing it up with other people and other dogs. Whether you're working or playing or walking, always try to bring her where she will meet others. The more comfortable she becomes with all situations, the happier she will be."

"What is the best activity?" Josie asked.

"You said you live in Los Angeles. Are you very far from the beach?"

"Just two blocks."

"Perfect. Find one that allows dogs, and go there every day. Twice a day if you can. Beaches are great because she will get comfortable with all manner of people and dogs."

Samantha frowned. "Mama, aren't there signs that say dogs are prohibited on the beach?"

"I think so, yes. But they're allowed on the walkway if they're on a leash."

The vet nodded. "Most beaches require that your dog is on a leash. So you should also find a place where dogs can run off leash. Usually there are dog parks and non-leash dog beaches. Maybe there are some woods or wilderness areas. I know you said she hasn't run. But still do it. Dogs need to explore. Find other people you know who have dogs. They will know these things."

Josie said. "Maybe I'll lose some weight walking the dog."

The vet made a little smile. "I've read studies that say that the single most successful tactic for changing to a lifestyle that helps people lose weight is to get a dog and exercise it twice a day. For many people, that alone will triple or quadruple the amount of exercise they get."

"How long is she likely to live?"

"Dogs of this size will often go to fifteen. So she's got a lot of years left."

Samantha looked at Josie. "It looks like we've got a long-term companion, Mama."

"Okay. Let's take her home to Los Angeles."

TWENTY-THREE

Thirty hours and another night in a motel later, they landed at LAX. The pets on the plane were unloaded separate from the regular baggage. So after they picked up their roller cases, Josie and Samantha waited for Unknown to arrive at the far end of the baggage pickup. The handlers hand-carried the various kennel crates in and set them on the floor.

Josie watched as Samantha ran to Unknown. "Baby, are you okay?" Samantha said as she stuck her fingers through the little square openings. Unknown sat, watching. There was no enthusiasm, no tail wagging. But she sniffed Samantha's fingers.

They showed their baggage tags to the airport employee and then let Unknown out of the kennel. The two women each pulled their roller bags, while Samantha carried the empty kennel and Josie held Unknown's leash. They went out to the access road. Their Uber ride showed up fifteen minutes later.

The driver dropped them off at their condo building in Santa Monica an hour later.

Samantha carried the kennel as they walked Unknown into their building. They usually took the stairs in an effort to get a little exercise. But with their luggage and kennel and dog, they took the elevator.

Once inside the front door of their condo, Samantha spoke with enthusiasm, "Welcome to your new home, Unknown! I think you're going to like it here." She set the kennel on the floor, then unlatched the kennel door and reached inside for the dog bed and blanket they'd included for Unknown. Samantha removed the blanket first. Unknown watched her, then lay down on the bed.

"Unknown, don't you want to explore your new house?"
Unknown didn't move.

"It looks like it's going to take some time for her to get comfortable," Josie said.

Unknown stayed inside the kennel, looking out, her eyes moving left and right, taking it in. Josie could see that the dog was not eager to embrace yet another living space. And this one was very far from home, with different light and different smells and different people. By comparison, Grand Marais, where Bill had lived, and the Gunflight Trail that went to the canoe outfitter, was much closer to what she'd been used to.

The next day, they took Unknown to the beach. Unknown walked with caution, carefully watching every person and dog. She was very focused, missing nothing.

"Not only do we have to have her on the leash," Samantha said, "but we can't even walk her on the sand. The vet said we need to find places where she can explore off the leash."

"We will, Sam."

When the walkway came closer to the water, Unknown stopped and watched each time a large wave crashed onto the sand.

"Look, Mama. The waves are a long way from the walkway, but she's still very wary."

"Pacific surf is a different order of magnitude from the waves on Quetico lakes."

Unknown watched as a woman on Rollerblades coasted past them, her Golden retriever running alongside. But Unknown showed no desire to speed up.

That evening, they fed Unknown as the Minnesota vet had recommended, and she ate well, if slowly.

The next morning, Josie decided to go to her office at UCLA. "Maybe you and Unknown should come with me."

"I think we should stay home. I want Unknown to get comfortable with her new home."

"You'll stay here?"

"Yeah. Or I'll take her on the beach walk."

"But no other exploring? No shopping?" The warm sun of Southern California gave Josie a sense of comfort. But a killer had tracked them all the way to the Canadian border. If he survived, he might well track them back to L.A.

"Mama, I think I can judge what is safe behavior and where it's safe to go."

Josie wondered if Samantha was right.

Samantha stayed home with Unknown while Josie took the bus to UCLA to prepare for classes, which began in three days. Once there, she walked to her office in Bunche Hall and tried to see it from a dog's point of view. It didn't seem inviting. There was her desk and reading table and bookshelves. All hard surfaces. If Unknown decided to bark or howl, the noise would be heard halfway across campus.

Perhaps, if Josie could slide the table over next to the window and put the kennel up on her table… Then Unknown would at least have something to see. Josie's office overlooked the Sculpture Garden, and there were always people there. Their movements would provide distraction.

Josie unloaded all the books off the table. She took the medieval crossbow and its quiver tube of bolts and set them on the bookshelf behind her desk. Once the table was unloaded, it was still very heavy. But with much effort, she slid the heavy table across the floor and over next to the window. It was the best she could think of.

Josie's next stop was the lecture room at the Renee and David Kaplan Hall. She hiked across campus and cut the corner over the grass of Dickson Court to the building and the room where her lectures were to be during fall quarter.

Her hope was that there was a place where she could leash Unknown out of sight from her students but within sight of her as she lectured.

One glance and she realized that it would not work. Every possible location for a dog was visible to the students. Unknown would be far too much of a distraction.

Josie went home, and she and Samantha and Unknown had a quiet evening. Samantha tried to engage Unknown, sitting on the floor next to her. But the dog remained reserved. Josie had the thought that the dog gave Samantha just a portion of her attention. The rest of Unknown's focus seemed to be elsewhere. At times, her eyes looked at the walls. Her ears went forward, then back. More than once, her right ear seemed to listen to Samantha while her left rotated as if to hear through the walls behind her. Josie didn't think Unknown could discern anything of substance. But the dog listened, nevertheless.

The next day, all three of them headed back to campus. Samantha carried the kennel and dog bed, and Josie took Unknown by the leash. They revisited Josie's office.

"Let's put the kennel up on the table," Josie said. "Now let's lift Unknown up on the table." Josie put her arms under Unknown's abdomen, and Samantha put hers around the dog's chest. When they released the dog on the table, Unknown immediately walked into the kennel.

"Maybe this will work out," Josie said. "Unknown has made it clear that she appreciates the familiar space of the kennel and the dog bed."

"It seems perfect, Mama."

"If she stays quiet when I'm lecturing, it could be perfect. Let's do a test. We'll close her in the office, and you and I will walk down the hall."

Samantha frowned. "I can see your point. But I get uncomfortable just thinking about leaving her. What if she freaks out?"

"We'll find out."

Samantha pet Unknown. "You be quiet, okay? You be a good girl." She shut the kennel door.

They walked out, closed the door, and headed down the hall.

As they got near the end of the hallway, a door opened next

to them. Josie made a little startled jump and put her hand to her mouth.

A big man with a dramatic head of silver hair stood in the doorway.

"Professor Silver," Josie said, smiling, glad that she hadn't slipped and called him by the nickname Silvermane, as the other history professors sometimes referred to him.

"Professor Strong. You're here early. Getting ready before classes start?"

"Early, yes. But not to prepare for classes. Have you met my daughter? Please meet Samantha. Samantha, this is Professor Tom Silver. He's dean of students and teaches the history of science when he has any time left." Samantha and Silver shook hands.

"You came and talked at our school last year," Samantha said.

Josie frowned as she looked at Samantha, then at Silver.

"I do a lot of school outreach," Silver said. "What's the name of your school?"

"Science and Art Prep Academy."

"Oh, of course. Off Wilshire, right?"

"You never told me that, Sam," Josie said.

"Oh, he just talked about college stuff. I probably didn't think to tell you, 'cause it was no big deal. He just told us what we needed to know for college." Then Samantha looked embarrassed. She turned toward Silver. "Don't get me wrong when I said no big deal. I definitely learned stuff. And I didn't know you worked with Mama."

Silver smiled. "Are you a history buff like your mother?" Silver asked.

"Not really. I'm more into, like, music and movies."

Josie tried not to wince.

A sudden unusual sound echoed down the corridor.

Josie turned to listen. It sounded like a high moan. "Sam! Could that be a cry from Unknown?"

Samantha inhaled. "I'll run and check." Samantha ran down

the hall toward Josie's office.

Silver looked at Josie, then gestured through his open door toward his office desk, in front of which were two big leather chairs. "You can wait for your daughter in my office, if you like. More comfortable than standing in the hall."

Josie nodded, walked in, and sat in one of the chairs.

Silver left the office door open and sat at his desk.

"Curiouser and curiouser," he said, "hearing a cry from the unknown right in our boring history department. Is the study of medieval history going metaphysical? Spiritual? Supernatural?"

"Sorry," Josie said. "This is much more prosaic. We just got back from a vacation in the Canadian wilderness. A guide we met died, and his dog was orphaned. They were going to send her to the animal shelter. Samantha realized that taking a dog to the shelter was a trip to be euthanized. So she begged me to adopt her."

"What do you mean by unknown?"

"That's the dog's name. It turns out that the man who died had found her lost and wandering two years ago. He took her in knowing nothing about her, including her name. So he called her Unknown."

"And why is her howl echoing through the Department of History?"

"Because we're test-driving her in my office."

Silver raised his eyebrows.

"Our condo is small, and Sam is at school during the day. I thought maybe I could leave Unknown here when I'm teaching. Do you think I'm breaking any major rule?"

Silver paused and narrowed his eyes. "As long as no one hears a cry from the unknown, no one would know she's here, right?"

Josie realized the man was attempting dry humor. "My daughter can be funny too," she said.

Silver smiled. With his big hair and white teeth, he looked like a celebrity. "What if she turns out to be a history book-chewing hound? I've seen your office. Lots of books."

"She's in one of those kennel cages."

Silver nodded. "My son William had a dog for a time. The poor thing couldn't stop jumping up, front paws on the dinner table, while we ate. So William got a kennel for the dog to stay in during our dinner. The dog actually grew to like it. A kind of dog house but made like a screened porch." Silver glanced over at a bookshelf with three, framed color photos. One photo showed a woman reading a book on the beach. Another was of two young men. One man was on horseback near a cabin that was perched on a steep, forested slope with a ridge behind it. The ridge had a rocky outcropping that seemed familiar to Josie. Next to the man on horseback ran a dog. It looked to Josie like a German Shepherd. The cabin overlooked the very blue Pacific far down below. The third photo was of a man sailing a small one-man boat out on that same plate of blue.

"Is William…" Josie hesitated, wondering if she was venturing toward a subject she should avoid.

"Yes, William is the son who died. He's the one on horseback."

"I'm so sorry," Josie said.

"These things happen," Silver said. "They crush your soul. But after some years, if you're still living, you begin to think you'll survive in some fashion."

Josie stood, walked to the bookshelf, and looked at the three photos.

The photos of Silver's sons were taken from some distance, but both young men looked athletic and very smart, a combination that had a kind of magnetism even to a bookworm like Josie. The photo of the woman reading on the beach was much more contemplative. She wasn't flashy like Silver. But she looked thoughtful, the kind of woman who Josie imagined to be judicious with words, a person who thought before she spoke.

Samantha reappeared in Silver's office doorway.

"Is Unknown okay?" Josie asked.

"Yeah. She's just—I don't know—getting used to the space.

Like, she keeps going through these huge changes. She's used to living in the woods on the Gunflint Trail. Now she's in a kennel up on a table in Los Angeles."

"Gunflint Trail," Silver repeated. "There's a name that conjures up a dozen stories. I wonder where it came from."

"Just ask Mama, and she'll give you a lesson about French fur traders in… When were they?"

"Eighteenth and nineteenth centuries," Josie said, "from the Great Lakes northwest across Lake Superior, all the way to Lake Winnipeg. One of the biggest industries in the Americas during that time."

"Yes, of course," Silver said. "The Beaver Wars come back to me. Native American tribes wielding significant influence in a business that Europeans considered very important."

Samantha looked from Silver to Josie. Her eyes traversed the bookshelves and stopped on the photo of the young man on horseback. She walked over and picked it up.

"Mama, look at this. This is beautiful!"

Josie took the framed photo and looked at it up close. "What's beautiful? The cabin and its view, the horse, or the young man riding?"

"All three! Why did we go to the Quetico wilderness? We could have gone to this horse riding place." Samantha turned to Silver. "Is this what they call a dude ranch?"

He grinned. "No. A dude ranch is a tourist attraction. That picture is my son William riding in the Santa Monica Mountains up near the top of Topanga Canyon. The horse belonged to a farmer up on the ridgeline. And the cabin is our summer hideaway. Been in the family for seventy years."

"Does your son take people riding?"

"No. He died several years ago." Silver pointed to the other photo. "But my other son takes people sailing. However, I wouldn't recommend it. He's a bit reckless. I'm sure he'll mellow in another decade or three. He's been enrolled at school here forever. His current focus is art. He wants to be a painter. But he seems to have more aptitude for carpentry. Fortunately, the art department hires him for a variety of projects. I'm hoping he'll be crossing over from sophomore to junior one of these years."

Samantha picked up the sailing photo and looked at it up close. "That thick hair is like waves of chocolate syrup."

Samantha's eyes seemed to widen.

Silver looked at Samantha and spoke, no pleasure in his voice. "I've seen that look of—what shall we call it—attention many times. Robert, especially, is susceptible to the attention his charms bring him. Actually, both of my sons would have been better off if they'd gotten less of that kind of notice."

Samantha turned to look at Silver. "That's funny. One of my teachers said that about a girl in my class."

"Who's that?" Josie asked.

"Clarice Angel. She was too perfect, from her hair to her name. And look how she ended up." Samantha said it as if she assumed the whole world knew about her classmate's murder, which, after the national media coverage, was probably true.

Silver made a slow, single nod and didn't speak.

Josie sensed recognition on Silver's part, but was pleased that Silver didn't ask about it.

Samantha set the photo back on the bookshelf. She was turning away when she saw a card with printed words leaning against some books. The card had a blue mat around it, giving it a framed look and emphasizing its importance. Behind the card was a blue bumper sticker that matched the matted card. Josie watched as Samantha looked closely.

Samantha carefully pronounced the words. "Ex historia est sapientia." Samantha looked at Silver. "What does that mean?"

"It's Latin. It means, 'From history comes wisdom.'"

"Is that some kind of famous quote?"

Silver smiled. "No. It's just something I preach."

"Do any of your students pay attention?" Josie asked.

"Truth be told? I don't think so."

They were silent for a moment.

"No more moaning from Unknown," Josie said, changing the subject.

"Yeah," Samantha said. "Maybe we should go back soon. That would help her learn that being stuck in your office doesn't go on forever."

Josie stood. Silver got up as well. "I'll follow you out."

"Good to meet you again, Professor Silver," Samantha said.

"You too, Ms. Samantha."

Josie got a jolt of pleasure out of her daughter's sudden display of manners coming just days after her ornery distress in the Minneapolis airport as she contemplated the guillotine dropping on her phone communication.

Josie and Samantha went toward Josie's office. Tom Silver went the other way to the stairwell.

Back in her office, Josie opened the kennel door and let Unknown out. "You can jump down on the floor, girl," she said.

Unknown stood at the edge of the table. She didn't seem eager to get down on the floor.

"Maybe she likes the view out the window," Josie said.

"But she's not looking out it," Samantha said. "She just seems sad to me. Don't happy dogs wag their tails?"

"I know some do. Maybe she will when she gets more comfortable."

"Should I carry the kennel home again?"

"I'm thinking we should leave it here. You are going back to school tomorrow, so I'll be coming here alone with Unknown. I can't walk her and carry my books and laptop and also carry the kennel. If we leave it here, that would solve the problem."

"Will it be okay having her at home without the kennel?" Samantha asked.

"It'll have to be okay, or we'll buy her another one."

TWENTY-FOUR

The next day, Samantha went to school while Josie did final paperwork in preparation for the beginning of Fall Quarter.

Josie and Unknown were waiting at Samantha's school when her classes were over. When Samantha came out of the building, she was with two other girls who, like Samantha, were wearing black clothes.

Samantha called out, "Mama, why are you here? Aren't you supposed to be teaching? Did someone die?" Samantha bent down and hugged Unknown. Samantha was wearing black nail polish and black eyeliner, makeup that was new to Josie. Makeup that her daughter hadn't worn when she left for school that morning. Was she losing influence over her daughter? Was she an ineffective parent? Or did it have to do with their terrible experience in the Quetico Wilderness?

"I just got done with work and thought I'd meet you after school," Josie said. "Is that okay? Am I interrupting an important goth affair?"

Samantha made a point of stopping and turning to give her classmates a long look as if to say, 'see what I have to put up with?'

The other girls had on so much heavy black cosmetics around their eyes, they looked ill. One of the girls wore a black bracelet with spikes. If she weren't careful and touched her face, she would gouge her cheeks. The other girl had black feathers arcing out of the sides and back of her shirt neckline. The feathers made a black arch around her head.

Samantha said, "What was that you said, Raven? That we are bound by dark cynicism? But I want you to meet my mother, who is the total opposite, all optimistic and happy."

Josie was surprised and pleased that her daughter didn't know the truth about her struggles with dark moods.

Josie said, "If it's too uncool to be seen with your mother, I'll just go home alone. I can probably get a single order of Chinese takeout, maybe take it and an eggroll out to the beach. After dinner, I can take in a show, go shopping, maybe go out on the pier and ride the ferris wheel and get an ice cream cone to watch the sunset. All totally uncool stuff."

"Got it, Mama." She made a little wave toward the other girls. "See y'all in the A.M."

She turned to walk with Josie.

When they were alone, Josie wanted to ask about Samantha's black makeup, but decided against it. She figured Samantha would tire of her goth phase in another month or two. It might be best not to comment.

They turned at the corner and headed toward the bus stop a block down.

"Look, the art lady has her security gate open," Samantha said. "What's her name again?"

"Shulu," Josie said. "Shuluwish Ojai. She told me that Shuluwish means the world of birds, and Ojai is the Valley of the Moon."

"It's Native American, right?"

"Yes. Although Shulu told me she thinks of herself as Indian. Part of the Chumash Indian tribe. She says she grew up a Chumash Indian and her Chumash friends feel the same way. I think they feel that the Native American moniker is political correctness run amok."

"So Shuluwish and Ojai are Chumash words?"

"Yes."

"Where did the Chumash live? You know, like back in the

past."

Josie loved that her daughter asked the question, a departure from her teenage focus on social media.

"The Chumash lived on the Channel Islands and on the coast from what is now Malibu up to Paso Robles."

"A long time ago, right?"

"Thousands of years from what they can tell. Far back before the time of Christ."

Samantha nodded, frowning, thinking. "How do you know this?"

"Because Shulu told me one time when I was walking by and she had her gate open. She doesn't talk much. But she's very smart."

They paused in front of the open gate in a chain-link fence. Behind the gate was a large area of broken asphalt that dated back decades. There was an old auto garage that Shulu had inherited and then converted to an art studio. The front portion had two large garage doors made of windows so that it was easier for auto mechanics to see to repair the cars years ago. The sides of the garage also had windows, which flooded the space with light, perfect for painting.

"They call her the baseball bat lady, right?" Samantha said.

"Yes. Although I don't think she wants to think of herself like that."

"How did she get the name again?"

Josie lowered her voice so that she couldn't be overheard.

"A guy broke into her studio. He had a gun, and he demanded money. He was shaking and clearly crazy. So she said she'd get him her money and that it was tucked down in one of a bunch of canvas rolls near where the guy was standing. What he didn't realize was that she had a baseball bat in that bin as well. She said she was going to reach for the money, but she instead reached for the baseball bat and swung it at the robber. He fired his gun and shot her in the side of her neck. But she survived, and she killed him with her baseball bat."

"Wow, that is so cool," Samantha said.

"I'm not sure we should think it was cool."

"Yes, it was! If some crazy with a gun breaks into your house, he should expect to get killed. It's like the psycho who tried to kill us. We should have killed him." Samantha was still looking through the gate toward Shulu's studio. She frowned. "Is it hard to kill someone with a baseball bat?"

"I don't think so. A bat will bash in someone's head pretty easily. The hard part is having the nerve to use it. I think most people don't. Either they can't bring themselves to swing a bat at a person's head. Or they only give it a tentative effort, which just wounds a person instead of kills them."

"Wounding a person isn't good enough." Samantha said it as if it were a simple fact of life when dealing with a bad guy.

"Maybe not," Josie said. "After she killed the robber, the media reported that the same man had previously used a knife to rob a store, and he got wounded when the store owner shot him. But he lived and sued the store owner for use of excessive force. The case got talked about in legal circles. After that case, some people said that if someone has a gun and breaks into your house, you should not only try to fight back, you should make sure you kill them so they can't sue you."

"Are you saying that the law allows you to kill an intruder but also allows the intruder to sue if you don't succeed?"

"Yes. The legal system is full of contradictions."

"That's totally dumb."

"I agree," Josie said. Josie thought of walking away but felt they should wait longer. She looked toward Shulu's studio and tried to appear casual. She didn't want Shulu to see them and then feel pressure to invite them in.

At the back of the studio space was a wall that closed off an old office and bathroom that Shulu had once showed to Josie when Samantha was a little girl. Shulu used the more private space as her living area. She'd also shown Josie the stairway that led to a loft and a small outdoor rooftop deck. They could see it now. There was a large blue umbrella above a blue table and two small, blue folding metal chairs.

The studio space was filled with many large paintings that were visible from the street. Most were landscapes of sea or beach scenes with many sea birds. The colors were bright and vibrant. Others were mountain scenes with soaring raptors and condors.

Because the paintings were obvious, city officials knew the place was used as an art studio. But Josie imagined that the city didn't realize the rear portion of the garage and the upper deck were being used as a residence. And if they did, perhaps the inspectors were kind enough to look the other way and allow Shulu some respite from the zoning demands and rules of bureaucracy.

Like the open front gate, the studio garage doors were also raised, blending indoors with outdoors.

"You can come in and visit." An old woman's voice seemed to float out from the studio.

Samantha looked at Josie. She spoke in a soft voice. "Do you think we should walk in?"

"Certainly. We've rarely seen the gate open. To ignore an invitation when the studio is finally open would be rude."

They walked through the gate and across the asphalt.

"Your daughter is now tall," the voice said.

It took a moment for Josie to see that the woman was perched on a high stool in front of one of two easels.

"Hi Shulu," Josie said. "So good to see you. This is my daughter Samantha. Samantha, this is Shulu Ojai."

"Hi, Ms. Ojai," Samantha said, smiling and exuding charm in spite of the gothic makeup and clothes. "I've seen your studio from out on the sidewalk. It's cool to see your bird paintings up close."

Shulu smiled and nodded. "Up close, you can see the details

of the birds. And up close, I'm called Shulu. Mrs. Ojai was my mother."

It took a moment for Samantha to respond. "Thank you," she finally said. Then she added, "Shulu."

Josie felt as if she were beaming inside as Samantha handled the situation so smoothly.

Shulu stood up and took a few steps toward them. The woman reached out and shook both of their hands. Her hands were gnarled as if she were a field worker, although Josie had no idea of the woman's past. Perhaps Shulu had always worked as an artist. It could be that her hands were simply gnarled with arthritis.

"And this is our dog Unknown," Samantha said.

Shulu nodded, bent over, and touched Unknown on her head.

Shulu had rich reddish-brown skin, like teak wood, and not especially lined for her 80-plus years. Her hair was white with streaks of gray, very thick, and pulled back into a long, thick bundle as long as an actual pony's tail.

Josie walked over and looked at three large paintings of eagles flying low over the ocean surf. They comprised a triptych. You could enjoy each image individually, but also hang them together if you had a room that was over 20 feet wide.

"Beautiful," Josie murmured.

Samantha was looking at a very small painting that hung in a corner. The painting, which was maybe six inches tall, was a portrait of a Great Horned Owl, surveying the forest landscape. The painting had a magical quality of making the owl look sweet even as its hooded eyes looked deadly.

"This is a totally beautiful painting," Samantha said.

"That's Hutash."

"Huta..." Samantha started to say as if unsure.

"Hutash is the Chumash goddess of the Earth. She protects all. I use the Great Horned Owl to represent Hutash because the owl is revered by my people for its power and intelligence."

Samantha looked at Shulu and then at the painting. "The Chumash god is female? That's cool. I love this painting," she said. "I'm a volleyball player, and this owl's eyes remind me of an athlete's focus."

The woman nodded. "Nothing escapes Hutash's focus. Would you two like a cup of tea?"

Samantha looked at Josie.

"Yes, that would be lovely," Josie said.

Shulu made a slight nod. She walked through a door, which swung most of the way closed behind her.

Josie and Samantha wandered the space, looking at paintings including one in progress on a huge oak easel. To one side of the easel was a rolling table with a glass top. The glass was nearly covered with dabs of paint in dozens of colors.

"This must be where she mixes her paint," Samantha said.

"I think it's called a palette," Josie said.

There were some brushes on the palette and dozens more in jars. With the brushes were other tools with wooden handles and metal ends so thin they would be bendy. Some of them were shaped like triangles, some diamonds, some just long rounded blades.

The door opened and Shulu came out carrying a tray with three cups. She handed it to Samantha. "If you please," Shulu said. Then she went back through the door and returned with a tea pot.

"Let's go up on the roof." She led the way up the stairs.

Josie noticed that the woman went up at a good speed and didn't use the handrail.

At the top, Shulu opened a door and went outside. Samantha and Unknown followed. Josie was last.

"Oh, wow, Mama, look! You can see downtown from here!"

Samantha set the tray on the table, then walked around the small patio. "And you can see the ocean, too! This is the best view ever. This is what it would be like for Shulu's birds, getting a great view."

Shulu poured tea, then pointed at the two chairs. "Josie, you and I can sit. Athletes like Samantha can stand."

They sat. Samantha came over, picked up a cup, and sipped.

"Shulu, how did you learn to paint?"

"I went to college at USC and then later at CalArts."

Samantha turned to Josie. "Mama, that's where Clarice's older brother went to school!" She turned to Shulu. "But he studies music. There's a special name for it."

"Musicology?" Shulu said.

"I think so, yeah. But you studied art."

"Right. After college, I taught at the San Francisco Art Institute, where I met an artist named Richard Diebenkorn. Twenty-five years later, my uncle died and left me his auto garage. Because Diebenkorn had moved to Santa Monica and taught at UCLA, I thought it made sense to come back down to L.A. So I quit teaching and turned my uncle's auto garage into my studio. Diebenkorn had gotten quite successful with his Ocean Park paintings, and that gave me the courage to be a full-time artist."

Samantha asked, "Were his Ocean Park paintings about the beach in Ocean Park?"

"They were abstracts, so not specifically about the beach and town of Ocean Park. But inspired by the beach and the colors."

Samantha looked at Josie. "Did you know all this, Mama? Diebenkorn art and UCLA and stuff?"

"Just a little. Diebenkorn was before my time."

"Did you and Shulu know each other?"

"No. We only met around ten years ago when she was setting up this studio and I was walking by to take you to daycare on my way to UCLA." Josie turned to Shulu. "I'm so glad you are still here and still painting."

Shulu made a slight smile. "Painters usually work until they drop."

"That sounds like a writer I know," Josie said.

They spoke about art and teaching while they drank their tea.

"We don't want to take up more of your time," Josie said, standing. "Thank you."

Samantha said, "Good to meet you, Shulu. Your paintings are cool. You're pretty cool, too."

Shulu nodded and looked down at Unknown. "Do you take your dog to the beach?"

"Yeah," Samantha said. "We just adopted her in Minnesota. So she's still learning about the beach. She seems to be alarmed by the waves."

"The next few days, the surf will be very heavy."

Samantha frowned. "Is that..." she trailed off.

"The Chumash learn to read the waves from the time we're born. I see the waves as communication from Hutash."

"Hutash is warning us?" Samantha said.

Shulu nodded. "I think so, yes."

TWENTY-FIVE

Back home, Josie opened the sliding deck door. Although they could only see a small slice of ocean and beach, the full roar of distant waves was even more palpable than it had been down on the street.

"C'mere, Unknown," Samanatha said. "You can see the ocean, smell the surf, look at the dog walkers on the beach."

Unknown didn't budge from her location in the corner. She sat in a corner and looked across the room toward the windows.

Samantha said, "Look, Mama. Unknown seems unsettled. Do you think she's afraid of the window?"

"I don't know. We're only on the third floor. She wasn't afraid at my office. And our deck has a substantial railing. So I would think she'd be comfortable. Maybe she doesn't like the sound of the ocean. That's probably the biggest difference between here and the Canadian wilderness." Josie closed the deck door.

Samantha fed Unknown some canned food. Unknown ate it, but not with any eagerness.

Josie fixed a dinner of bean soup, steamed broccoli, and salmon fillets. No salt, in keeping with doctor's orders.

After dinner, they sat together on the couch and looked out the window. Samantha left her phone on the kitchen counter. Josie was surprised. Her daughter normally held her phone constantly, as if it were her air supply. If that was because of the trauma in Canada, then maybe the experience wasn't all terrible.

"Do you think the assassin is dead?" Samantha asked.

"I want to think so. Of course, it really bothers me that the sheriff said they couldn't find him. Maybe he survived his burns and escaped. Or maybe he crawled off and died someplace else."

"If he's not dead, he could come here and try to kill us again." Samantha's voice wavered. "Will we have to be afraid forever?"

Although Samantha sat taller than Josie on the couch, Josie put her arm around Samantha's shoulders and pulled her down next to her. "I don't know, Sam. I'm so sorry, but I don't know. I'm guessing that something will happen to the man, if he's still alive. He'll make a mistake. He's obviously really unhinged. He'll assault someone else who gets in his way. Or he'll cause some kind of problem that makes the police pick him up on a different charge. They could identify him by his fingerprints from the canoe or paddle."

The next morning, Josie walked Samantha to school. Samantha held Unknown's leash. Once at the school, Samantha squatted down and gave Unknown a long hug. "You be a good girl, right?"

Then Samantha stood, handed Josie the leash. "Bye, Mama."

"Don't I at least get a hug like Unknown?"

Samantha briefly looked at the sky. "Unknown is a poor helpless dog. You're the big shot professor. Professors don't need regular stuff like hugs, right?"

"Sam, professors need hugs more than anyone."

"Okay."

They hugged. Samantha's friend Alaysia walked up. They all said hi, and Alaysia pet Unknown. The two girls turned and went into the school. Josie and Unknown walked two blocks over and got on the bus to UCLA.

During the ride, she thought again about what she could have witnessed that would result in someone sending a killer after her.

Her best guess was the party she mentioned to Samantha. It was probably a dead end. But she felt desperate with the possibility that a killer was still out there and that he might intend to complete his mission.

Josie got off the bus, turned at Dickson Court, and headed toward Bunche Hall and her office.

She took the stairs to her office floor, walked down to Professor Silver's office, and knocked.

He called out from the other side of the door, "'Abandon hope, all ye who enter here.'"

Josie opened the door. "Hey, professor," she said. "I love the way Dante starts his Divine Comedy with his treatment of hell."

Tom Silver looked up from his desk. "Dante lives on. Come on in."

"Is it okay to interrupt your work?"

"As I tell my students, if I'm approached with respect for my time, of course. But students don't respect my time, so it's a moot concept."

"Maybe a title would help get their respect. Sir Thomas?"

"Considering my skepticism about the accuracy of recorded history, I'd say Sir Doubting Thomas would be more appropriate."

"Ah," Josie said. "Jesus himself wanted his apostle Thomas to doubt the concept of a messiah, right? But what would your students think of that name?"

"They'd think the same as always. That we teachers live in an unreal world, disconnected from anything of real value. They probably think the resurrection of Jesus is a video game."

"I bet you're right. In fact, maybe there is such a game. Anyway, I have a question."

"Hmmm?" He held out his hand toward Unknown. "What's your dog's name? Oh, I remember. Unknown. C'mere, Unknown." He gestured at the dog. "Don't worry, I don't bite."

Unknown looked up at Josie, the first instance Josie had noticed of the dog checking with her in that manner.

"It's okay, girl. Go on." Josie waved her hand toward Silver.

Tom gestured again.

Unknown took a few steps toward him, lifted up her head a little and sniffed the air, her nostrils flexing. She didn't stand close. Tom leaned forward in his chair, reached out, and let her sniff his hand.

"C'mon, Unknown. I'm dogless at the moment, but I'm a dog person. Honest."

Unknown took another step. Tom rubbed her neck. He was kind and gentle.

Josie said, "Remember the big bash in Bel Air for Lawrence Winston Underwood, the man who made the extravagant donation?"

"Yes, indeed. A kind of quid pro quo. An extravagant party befitting extravagant generosity, complete with the paparazzi who spread such news with photographs of recognizable people in recognizably compromising situations."

Josie laughed. "Right," she said. "I want to contact a woman I saw at the party. But I didn't get her name. I thought you might know. She is around fifty years old, very thin and elegant, has the looks and demeanor of a film star."

There was a short silence before Silver answered. "A white lady?"

"Asian, I think," Josie said.

"I don't know that woman."

"But by your phrasing, I can tell you noticed her."

"I'm a widower. The woman you speak of is of the appropriate age range. And she is—how shall I phrase it—quite noticeable. Your word choice was 'elegant.' I've always appreciated elegance. Your question makes me curious about why you are interested in her."

Unknown was now leaning into Silver's pets. Josie was

surprised at how pleased it made her to see Unknown's response to the man's affection.

"I suppose it's an obscure fishing expedition," Josie said. "I'm curious about a man I've met. It was a brief meeting, but it was memorable. I never got his name, either. But I have reason to think that the woman I refer to might know him."

"And she could be your matchmaker," Silver said.

"Maybe she could just tell me his name."

"How could I help?" Silver asked.

"I assume, perhaps wrongly, that someone else who was at the party must know the woman's name. The only people I knew there were other professors or UCLA administrators. I'm reluctant to call on them because…" Josie trailed off.

"Because you want your personal life kept private from the prying eyes of your colleagues," Silver said. "Yet you're talking to a colleague."

"A doubting Thomas colleague who is highly skeptical of the things he hears, whether those things appear to be simple facts or salacious gossip. Am I right?"

"True, true," Silver said. "How would one navigate life without a code of ethics to reign in gossip and innuendo? Let me think."

"Take your time."

"There's a graduate student of mine who works an internship with Roger Lopez."

"The professor who put on the party," Josie said.

"Right. The student's name is Emily Brusse. She's working on her Masters' thesis. Studying the ancient Greeks. Anyway, she's very sharp, misses nothing. Someday she'll be president of something important. If anyone would know the lovely woman, Emily would."

Josie smiled. "The 'elegant age-appropriate woman a widower would notice' as a matter of course has now morphed into a lovely woman," she said.

"You brought her up and got me thinking about her elegance. Morphing follows. Hold on while I look for Emily in my contact list." Silver opened an address book on his desk and flipped pages.

Josie was pleased to see that she wasn't the only person who still wrote addresses in a book rather than typed them into a phone.

"Here we are," Silver said. "Emily Brusse." He wrote on a Post-it note. "I'll write down her cell, which, of course, people of Emily's generation won't answer. I'll also put down her email, which, of course, people of Emily's generation consider archaic."

"You're saying I should text her."

"Or you could call Roger Lopez's office. Answering his phone might be a required duty when she's doing the intern thing."

"Do you know when she works there?"

"No."

"If I can reach her, may I tell her I got her name from you?"

"Sure, why not?"

"Shall I refer to you as Professor Silver, Sir Thomas, or Sir Doubting Thomas?"

"Professor Silver will ring the bell louder than the others." He wrote another number. "I added Roger Lopez's office number." He handed the Post-it note across the desk to Josie.

"Thank you very much. I'd like to return the favor someday."

"You know I'll accept that when I have a need. Courvoisier, Remy Martin works as well."

Josie said goodbye, and she left with Unknown.

TWENTY-SIX

Once Josie was in her own office, she dialed Roger Lopez.

"Professor Lopez," a young woman answered.

"Hello, this is Professor Josephine Strong calling. I was given this number by Professor Silver. He suggested I call Emily Brusse."

"Speaking." The woman said.

Josie thought the woman's voice was a bit clipped, though not from brusqueness so much as efficiency. The world of academia did not countenance much small talk.

"Emily, I'm trying to get in touch with a person who was at the Bel Air party for Lawrence Winston Underwood."

"The man who gave the UCLA History Department twenty million," Emily said.

"Yes. A very fine gift. The person I'm looking for was a woman I saw briefly, upstairs in a study. She was about fifty years old, Asian or Asian American, thin, elegant. Is there any chance you know the person? Or perhaps Professor Lopez had a list of attendees? Maybe her name was on the list."

"Oh, I think I know who you're referring to. But I don't know her name."

"Can you think of anyone who would?"

"Not really. But I didn't circulate much. My job was basically acting as a liaison between Professor Lopez and Mr. Underwood. And I answered questions about the UCLA History Department."

"Who else would I call?" Josie asked.

"Well, I suppose you could talk to the catering company. The food service crew and the bartenders… They talk to everybody. Or you could talk to the parking valets."

"Good idea," Josie said. "Any chance you know the names of those companies? Or anyone who worked as a caterer or car park at the party?"

"Let me look in the file."

Josie waited. After a minute, she heard a file drawer close.

"Here are the names of the businesses at the event."

Emily read off names and phone numbers.

"Thank you very much, Emily. I appreciate your help. And I'll put in a word of thanks to Professor Lopez."

Josie spent the next two hours on the phone, calling the catering and parking valet services that Emily Brusse had referred her to. No one was able or willing to help her. Most made it clear that she was an unwelcome interruption to their busy schedules. The only useful information came from one woman who said she didn't know anything about the party because they hired temp workers for that kind of special event. When Josie asked what temp company they used, the woman said that the catering owner knew but that she was in Hawaii on vacation and no way could she be contacted.

Josie hung up feeling dejected.

She took Unknown down the stairs, across campus, and rode the bus back to Santa Monica. They headed over to the Beach Walk. They went south a mile toward Venice, then back. The waves were abnormally loud. More warning that Shulu spoke of? But the tourists going to and from the Santa Monica Pier only saw sunshine and blue Pacific. Their world seemed to Josie to be blissfully happy. None of them seemed to be in danger. Maybe none of them worried that a killer was out there, waiting to strike again.

After Josie and Unknown climbed the stairs back to their condo, Josie searched online for temp services in Bel Air. She dialed the first one that came up.

"Bel Air Job Staffing," a male voice said.

"Hi, my name is Josephine Strong, and I need catering and car parking for a large party our university is planning. I was at a party in Bel Air some time back. I really liked the service at that party. I don't know the name of the company that set it up. But I do know they used a temp agency. If I could establish that the temps came from your company, I would be interested in hiring you to work our party directly, no catering middleman at all."

"Where and when was the party?"

Josie gave him the address and date.

"Oh, was that the UCLA gig? For a bunch of professors?"

"Yes."

"That was us," the man said.

"Perfect," Josie said. "Before I do any further planning, I'd like to talk to a couple of the people who worked that party. Can you please refer me? Perhaps one of the car parkers and either a bartender or one of the wait staff."

"I don't know if we can give out that information."

"The job would depend on me talking to a couple of staffers. It's a proforma thing our department requires. We don't need any personal information. We just have to ask a few questions."

"Okay. Hold on, please."

The man got back on the line in a minute. "My boss says it's okay. But he will coach our people not to reveal anything personal. He also says we have to call you. So if you can give me your number, I'll see who I can find to answer questions."

Josie gave him her cell number.

They said goodbye.

Josie's phone rang fifteen minutes later.

"Yo, Antonio calling for Josephine."

"This is she."

"My boss says I'm supposed to talk sweet to you about car parking."

"Thanks, Antonio. I just have a few questions."

"Sure, hon. You want a fiesta, we'll make it killer."

"Did your boss mention the UCLA party your company staffed?"

"Right on. I ran the valet. We roll with six of L.A.'s finest drivers. We handle all rides from super cars to limos to Harleys. We have your back."

"Could you bring the same drivers to another party?"

Antonio paused. "I don't know 'bout that. My guys, we're in so much demand."

"The reason I ask is, one of our patrons brought a friend to the last UCLA party. I want to impress that friend. You know how it works. If you keep the big money happy, they're more likely to spread it around. You probably remember her. About fifty. Asian American. Very elegant. She wore a black skirt and a white blouse."

"Oh, you're talking about the sunset orchid?"

"Maybe. What does that mean, 'sunset orchid.'"

"Just, you know, real easy on the eyes?"

"She's attractive, if that's what you mean."

"Uh, huh. That's the orchid part."

"What's the sunset part?" Josie asked.

"You know. Like an old flower. About to drop off the plant."

"But this woman is only about fifty years old," Josie said.

"That's what I said. Old."

"Do you know her name?"

"Nope."

"Would any of your drivers know?"

"Pretty sure they don't."

"Would anyone else in your agency know?"

There was a pause.

"Well, Maria would know," he said.

"Who's that?"

"My chica Maria. She rocks names. She's got one of those memories. Remembers everyone she's ever met in her life."

"Was she at the party?"

"She carries the snack things."

"What does that mean?" Josie asked.

"We call them our latina express. Maria and Gabriela carry the trays. Fancy snacks."

"Hors d'oeuvres?"

"Yeah. That's it."

"Could I talk to her before I get to the details of hiring your company?"

"Let me ask."

Josie was taken aback. Antonio had someone with him the entire time.

"Hola."

"Hello. Is this Maria?"

"Sí."

Josie briefly explained what she'd already told Antonio. "So I'm just looking for the name of the woman who was at the party. Antonio called her the sunset orchid. Do you know her name?"

Josie heard Maria talking in Spanish.

Antonio came back on. "Maria is worried. She says she can get in so much trouble talking about the people she serves."

"The party attendees?"

There was a pause.

"The clientele?" Josie said, clarifying. "The customers?"

"Right," Antonio said. "I shouldn't have mentioned the sunset orchid."

"Trust me. I will never say a word to anyone. I just would like the woman's name."

Josie heard more Spanish.

Antonio was back. "Lena."

"Lena?" Josie said. "Thanks. Does Maria know Lena's last name?"

"Let me ask."

More Spanish.

This time Maria came back to the phone. "Dos nombres. Dos Cartas. Li. L I. Then Na. N A. Chinese. The family name is Li. Her name is Na."

"Thank you very much, Maria. You have helped me."

Josie disconnected. She Googled Li Na. Most of what she found was about a professional tennis player. But she also found an article about a woman named Li Na who had been indicted by a grand jury in a racketeering and money laundering business. There was a picture of a woman. Josie was certain it was the same woman she'd seen at the UCLA party.

The article said that the woman was involved in a birth tourism scheme, whereby she charged Chinese couples $200,000 each to help them come to the U.S. to give birth and thereby have a baby with U.S. citizenship. Li Na then laundered the money through her chain of 26 nail salons that operated under the name of Stiletto Nails by Li Na.

Li Na's troubles expanded when a sophisticated Hispanic gang hired a hacker to breach her website server and intercept payments totaling $19 million. Li Na fought back. She hired her own hackers—computer science students at USC—and identified the hacker and the gang members responsible. Then she reportedly hired an assassin who killed two of the gang members and the hacker who had targeted her. She was indicted on three counts of murder. But the charges were later dropped for lack of evidence. The assassin was never identified, although it was rumored that he had an association with the Men's Workout Gym in Hawthorne. The article on Li Na also referred to her two bodyguards, both of whom were also associated with Men's Workout Gym.

The article left Josie with many questions. Josie had seen the woman named Li Na at the UCLA party in Bel Air. She was with a young man who looked athletic. Was the man a killer for hire? The woman named Li Na seemed to be staying out of sight. Was it possible that the mere fact Josie had witnessed the man with Li Na meant that Josie was a threat and should be removed?

Josie Googled the address of the Men's Workout Gym and it came up in a neighborhood just east of the 405.

Josie took Unknown with her. She drove and parked her Prius

on a rundown, urban street. The street was lined with dilapidated brick warehouses. Some were boarded up. Some were so broken that they were missing portions of their outer walls. Young men stood in groups on the street.

Josie would have hoped that having Unknown at her side would give her comfort as she walked through what seemed like a tough neighborhood. She believed there was no cause for fear. She wasn't wearing noticeable clothes. She didn't think anything about her telegraphed money. The neighborhood was only threatening to young men who might belong to the wrong gang. But she was still nervous. She could turn around and go back. But how would she get the information she was seeking?

Two blocks down, she came to the address. On a brick wall, six feet above the broken sidewalk, was a plywood sign with peeling paint. It said, 'Men's Workout Gym' in red block letters that were poorly formed. The sign looked like it had been painted by an ambitious seven-year-old.

Under the sign was a windowless steel door. Josie realized that a glass door was perhaps the most common aspect of a commercial establishment. But not here. Josie looked for a doorbell. Nothing. The door was ajar an inch as if its latch didn't work.

Josie felt very uncomfortable opening an opaque steel door. Still, she pulled it open, and she and Unknown stepped inside.

She was in a single large room about the size of a basketball court. The walls were rough brick painted black, and the floor was concrete painted brown. Like a basketball court, the ceiling was high, and the lights were harsh. There was no decor of any kind. It immediately seemed to Josie to be as dreary a place as she'd ever been.

Near the door was a counter that looked as if it might be where someone on the staff would talk to customers or write up sales receipts. But there was no apparent staff.

The gym space consisted of multiple weight benches and exercise bars, and floor mats and angled, padded boards. There were large racks that held long barbells and circular weights to put on them.

Josie was not familiar with the current fitness trends. But even she understood that this gym was very different. There were no bicycles or treadmills or stations designed for ten different kinds of exercise. Indeed, there were no machines with moving parts. Men's Workout was simply a place to lift weights.

She counted eleven men, mostly Hispanic, mostly under 30. Some lay on benches, pressing barbells with so many weights on them that the bars curved. For each man pressing the weights skyward, there was another man standing at the prostrate man's head, hands out, ready to grab the bar and assist if needed. Josie had seen that on TV. She believed the helper assistant was called a spotter. Two men stood alone on widely-spaced mats, holding long barbells across their shoulders, behind their heads, squatting down part way, then straightening back up. When one of them tired, he moved back a step to a tall stand, and lowered the bar onto the supports. There was a single white guy over in a corner, doing pullups on a short bar that was mounted about 8 feet above the floor. Near him, a Black man was lying on an inclined board, his head downhill, doing sit-ups.

None of the men wore stylish or even colorful clothing. Every man had on loose shorts and a T-shirt or sleeveless jersey. They all wore over-sized athletic shoes. All of the men were big and strong, but none looked sculpted like what Josie had seen at Muscle Beach. This gym wasn't about bodybuilding for looks. These men were pursuing exercise only for its own sake. It wasn't about catching the eye of any observers. And, of course, except for Josie and Unknown, there were no observers.

The air was filled with an acrid body odor of men who were overdue for showers. Yet, Josie could see no showers. At the far corner of the gym, a small room had been built out into the main space. There was a door. Josie thought it was likely a restroom. But there wouldn't be room for showers. And there certainly wasn't room for women's facilities.

Josie stood near the door, wondering if anyone associated

with the gym would notice her. A couple of the men glanced her way, but it was as if they didn't even see her. She noticed the rhythm of two men at a bench press. As one finished a set of repetitions, he stood, and the other lay down to take his place. At the end of a cycle, Josie walked up.

"Excuse me, please?"

The two men turned and looked at her, frowns on their faces.

"Is any staff member here, today? I'd like to ask some questions."

One man shook his head. The other turned to adjust the weights on the bar.

"Does a staff member come in at a certain time?"

The man shook his head again. "No, ma'am. Just us." The man enunciated well and spoke crisply. He had a weak Hispanic accent. He had chestnut brown skin. He was short, and his neck was as wide as his head, maybe wider. He was not especially muscle bound, but no doubt very strong. He looked like he could lift cars.

"Maybe you could answer some questions for me? I'm happy to pay for your time."

The man had a rolled towel draped over his shoulders. He pulled it off, used it to wipe down the barbell, then spread it out on the weight bench. He picked up a small white bag that was sitting on the edge of the weight rack. He massaged the bag with both hands, then set the bag down. His palms were now white. Josie understood that the white was some kind of chalk powder, probably to aid gripping.

"Are you a reporter?" the man asked as he sat down.

"No," Josie said. She realized that the news story on Li Na's bodyguards and the Men's Workout Gym had probably generated a great deal of interest in these men, interest they hadn't wanted. She had thought she could approach them as a writer, a presentation that technically described much of what professors do. But his question made her appreciate that he was sensitive about reporters.

"I'm not a reporter, I'm a professor. I'm working on a project that requires the kind of expertise you might have. Maybe we could talk after your workout?"

"How much?" he said.

The question surprised Josie. She wasn't used to such a direct manner of speaking. "Well, I suppose it would depend on your answers." Josie paused. Could she trust this guy? Her gut instinct told her she could.

"How about I pay you one hundred to start?" she said. "We'll go someplace where we can sit and talk. As you tell me more about the things I'm interested in, I'll pay you another hundred. Maybe that process would repeat. If at any time, you want to stop, you walk away with the money I paid you, along with my thanks. But first, I would need to know if you have the kind of expertise I'm looking for."

"What's that?"

"I want to ask questions about soldiers."

"You're interested in soldiers?" The man seemed wary.

"Yes. Mercenaries, in particular."

The man raised his eyebrows. He didn't speak.

"You don't have to have personal experience to answer my questions," Josie added. "If you know of men who are veterans, men who have worked as soldiers, especially soldiers for hire, then you probably know enough to help me. From what I read, that applies to some of the men here."

The man glanced up at the wall.

Josie followed his gaze to a wall clock. It said 2:35.

"I'm done at three," he said. "We don't have showers. But I can clean up a little in the washroom."

"I'll wait outside," Josie said.

TWENTY-SEVEN

Twenty minutes later, the man and three others walked out. They exchanged some words, and the man separated himself and walked over to Josie.

"Thank you," Josie said. "I appreciate your time. Where would be good to talk?"

"The taqueria next block down serves beer."

"That sounds good." Josie waited to see which way the man would walk.

He hesitated.

"Oh," Josie said. She'd previously stashed some hundred dollar bills in her front pocket as a safer way to carry cash than in her purse. She reached into the pocket, managed to separate a single bill, then pulled it out and handed it to him.

He took it without looking at it and stuffed it into his own pocket.

"I'm Josie Strong."

"Manuel Castro. My friends call me Manny." He started walking down the sidewalk.

Josie walked along, with Unknown dutifully at her side. She didn't pull on the leash. Josie didn't know if that was because she was well-trained or because she had no enthusiasm.

"What do you do for a living, Manny?"

"I'm an ESL teacher at the Hawthorne Neighborhood Center."

"English as a Second Language."

He nodded. "And I'm a financial counselor for Latin American immigrants."

"Wow," Josie said. "You're... Sorry, I don't mean to sound patronizing. But you are quite young. So I'm sur... I'm glad to know of your focus."

"Go ahead and say it. You think most Latinos you see on the street are probably gangbangers and that the ambitious entrepreneurs among us are running taco trucks."

"Well, a little bit, maybe."

"My mama raised me right. After I got back from my second tour in Afghanistan, I helped our center write a three-year grant application for the center's rent, which is two thousand a month. My own salary was part of the proposal. I get fifteen hundred a month for my teaching and another fifteen hundred a month to teach Hawthorne residents how to budget and plan their finances. The center was awarded a three-year funding grant. We had enough extra to get wifi and buy ten laptops that neighborhood kids can use at no charge. We allow those kids to check out the computers and take them home for school work and such."

"How did you learn finances?"

"I have an aunt who is smart about money. When I complained about high rents, she explained how my sister and I could buy a rundown double bungalow. The key is that you find a house so bad that the owner can't sell it at any price. So we found one. The word was that a city inspector was going to have it condemned. It had a swayback roof and bad plumbing, and it was infested with rats and mice. There was even an opossum living in the attic. So we made a rock-bottom offer. Fifteen thousand down, a ten-year contract that the seller would carry, a monthly payment based on half a percent of loan value, and a balloon payment at the end of ten years. We started by getting rid of the vermin, then cleaning and repainting. Then we did basic repairs to the plumbing. Nothing fancy, because we couldn't afford that. We rented out one side to an older immigrant couple. A couple of months later, we invited the inspector over for cupcakes. He took one look at what we had done and said he would use us as an example of how to transform neighborhood housing. We're now four years into the contract, the house has doubled in value, and we're looking at finding another house."

"That's so great, Manny. I'm going to tell my daughter about you. She could use some of your focus."

"So where do you do your professoring?"

"UCLA."

"What subject?"

"Medieval history."

Manuel walked in silence for awhile.

"That means the Middle Ages, right? Knights on horseback."

"Yes, exactly."

More silence. "You probably get more than three thousand a month."

Josie wasn't sure how to respond. "Yes."

Manuel said, "Do you have a Ph.D.?"

"Yes."

"Did you go to UCLA for college?"

"No. I applied, but I didn't get accepted."

"Where did you go?"

"UC Davis."

"The wine school."

Josie grinned. "Some people think of it as the wine school. Others think of it as the veterinary school. Davis has a good rep. I was lucky to get in."

"I couldn't have," Manuel said. "I wasn't a good student."

They walked in silence for a minute.

"If you took your big paycheck and divided it by all the years you spent learning and getting your Ph.D., it wouldn't look so big, huh?"

"You're smart about numbers, Manuel," Josie said. "I'm pretty sure you're going to continue to be a big success."

He made a small nod.

They came to the taqueria. "I've been exercising," Manuel said. "So we should take an outdoor table. Better ventilation." He grinned.

Josie let him pick a table. They were round and made of metal, painted brilliant colors, yellow and red, orange and green. They sat on high chairs and ordered cervezas. When their beers came, Manuel said, "Why would a professor want to know about mercenaries?"

Josie didn't know how best to phrase it. She decided to take a hypothetical approach so that it could largely be true. "Let's say I'm writing a novel. I have a hired killer who intends to murder a woman." She proceeded to explain what had happened to her in terms just vague enough to fit the possibility of a novel.

When she was done, she said, "What do you think?"

Manuel was shaking his head. "It's all wrong."

"What do you mean?"

"Everything. You're talking about someone who kills for money. An assassin. But you're describing a clown. Professional assassins don't engage with their target. They stay away. They don't allow themselves to be noticed. They are the essence of normal. They might be strong, but they don't show off their muscles. They keep their bodies covered with loose shirts so no one notices. They never travel with their weapons or check them on planes. It's too risky because any number of TSA inspectors might discover their weapons, which would blow their cover. They arrange to pick up their weapons in another fashion. They wear ordinary clothes and have boring haircuts. A target never sees his assassin coming. A target especially never meets and talks to his assassin. A professional assassin never shows up on security cam video footage. An assassin is a phantom. After a kill, the assassin leaves no trace of where he was, where he came from, or where he went."

"So my entire exper... presentation is false," Josie said.

"If you want your assassin to be a believable professional? Yes. The killer you describe is someone whose only information came from watching movies. Someone who thinks of himself as the cliché of the dramatic lone wolf. Someone who wants to be noticed and feared. That's nothing like a professional. A professional measures his success by the fact that no one knows what his job is, how he does his job. A professional is someone who is never feared because he's never noticed."

"This is very helpful," Josie said. She felt awkward pulling out another hundred dollar bill, but it seemed appropriate.

As before, Manuel slipped it into his pocket without looking at it.

"When I was a boy," Manuel said, "my mother taught me something very valuable. Question your assumptions. Things are rarely as you expect. And often, things are the opposite of what you think."

Josie thought about it. "You're right." She was thinking that she should go back through the last many days, identify her assumptions, then question them.

"If a person wanted to find a mercenary, where would you look?" Josie asked.

"It doesn't work like that. You can't look for them. You put the word out, and they will find you."

"How would you put the word out?"

"There are some internet boards where people post. Or you mention your needs in places where veterans get their libations. Or maybe you talk to someone at, say, a local gym."

"Then how does the mercenary contact you?"

"In a way that can't be traced. An anonymous text from a burner phone. An email from a Tor account."

"What's a Tor account?"

"It's a type of internet browser that can't be traced. It was created by the U.S. government."

Josie thought about it. "So you wouldn't meet a

mercenary?"

"Not a professional, no. That's one of the ways you know he's good. Because his identity always stays secret."

Josie nodded. She sipped her beer. It didn't fit her assumption about the sunset orchid at the party for the donor. She was with the man, talking to him. "And the lone wolf-type guy you mentioned... The non professional. Where does he hang out?"

"That kind of guy is an idiot. So they could be anywhere. The mall. The beach. The local coffee shop."

"But they are still dangerous?"

"Of course. Anyone can kill. But unlike the professional, they get caught. And they either go to prison or they get killed, themselves."

Josie pulled out another bill and gave it to Manuel. "Thanks. You've been very helpful."

"Any time. And when you want to invest in a struggling community, you call Manuel at the Hawthorne Community Center."

"I will. Thanks again."

Josie and Unknown walked back to her car and drove home.

By the time she and Unknown were inside, it was late in the afternoon. Samantha would be nearly finished with the after-school math tutoring class she taught.

Josie made some tea and thought about what Manuel had said, especially about assumptions. Manuel was young, but he was smart. He'd made it clear that everything about the man who'd tried to kill them was unprofessional. Now Josie wanted to reassess everything she thought she knew.

TWENTY-EIGHT

Josie got out a pad of paper and listed everything she could remember about the killer, from his first contact with her and Sam in the Minneapolis airport to the moment they paddled away from his unconscious body lying on the shore of the wilderness island.

When she was going to make notes about his possible motivation, she recognized the obvious assumption she'd made about him may have had no basis in fact. From the beginning, she and Samantha talked about the reason why someone was trying to kill them as being some kind of response to something Josie had seen or experienced.

But what if it wasn't about Josie at all? What if it was about Samantha?

What if Samantha had witnessed something that made her a risk to the killer?

To Josie's recollection, there was only one extraordinary thing in Samantha's recent experience.

Her friend Clarice had been abducted and killed.

Josie looked at the time. Samantha would be about to get on the bus to come home.

Josie picked up her phone and dialed Samantha's number.

"Hi Mama," Samantha answered.

"Sam, where are you?"

"I'm walking from our school to the bus stop. What's up?"

"I have a question. What are the last things you remember about Clarice?"

"What do you mean?"

"For example, where were you when you last saw her? What happened? Did you notice anything unusual? Was she with anyone?"

Samantha didn't immediately respond.

"Sam?"

"I'm thinking, Mama. The last time I saw Clarice was the night I stayed over at Melinda's house. It was several days before her body was found. Melinda and I were out getting frozen yogurt at the Your Yogurt shop. We thought it was weird. Clarice was walking down the sidewalk. She didn't see us. She walked over to a black car and got in the passenger side. I think it was her mom picking her up."

This was news to Josie. Her first reaction was anger that Samantha had been out at night when she'd promised Josie she and Melinda would stay inside during their sleepover. But now was not the time for Josie to deal with that.

"Did you tell the police about it when they interviewed you?"

"Yeah."

"What did they make of it?"

"Nothing. Like it was no big deal. They made a call and found out Clarice's mom has a black Lexus. It was obviously fine."

"Did they ask her mom if she picked up Clarice that night?"

"They couldn't. Because the day before they talked to me about it, her mom had to go to Japan on a business trip. But Clarice's dad thought her mom probably picked her up."

"Did the car you saw seem like it could have been a Lexus?"

"Sure. At least, I suppose it was. That's what the cops asked, too. I just remember that the car was nice. You know how fancy cars that are black are always shiny and polished. If a black car is grubby, it's usually an old car. This one was shiny."

"When Clarice got into the car, did you see the driver?"

"No. Like I told the cops, I'm pretty sure the car had tinted windows. And her mom's car has tinted windows. So I didn't really think about it."

"Did the driver see you?"

"I don't know. I suppose she could have."

"Were you in a place where you were easily visible?"

"No. We were sitting at one of the outdoor tables. There are trees that kind of drape over the area. And there's a hedge that pretty much blocks the view from the street." Samantha paused. "But now I remember that when I saw Clarice get into the car, I stood up and walked over to the street. I was on the sidewalk when the car drove past me."

"Is there any chance the car wasn't Clarice's mom's? Could it have been something other than a Lexus?" Josie asked.

"I suppose. Like I said, I didn't notice."

"Was there anything at all that you noticed about it?"

"No. Lots of parents have black cars. You know that about our area. Wait. Let me think. I remember it had a bumper sticker. A blue bumper sticker. I remember because I thought that nice cars don't usually have bumper stickers."

"What did it say?" Josie asked.

"I don't remember. It wasn't something that stuck in my brain. It just flashed by my eyes and I didn't process. Like if it was in another language."

Josie's heart seemed to hit the inside of her chest. An ache spread through her.

"Sam, could the bumper sticker have been in Latin?"

"I don't know. I don't know what Latin looks like."

"Ex historia est sapientia?" Josie said. "You just read those Latin words in Professor Silver's office."

Samantha paused. "I don't know. Maybe."

"Where are you now?' Josie asked.

"I'm still walking toward the bus stop."

"Stay near friends. Don't go anywhere alone."

There was a longer pause after Samantha spoke.

"Sam, are you there?"

"Yeah. That's funny. Here we are talking about fancy black cars, and one just pulled up across the street. It's a Mercedes with tinted windows."

"Sam, stay away from that car."

"I'm just walking over so I can see if this Mercedes has that bumper sticker.

"No, Sam, don't do that! Stay with other people. Don't go near that car!"

"Something's wrong..." Samantha said.

'What is it?'

Josie waited. Samantha didn't reply.

"Sam, talk to me. Are you okay?"

Another pause.

"Sam! Talk to me."

But there was nothing.

Then Josie's phone chimed. A photo began to load.

Josie held her phone up, squinting. It was a blurry photo. A black car. The shape of a large man stepping from the car and reaching out toward Samantha.

"Sam!" Josie yelled, but the phone was dead.

Josie texted her. 'Sam! What's happening?'

Again, nothing.

Josie dialed Samantha's. It rang several times, then routed to Samantha's voicemail.

"Sam, call me." Josie realized she was shouting. "Please! Let me know you're okay. Call me now! I'm worried."

As Josie disconnected, she had the powerful sensation that Samantha had just been kidnapped.

TWENTY-NINE

Josie dialed 911.

A woman answered. "Nine, one, one emergency. Please state your name and address."

"Josephine Strong." She recited her address. "I was just speaking to my daughter on the phone. I believe she's been assaulted. Or kidnapped. She said something was wrong, and the line disconnected. Then she sent a photo of a man reaching for her."

"Where is she?"

"She's near her school, the Art and Science Prep Academy."

"What is her phone number?"

Josie told the dispatcher.

"Please stay on the line. I'll contact the Santa Monica Police. They can ping the phone for its location."

Josie held.

A few minutes later, the dispatcher came back on the line. "The police get no ping from your daughter's phone. And they have no report of any criminal activity near your daughter's school. They're still checking. Stay on the line, and I'll let you know as soon as we hear anything."

"Thank you," Josie said. It was an obvious dead end. So she disconnected.

Josie couldn't breathe. She was hyperventilating. It felt like she was going to black out from lack of oxygen. A wave of dizziness swept over her. Unknown stood next to her.

"What am I going to do, Unknown? I don't know what to do!" She gripped Unknown with both hands and leaned on her for support. Unknown wavered under the weight.

Josie had never felt so alone in her life. Her daughter was out there somewhere. When a girl like Samantha—someone who connects to the world with her phone—doesn't call or text after something bad happens, she's obviously compromised in some major way. Maybe kidnapped. Maybe tied up in a speeding black car.

Think! Josie told herself. You don't have time to collapse! Even Samantha would tell you to think. Do the professor thing! Analyze!

Josie rocked back and forth, crying, gasping, squeezing Unknown hard. She tried to organize her thoughts. She didn't need a comprehensive plan. She didn't even need to know her top priority. What she needed was to identify any priority. Any useful move and do it.

Josie found Tom Silver's phone number in the UCLA directory that Samantha had installed on her phone. She pressed the call button. It rang several times, then went to voicemail.

Josie listened to his outgoing message. As she was about to leave a message, she paused. Maybe she should wait until she could talk to him in person. In person, one can read body language and attitude and inflection. On the phone, it's easier for a person to dissemble.

She hung up. Silver would now have her number on his caller ID, but she didn't think she'd called him before, so he might not. And if he did, he might simply think she was asking another question about leaving a dog in her office.

It was rush hour. An impossible time to drive.

Josie took Unknown down to the street and ran to the bus stop. She got on the first bus, rode several blocks, then transferred to another bus line and rode to Venice, where Tom Silver lived on one of the canals.

As she planned what she'd say to Silver, she thought again about the killer's motivation. If the killer thought Samantha could identify him as Clarice Angel's killer, it could explain the extraordinary lengths he went to in his effort to silence her and her mother.

Josie was distracted by a whirlwind of thoughts and worries and confusions. Somehow she arrived in Venice without remembering anything about the ride.

It was early evening when she started walking toward where she thought Silver lived. As she came close to the waterways, she recalled that the road layout was confusing.

Venice was created by a planner who dug canals in an effort to bring a taste of Venice to Southern California. The neighborhood was not especially charming or attractive, and most of its houses were not fancy. But it was a very popular place to live, near the beach and close to LAX airport. The houses fronted on the canals, which were accessed by walking paths along the waterways. The few narrow roads were designed more as alleys than streets. It was the rear of the houses that faced the alley roads.

At one point, Josie glanced down at Unknown walking beside her. The dog looked enormously sad. But Josie didn't know what to do. All she could think of was Samantha. She reached down and pet Unknown's head and neck. "I'm so sorry, Unknown. I'm worried as hell about Samantha. But you're probably worried, too."

Josie and Unknown went along a canal and turned and went up and over a walking bridge to another canal. Eventually, she came to a house with Silver's number. It was an angular design that would have been considered modern in the 1950s and still looked interesting. It had large sloping roofs, big planes of shingles that angled just one way. The windows were triangular and trapezoidal with white frames that stood out from the dark-brown cedar shake siding.

Josie walked up and pressed the bell. It was the time of day when people started turning on lights inside. Silver's windows were all dark, so she didn't expect an answer. She waited on the doorstep. A small wall sconce sent a wash of yellow light that was too low to illuminate faces but was designed just to let a visitor know the location of the front steps.

A bird called out from down the canal, a forlorn cry that sounded lonely.

Josie pressed the bell again.

After a minute, she walked down the steps and worked her way around to the alley and the back of the house.

The door at the adjacent house opened. A woman came out, facing backward, hauling a chair. She went down her walkway toward the alley. She dragged the chair over to a small Nissan and lifted up the hatchback. It was immediately clear that the chair would not easily fit into the space.

The woman glanced toward Josie, who was standing at the back door of Silver's house.

"Maybe I can help you with that," Josie said, the words coming with difficulty as she fought back images of Samantha being held prisoner.

"I'll take you up on that," the neighbor lady said.

Josie walked over and draped Unknown's leash over a bush. "Stay here, girl."

The two women wrestled with the chair, but it didn't seem to fit.

"I think it's an illusion," Josie said. "Your chair looks wider than it is deep. But I think that's not the case. Let's turn it ninety degrees."

They did as Josie suggested. The chair slid into the Nissan, and the woman was able to shut the hatchback.

"Wow, that was a good call," the neighbor lady said. "You must be some kind of engineer or something."

"No. But I'm a professor. We have a personality flaw that makes us analyze everything. It's the hazard of my profession." Josie reached out to shake the woman's hand. "I'm Josie Strong. I teach medieval history at UCLA."

"That's like my neighbor. He's also a history professor at UCLA."

"That's why I'm here. I had a question for Tom. I was in the area, so I stopped by. But apparently he's out."

"I can tell Mr. Silver that you came by," the other woman said.

Josie tried to think quickly. "I just wanted to ask him something about his Mercedes. The question can wait."

The neighbor woman paused. She lowered her voice a bit. "We call it his professor car," she said with a small grin.

"That's curious," Josie said.

"Do you know him well?" the neighbor woman asked.

"Not really. But our offices are near each other in the history department. We've talked most every day for the last ten years."

"Well, then you probably know that his life isn't as fancy as his title. Us ordinary people think UCLA professors probably live on a cloud. And maybe some of you do. But Professor Silver's world is all about struggling with his sons. Ever since his wife died, his sons were more than he could handle. And then, when his first son died, the younger son completely fell apart."

Josie had known that Silver's grief about his wife had been obvious and severe. But he hadn't spoken of the problems with the second son. At least not when Josie was around. She decided to play along. "I know it's been hard. Having a son get in trouble is probably one of the hardest things to deal with."

"You know it," the woman said. "After William died and Robert went off the deep end, the professor tried hard to help. He got Robert carpentry jobs in the art department, where the boy goes to school, but that didn't go well. Robert is quite a bit older than most of the students, so he doesn't fit in very well. So Mr. Silver pushed the theater department to hire him for their set designs. You probably know that the theater department is right next to the art department."

"Sure," Josie said. "Just north of the sculpture garden."

The neighbor woman nodded, obviously familiar with the campus. Probably from talking with Silver, Josie thought.

The woman continued, "But I don't think carpentry is the best job for him, because he's been acting injured. I saw him recently, and he moves carefully, like he cut himself with a saw or something."

Josie tried to think fast. "Oh, I saw him favoring his hand," Josie said, tempting a response.

"Yeah. But it's not just his hand. He moves like he got stabbed in his stomach or something. Anyway, Professor Silver's idea was that a job of any kind would bring structure to his life. And he no doubt thought that Robert's studies would be less disrupted if he worked on campus. I think he also imagined that he could keep better track of Robert if the boy was almost in view from his office. So then he hired Robert to be his driver when he went out to do his school talks."

Josie nodded, continuing to play along. "I wondered about that."

"Some people—like me—would think it was nuts to let that young man anywhere near high school girls. But I think Silver thought the whole business that got Robert in trouble was over and done with. But then Robert did that joyride thing with the professor's Mercedes, taking Silver's car all over hell and back at a hundred miles per hour. When the cops finally caught him, Professor Silver found out and practically exploded with rage."

"That would be embarrassing, what with him serving on the volunteer patrol," Josie said.

The neighbor nodded her head. "You know how Silver is sort of rigid about doing the right thing. That's part of the LAPD volunteer stuff. Give back to the community. So when his kid ran off and got in trouble in Silver's car, the old man was more than bent out of shape. Plus, you probably heard about the weird side."

"I don't remember," Josie said.

The woman looked left and right as if to see if someone was listening. She lowered her voice. "When they caught Robert speeding on the four-oh-five, the boy was playing dress up."

"What does that mean? Was he in drag?"

"Oh, no. Not that. He was wearing theatrical disguises. Wig and moustache. Stuff like that. Like he was trying to pass himself off as someone else."

Josie choked. She thought of the assassin after they'd hit him with the onager and the Greek Fire. His short hair was singed, and his scalp looked mottled. The scalp had an unusual texture. Could it have been a wig? And the way his nose was so blackened, it wasn't even recognizable as skin. The black area almost seemed to have edges. Maybe it was his real nose. Or maybe the nose was part of his disguise, like some kind of glue-on prosthesis. Could it be that the disguise protected Robert from the worst of the fire? Was he wearing contacts as a disguise? Could contacts protect someone's eyes from fire? But their assassin was blinded! It couldn't have been an act! Then again, maybe the contacts were severely burned and dried, stuck to the man's corneas. Maybe moisture from his eyes would gradually seep through. Would that allow the burned contacts to peel off?

Josie struggled to maintain her composure. She thought of a way to solicit more information. "Last I heard, Robert still lived here with Tom," Josie said. "But then another professor said the boy was staying someplace else."

"I don't know. I think living here at home is the official story. But I think the boy spends most of his time up at the cabin."

"The one up Topanga Canyon," Josie said.

"Yeah. That's where William had his accident."

Josie felt dizzy. The ground seemed unsteady. "He fell when he was horseback riding, right?"

"That's what they say."

"What do you mean?" Josie started to feel nauseated.

"Just that the cause of death was never determined beyond

injuries received in a fall. William's body was down in a ravine. His horse was grazing nearby. That's circumstantial evidence, right?"

Josie frowned. "Circumstantial?"

"Sorry," the neighbor lady said. "I'm kind of a courtroom procedure buff. Circumstantial evidence connects to circumstance, right? It suggests certain things and it adds to a case. But it's not direct evidence."

"I'm not sure I follow," Josie said.

"In this case, the evidence all indicated that William fell from his horse. And that conclusion is probably accurate. But that doesn't indicate why he fell."

"Oh," Josie said as the realization came to her. "A fall from a horse can be an accident. And maybe it usually is an accident. But it doesn't have to be an accident."

"Right." The neighbor lady looked off as if visualizing. "And Robert always seemed to hate the way everything came easier for William. Those two fought like angry dogs their whole lives. And, of course, the worst came after William got interested in the girl Robert favored. I think that fueled Robert's anger toward women."

The women looked at each other. Josie couldn't breathe.

"Oh, of course," Josie managed to say in a choking breath. "The girl whose name was..." She stopped to see if the woman would confirm what Josie suspected.

"Clarice," the woman said.

Josie felt crushed by dread.

"I suppose I should be going," Josie finally said, her voice sounding like she was choking.

"Sorry I talked your ear off. Being a nosy neighbor is in my DNA. You want me to give Tom a message?"

"No. It's not important. Classes start the day after tomorrow. I'll talk to him then." Josie started to back away, she started to sway from dizziness.

"Hey, are you okay?"

Josie put her hand on the woman's Nissan. "Yeah, thanks. I'm just tired."

"Okay." The woman made a little wave. "Thanks for helping me get the chair into my car."

"You're welcome."

"By the way. You said you had a question about Tom Silver's Mercedes."

"Oh, right. I saw a car that looked like his, and it even had a bumper sticker in the same place. But someone else was driving it. I've always had a soft spot for a car like that and wanted to tell him to keep me in mind if he ever sold it. So I wondered if it was his car I saw and if he'd sold it."

"As far as I know, he still owns it. But I think he's sort of given it to Robert. Personally, I think that's misguided. I think a kid should earn his car. But Tom is kind of desperate to help get that kid onto the straight and narrow. I believe he's hoping the car will give Robert something to feel responsible about."

Josie gestured at the empty parking space behind Silver's house. "So Tom must be commuting by bus."

The neighbor nodded. "He often said that it didn't make sense to drive to work."

"Yeah, we all think that when we get stuck in L.A. traffic," Josie said, forcing a wan grin.

"Tell me about it," the neighbor said. The woman turned to Unknown, who was still sitting by the bush. "Hey, that dog of yours is really well behaved. She doesn't want to run around and get into trouble, does she?"

"No. We just adopted her. She's been very easy so far." Josie didn't want to say that she thought the real reason Unknown wasn't running around was that she was really depressed.

They said goodbye. Josie picked up Unknown's leash, and she began running as fast as she could.

THIRTY

Josie felt an overwhelming sense of fear and confusion as she ran back to the bus stop. While she waited for the bus, she called the Santa Monica Police on their business line. It took several minutes to get through the phone menu and the layers of bureaucracy. Two people explained she'd have to wait until Samantha had been missing for 24 hours, and then she could come in and fill out a missing persons report. She pleaded and cajoled and finally told them that she was a good friend of Professor Tom Silver, one of the LAPD volunteer patrol drivers. After she implied that brushing her off could have repercussions throughout UCLA and a hundred contacts between the university and LAPD and Santa Monica, they finally let her talk to a sergeant named Menendez.

Josie explained that she thought her daughter had been kidnapped at her school in Santa Monica and how it connected to the attack in the Canadian wilderness. Even as she tried to minimize the drama and not even mention the onager weapon they'd built, she realized how unbelievable it sounded.

"Let me see if I've got this straight," Menendez said. "You're saying you and your daughter were attacked by a hired killer in Canada, possibly by a man who followed you from L.A. You don't know for certain why he targeted you. Although you suspect it was because he knew that your daughter witnessed him kidnapping Clarice Angel, the poor girl who was murdered at the cliff beach. So he wanted to silence your daughter and you. But when he came after you in Canada, you managed to wound him and then get away. Yet the suspect lived and killed your guide and stole his canoe to come after you again. I mean no offense, ma'am, but this sounds…"

"I know. Like a Hollywood movie. But it's true." The man's doubt about her story had her voice shaking. "You can call the county sheriff on the Minnesota side of the border. His name is Denser. He'll corroborate my story."

The sergeant's breathing was audible over the phone. He continued, "And now you believe the suspect has followed you back to L.A. and has kidnapped your daughter."

"Yes."

"But you have no evidence."

"My daughter texted me that something was wrong. Then she sent a photo of the man reaching for her. The photo is blurry. But I can get you a picture of the man after we wounded him in Canada." As she said it, she realized that Samantha hadn't emailed it to her, only to the Minnesota sheriff. Josie couldn't get it off Samantha's phone, because her kidnapper, no doubt, had that. Not only that, but if the kidnapper really was Robert wearing a disguise, the photo wouldn't look like Robert. Josie added, "Although the kidnapper may not look like the photo."

"I don't understand."

"Robert Silver was recently caught speeding, and he was wearing a disguise wig and moustache, which is reason to believe he was wearing a disguise in the Canadian wilderness. Anyway, right after my daughter sent the photo, her phone disconnected, and I haven't been able to reach her since. My daughter is level-headed. She's not given to hysteria. I'm certain she's been attacked and probably kidnapped. The killer wanted us dead in the Canadian wilderness, no doubt so our bodies wouldn't be found. So it's reasonable to assume that he would take Samantha, wait until the middle of the night when he wouldn't be observed, and then dump her body where it wouldn't be found."

"I'm sorry, ma'am," the man on the other end of the line said. "I realize you are upset. But police departments everywhere have learned that most of the time when a parent is certain that their child has been kidnapped, it's not so. The kid turns up the next day or two. We don't have the budget or manpower to chase down every report. That's why we need some kind of evidence. An eyewitness who saw your child taken. Somebody who recorded the incident on their phone. Or a threat from the kidnapper, whether phoned or emailed or texted."

"What will you say if you find out that my daughter really was kidnapped?"

"We'll say we're very sorry this happened, and we'll do everything in our power to find your child."

Josie felt like she was being strangled. Her baby was kidnapped. She was sure of it. Just because law enforcement had rules about evidence didn't make it untrue.

"When Samantha witnessed Clarice Angel getting into a black Mercedes, the car had a bumper sticker that had Latin words."

"Do you have some evidence that this event or car is connected to the girl's murder?" the sergeant asked.

"No." Josie was exasperated. Like Silver's neighbor had said, it was circumstantial. Josie felt about to implode. "A colleague of mine, another professor at UCLA, has a black Mercedes with a Latin bumper sticker."

"Are you accusing your colleague of kidnapping Clarice Angel?"

"No. He's a good guy. He even participates on the LAPD volunteer patrol."

"So you don't think he kidnapped your daughter Samantha?"

"No. Of course, not. But I think the kidnapper may be his son. Or maybe the perpetrator is a friend of the son. The son majors in art at UCLA, and he works as a carpenter. The art department is next to the theater department, and he's done work for them as well. So it would be easy for him to get theatrical makeup or disguises."

"You mean wigs and such?"

"Yes. And a nose prosthesis."

The sergeant made a long sigh. "I've got your number," he finally said. "I'll put my people on notice. If we hear anything, anything at all, I'll be in touch. Does that help?"

Josie felt defeated, pushed up against a hard wall of resistance.

"Yes, sir," she said. "That helps. Thank you very much."

The bus came. Josie and Unknown got on, walked to the rear, and sat. Josie tried to maintain her composure. If Samantha had been there, she would have said, 'Think, Mama. That's what professors do, right? Think and analyze. Make like Dante.'

Josie tried. She was exhausted and leaned forward, elbows on her knees, forehead against her hands. Then she realized that was the posture of Rodin's The Thinker, the well-known sculpture that was based on Dante. She straightened up and leaned her head back against the bus seat. Just think, she told herself.

In the last few years, she'd noticed that her history students had been fixated on a spate of super hero movies. So Josie told her students that success at thinking was like success at anything else. It was all about focus. If you gave your undivided attention to a problem and kept that focus turned on like a spotlight, that was as close to superhero thinking as one could get.

A few basic thoughts seemed clear.

Josie thought—but didn't know—that Professor Silver's son Robert was Samantha's kidnapper. He had a likely opportunity in that he lived with his father and could probably borrow his father's Mercedes. Or simply take it without asking for his father's permission. If, in fact, Samantha could identify Robert as a suspect in the murder of Clarice Angel, then he had motive. If Robert had been staying at the Silver family cabin and could come and go without anyone witnessing his actions, that gave him even more opportunity.

Josie didn't know how law enforcement looked at past transgressions of a suspect. But whether they factored into the situation in a legal way or not, the Silvers' neighbor lady in Venice referred to a couple of them. The main one was some kind of trouble that Robert had with girls. Josie didn't know what they were. But the neighbor expressed surprise that Tom would hire Robert to take him to schools or—as the neighbor said—anywhere near girls. Was Robert a serial predator?

Another past transgression was when Robert took a joyride in Tom's Mercedes, something the neighbor lady hadn't described other than to say the police found Robert Silver in his father's car, and Robert was wearing a disguise.

There were additional issues, even if they didn't qualify as circumstantial evidence.

According to the neighbor, Tom Silver had made desperate efforts to get his kid straightened out and get him jobs. The young man had been dealing with great stress, with both his mother and his only sibling dying in recent years. The neighbor also alluded to the possibility that William Silver's death had not been an accident. The unspoken suggestion was that Robert, who had fought with William as a child, could have been involved. How? Scaring William's horse while William was riding at the edge of a drop off?

Josie now knew that Robert had access to theatrical disguises. He had a free and private place to live. He had a vehicle that would allow him to pass as a respectable person, a vehicle that might even make it easy for him to attract girls into his orbit.

Josie choked back her sobs as she considered whether or not Robert had already killed Samantha. She focused with all of her heart and soul on something other than images of Samantha being held prisoner by a psychopath.

She didn't know what to do, how to proceed. If only she could get some advice. Someone who was very wise would no doubt have an idea of how to proceed.

THIRTY-ONE

Josie's bus came to the transfer stop. She got out. While she waited for a bus from the other line, she got back on her phone. It took some phone tag before she spoke to Shulu Ojai. They agreed to meet at Shulu's studio.

A half hour later, they spoke in Shulu's back room. They sat on two rickety wooden chairs. Josie was shaky as she explained what had happened. Shulu wanted the details.

Josie told her what had transpired, how it started with their attempted murder in the Quetico Wilderness in Canada and how it culminated with Samantha's kidnapping.

As Josie spoke, Shulu reached down and patted Unknown. "This is how you adopted Unknown."

"Yes. Her owner was murdered. Indirectly, the cause traces back to when Samantha saw Clarice Angel get into a black Mercedes the night she was murdered. The killer knows that Samantha saw him, so he followed us to Canada to kill us. Unknown's owner Bill became an obstacle of sorts, so the killer murdered him as well."

Shulu was making a slow shake of her head. "And now, Clarice's killer has Samantha."

"Yes. I'm guessing he's taken Samantha to his family's cabin up at the top of Topanga Canyon."

"You called the police?"

"Yes. They said that without any evidence of kidnapping, they can't do anything. They won't even act on a missing person's report until twenty-four hours have passed."

"What will you do?" Shulu asked.

"I don't know. I'm hoping you can give me advice about what to do."

Shulu had a glass of fizzy water with a lemon slice in it. She took a sip.

"Do you know where this cabin is?" Shulu asked.

"No. But I think I know someone who can figure it out."

Shulu sat in silence. She took a deep breath, shut her eyes.

Eventually, she spoke. "The Chumash were peaceful people. They had lived without substantial conflict for a thousand years or more. Then the Spanish came and claimed they were missionaries. They took all the Chumash as slaves, made them work the fields and tend livestock. And the Chumash girls... Well, let's just say, they endured the worst."

"What did the Chumash do?"

"People who only know peace are not good at war. But our oral tradition includes some stories that suggest that some of the Chumash studied how the Spanish acted, watched how their weapons worked, realized how to think strategically and fight back. Maybe it was Hutash who finally told them to ignore peace and fight for their lives. Whatever the reason, when the Spanish went too far with the Chumash girls, some Chumash men became very effective warriors. They turned Spanish violence against the Spanish. In the end, of course, the Spanish and later, the American Army from the east, overwhelmed all of the Indian tribes in California. But in the process, many Spanish died."

"What are you saying I should do?"

Shulu took another sip of her lemon water. "You've tried to run. You've tried to hide. You've called the cops. And now the bad man took your daughter. Hutash says, when you've exhausted all other approaches, it's time to fight violence with violence."

"You think I should go to the cabin where I think the killer has taken Samantha?"

"Yes. You should go there and kill him."

THIRTY-TWO

Josie thanked Shulu, left, and walked toward home.

An idea formed. It was a stretch but not as outlandish as building an onager on a wilderness island. But this particular idea would require some specialized help.

Josie remembered a student she had the previous spring, a person who only took her class to fill in a distribution requirement. He was a tall, handsome kid with good teeth and clear skin who could have been a model. He also could have had a great social life if only he'd had the tiniest bit of charisma and charm. Instead, he lived in the clichéd geek/nerd world, barely able to speak to another human in person, apparently unable to connect to anything that wasn't run by software. Even his name labeled him as a social misfit. Cumberland Durand. The main reason Josie remembered him was that he was briefly celebrated for being a hacker who had broken into a couple of the giant tech companies. Companies such as Microsoft and Google were known for paying large rewards to hackers who could expose security bugs or flaws in their software. Cumberland had been written up for earning 'bug bounties' of several hundred thousand dollars for his legal hacking.

Once she and Unknown were back in their condo, Josie sat on the couch and patted the cushion. "Come sit, Unknown."

Unknown hesitated. Josie coaxd her again.

Unknown slowly put one paw on the couch, waited to be certain it was okay, then climbed up slowly, moving like a cat.

Josie pulled Unknown over next to her leg.

"Sam is gone, Unknown," Josie said through tears. "She's

gone, and we have to save her. Will you help me?" Josie leaned over and hugged the dog.

When Josie lifted up, Unknown looked at her, her focus on Josie's eyes individually and then moving back and forth like the way some people look at faces.

Josie found a phone number for Cumberland Durand in the student directory. She dialed.

A voicemail message said to leave a number. Josie started talking.

"Hi Cumberland. I'm sure you don't remember me. I'm Josie Strong, and I teach the Medieval Weapons class you took last spring. Anyway, I have a serious problem that could use your expertise. I'm trying to figure out how to get some kind of recorder that…"

"Hello?" A male voice interrupted her. His voice was deep, but it cracked and warbled. He sounded very tentative. "This is Cumberland."

"Oh, thank you so much for answering. I'm Josie Strong. I don't know if you remember me."

"Sure. Um. Professor Strong. What do you need?"

So Josie told him much of the story. She believed her daughter was kidnapped. The police were unwilling to do much until 24 hours had passed. Josie thought she knew where her daughter was being held up in Topanga Canyon. She wanted to go there, but she needed some technical expertise.

"So I'm wondering if you would be willing to help me," she said.

"Um. You mean like, could I answer questions? I know tech stuff, but not much else."

"That's what I need, Cumberland. Someone who knows tech. Could I come over? I'll pay whatever your going rate is for tech advice. Wait, what am I thinking? I'll pay whatever you want. Twice your rate. Ten times your rate."

"Um. Thanks. I don't really have a rate."

"Can we meet? Any place you want. The sooner the better. I think her life is in danger."

"You could… Um. You could come to my mom's house. That's where, you know... where I live."

"Of course. Where should I go?"

"It's on Benedict Canyon Drive. Not far from the university."

"Beverly Hills?"

"Yeah." He gave her the number.

"I'm in Santa Monica. So it'll take me a bit to get there."

"I'll be here," he said.

Josie grabbed Unknown's leash. She ran down the stairs to the underground parking level. She pulled on Unknown's leash. The dog matched her speed. This time Josie drove instead of taking the bus.

Josie let Unknown in the back car door, pushing aside some drycleaning that she'd picked up but hadn't yet brought up to the condo.

The evening traffic was thin, especially for Los Angeles. But the seven-mile drive still took 25 minutes. Josie found the number on a stone light post next to signs that said 'Armed Security Response.' She pulled into a drive that was mostly dark despite multiple low lights that illuminated flower beds thick with fall blossoms. Josie got out feeling insecure. After all her years at UCLA, she still felt out of place in the land of the wealthy. She opened the back door of her car. "C'mon out, Unknown. If I can do this, you can too."

Unknown was tentative. But she accepted Josie's tug on the leash.

THIRTY-THREE

The two of them walked up to a front entry that was vaguely like a medieval castle gate with an arched stone entrance. Josie pressed the lit button.

The door opened in ten seconds. Cumberland was taller, bigger, and handsomer than she remembered. But he still telegraphed extreme awkwardness. He didn't say hi. He just said, "We can talk, you know, by the pool or something." He turned and walked into the house.

Josie followed, still holding Unknown by her leash. She had expected to ask if it was okay to bring her dog. But either it was fine or Cumberland didn't even notice.

The young man walked through an entry, across a large living room with a marble floor and what looked like Moroccan rugs, and out through a sliding glass door to a swimming pool.

The pool was a kidney shape, 40 feet long, and it glowed turquoise from underwater lights. The water was surrounded by dark slate lit by low yellow lights at intervals around the perimeter. There were artful plantings with more flowers, some with heavy, aromatic blossoms.

Cumberland sat on a chaise lounge. He didn't invite Josie to sit, but she understood that was what he expected. She sat on a lounge five feet from the young man. She held Unknown close.

Cumberland said nothing, which was no surprise to Josie. She had met several students like him over the years. So she started telling him what she wanted.

"I'm thinking about two concepts. For the first, imagine that a man is inside a cabin, and he has kidnapped my daughter and is holding her in his house. What would get him to walk out of that house? I don't know. But I'm thinking things like, what if he thinks he heard a litter of young kittens? They are out on his back porch, meowing in distress. Maybe they've wandered over from the next house. Or maybe someone has snuck up and left them there in a basket. Either way, the young man won't be on his guard, right? He won't come out of the house with his weapons blazing. He'll open the door and look and then step out investigating."

Cumberland was nodding. "That's good. I can see that. I can make that happen."

"Okay, good. Now for the second scenario. Let's say that the man hasn't succumbed to the cries of kittens. So imagine that a bunch of cops pull up near the suspect's house. It's late at night. The air is filled with cop sounds. Maybe there's a few blips of sirens rising and then turning off. Car doors open and close. Someone shouts commands. Someone asks questions. Both men's and women's voices. It's very official. There is a backdrop of radio chatter. Crime talk. Number codes. Little snippets of info about the suspect. And cop car lights."

Josie stopped. She'd probably said more than enough. Or maybe, she hadn't said enough. She couldn't tell. Cumberland hadn't said a word.

She waited.

"This is what you'd like at this Topanga Canyon place where your daughter is being held prisoner," he said.

"Yes."

"But there won't really be cops there," Cumberland said. "You just want the kidnapper to hear kittens outside his place. And if that doesn't work, you want him to think the cops have dropped on him like some kind of final battle between good and evil. Like armageddon. And when the bad dude makes his escape, you'll be there with your private army to take him down."

"Yes, exactly," Josie said, nodding in the turquoise-lit darkness. "Thank you so much for understanding. That's what I want," she said in a soft voice. She didn't know how to tell Cumberland that she had no help. That she was a single mother with no close friends. That she was thinking of going up there with nothing but her orphan dog and a medieval weapon or two. Josie blinked her eyes against the tears. She tried not to make noise as she cried. She hoped Cumberland wouldn't see her tears in the pool light.

He was silent for a long time. He stared at the pool.

Josie couldn't tell if he thought she was crazy. She grit her teeth. Maybe she had lost her perspective. But she felt as if Samantha's very survival, and her own, were dependent on this awkward, silent young man.

Cumberland was lying back on the chaise lounge. It seemed as if his head had sunk down into his chest. For all Josie could tell, he had fallen asleep.

"You'll need a system with good sound quality," he finally said. "And there's, you know, a start-time issue. You can't just put a timer on your stage production. You need to be able to control all parts of it. But that can be arranged. I could get the sound bites by sampling online. I also have a light bar that I can program for color and strobe. If your dude looked out the window and saw a blue and red flashing up the road, that could be helpful."

"Yes, it would," Josie said. Her voice felt unnaturally small.

"I could also plan for some variability. Like, maybe the bad dude responds one way, we stay with the kitten sounds. If he goes a different way, we switch to a full-on SWAT team assault."

"Sure," Josie said, not really understanding what he meant.

"Is this dude really bad?" Cumberland asked.

"He's killed at least two people, a young girl and a wilderness guide. He's already tried to kill my daughter and me. We escaped. But he's very tough. Very mean."

Cumberland paused for a long minute.

Josie waited.

Eventually, Cumberland spoke. "All my life, I got beat up almost every day. Most bullies were just idiots. Mean and stupid. But a few were smart and twisted. They got kicks from hurting anyone smaller than them. Guys like me. Girls. Small dogs. It sounds like this guy might be one of those."

"I think so," Josie said.

"I should come with you and help. You know, um, on location."

"Oh, Cumberland, I just want technical expertise. I could never ask you to put yourself at risk."

Another pause.

"Even after I grew tall, I still got pushed around. Last winter, some guys—jock types—slammed me to the ground on Dickson Court. They kicked my books away and spun my laptop across the grass like they were skipping a stone across the water. I didn't do anything wrong. But they were looking for someone to abuse. I was there. They thought it was funny, humiliating me. I've always telegraphed that I was a target for abuse. Like, um, there's the proverbial sign on my back."

"I don't know what to say," Josie said. "I'd love your help. But it would be dangerous. You could even get killed."

"Yeah, I could. You could too, right?"

It took a moment for Josie to face the truth. "Right."

"So this is my chance for payback. This is my chance to finally help take one of these guys down. And if you get killed, maybe I could still try to take him down. At least I would have finally done something worthwhile in my life." Despite the brave words, he said them with fear in his voice.

"Cumberland, I'm sure you've done uncountable worthwhile things."

"No. My mom doesn't understand me. She thinks if only I could have a job, or be a surfer and date girls, life would be good. I grew up with a swimming pool, and I don't even like the water. I had a cat, and he died. My dad's embarrassed by me, and he left both of us. I think the main reason he wanted out of mom's life is that she won't kick me out of the house. I don't like school. I only got into UCLA because my high school counselor knows some people in the admissions process. I've never done anything successful."

"Your hacking to expose security flaws pays good money. So obviously, coding is very worthwhile."

"It pays, but that's like, um, in the old west when the town marshal buys off a killer so he leaves your town alone. No one cares about benign coding. Just like no one cares that the town barber obeys the laws. Even if you want to work for Silicon Valley and you have the skills, you still have to have an approach to get noticed. Why would they hire me? I'm just one of millions. Maybe I could get, like, serial temp jobs. But the only way to go anywhere with coding is to create a startup. I'm pretty smart. But I don't have the chutzpah to make something new out of nothing."

Cumberland's low self image permeated his demeanor. Josie thought he might be wanting to help her as an antidote.

"Helping me would be very hard. Success might be very unlikely. And you'd be doing it tied to a middle-aged, out-of-shape professor."

"True. And I'm not a warrior. But you'd make me brave. Well… maybe a little braver than a total coward."

"How could I do that? I'm the kind of person who carries a spider down two stories to put it outside where it'll probably be eaten by a bird anyway. All because I'm not brave enough to squish it."

"Maybe. But you do something far braver than anything I could ever do, even if my life was at stake."

"What's that?"

"You get up in front of a huge lecture hall and talk to hundreds of students. That's the hardest thing there is. Public speaking. I almost vomit just thinking about it."

Josie didn't know what to say.

Cumberland sat up on his chaise lounge. He suddenly spoke in a louder voice. "With Professor Strong having my back, I could kick some butt for the first time in my life." He made a fist and pumped it.

But it was a weak fist and a soft pump.

THIRTY-FOUR

Josie realized there was no point in protesting Cumberland's desire to help. "So how would you do this sound and light show?"

"I think I can do it all in my studio. It will take some time."

"Could we go there now?" Josie said, hoping to push him toward her needs.

"Yeah." Cumberland stood up and walked toward the house, once again acting as if Josie weren't even there.

He slid open the living room slider, walked in, turned, and walked down a large curved staircase that circled around a huge chandelier made of art glass.

Josie followed with Unknown, shutting the pool door behind her.

The main room in the lower level was a movie theater with a dozen large upholstered chairs facing a large screen. Cumberland walked to the rear of the room, went down a wide hallway, and turned into a room.

As Josie followed him into a dark room, it was immediately obvious that Cumberland fit the cliché even to the point of living in his mother's basement. There were no windows. Over on one wall was a twin bed with rumpled sheets and a blanket. At the foot of the bed was an armoire with its doors open and clothes spilling out.

The room was not just Cumberland's bedroom, but his studio. It was filled with computers and monitors and shelves with odd electronic components. Everywhere were glowing LED lights, dozens of dots of red, with several blue and white lights and a few green and lavender added in. Many of the lights blinked slowly as if indicating electronics in sleep mode. Cables stretched everywhere. There was a large built-in desk with multiple computers and screens. In the middle of the room was a separate table with more computers. The room was filled with the soft whir of fans cooling the electronic components. One fan made a fast, repetitive tick as an out-of-balance blade struck its housing.

Cumberland walked over to a shelf. He picked up a small, black metal box the size of a hard-bound novel. The box had a couple of rocker switches, and three knobs. He set it on the table in the middle of the room. Next, he lifted two cords off a clothes hook. There was a set of drawers in a rolling cart like what Josie had seen mechanics use in auto garages. Cumberland pulled open the second drawer. Moved some of the contents. Shut it. Opened the third drawer. Pulled out another metal device about the size of a cigarette pack. It was also metallic but bright red.

Cumberland took a step to the side, pulled a chair out from under the table, sat down, and reached for a mouse. He wiggled it. A computer screen came to life. Cumberland typed on a keyboard. Several small rectangles appeared on the screen. It looked like some kind of program, but one that Josie had never seen before.

Through all the motions, Cumberland said nothing to Josie. It seemed clear to her that she should let him be. So she stood off to the side of the room with Unknown. If he had a question for her, he would ask.

Cumberland plugged a cord into another computer. He pulled on headphones, brought up a Google page, typed some terms. In moments, he visited several web pages and clicked on some links. Some brought him to videos with cop cars racing down roads, emergency lights flashing. Josie could hear just enough distant sound to think that the sound was loud in Cumberland's headphones. She saw what looked like blog explanations and lists of comments below. Other links brought him to pages that made no sense to Josie. It was like watching a pilot in a jet cockpit, working controls the purpose of which one could only guess.

Twenty minutes later, Cumberland pulled a memory stick out of a computer, clicked off two monitors, unplugged and pocketed a device the size of a cigarette pack. He set the hardback-sized metal box and one of the cords into a large plastic toolbox, then added another device the size of a small bread loaf. It was perforated with tiny holes. Josie guessed it was a speaker.

He pushed back his chair, stood, and picked up the toolbox and light bar. "Oh, I almost forgot the battery pack." He reached for a red item the size of a cell phone and added it to the toolbox.

"Okay. I'm ready."

Josie didn't know what to say. "Does that mean you can make it sound like cops are outside of a house?"

"Yeah. Kittens, too." Cumberland said no more. Josie thought it was both the mark of a genius and of a person so socially awkward that they don't even have a full perception of their awkwardness.

Cumberland handed Josie two small, rounded plastic objects. They had buttons on them.

"These look like key fobs for cars," Josie said.

"They are. I just gave them a different purpose. The gray one is for kittens. The unlock button makes them meow. The lock button makes them go silent. If you're working by feel, the lock button dips in. The unlock button has the bulge sticking out. The black fob is for cop sounds. It's like the kitten fob. The unlock button also turns it on, lock turns it off. Both kitten sounds and cop sounds will run for about four minutes and then repeat."

Josie put the cop fob in her left front pocket and the kitten fob in her right front pocket.

"Let's say we get separated. How will I know when you've got your gear in position and I can turn on the sounds?"

"Put this old phone in your pocket. It's on mute and vibrate. When the gear is ready, I'll ring it. You'll feel it vibrate."

"Good idea," she said as she took the phone and put it in her pocket. "You could be a spy or something. There's one more thing I'm hoping you can help me with," she said.

Cumberland didn't respond other than to look at her.

"I don't know the location of the house where I believe my daughter is being held. I know it's near the top of Topanga Canyon. And I know it's owned by a man named Tom Silver. He's a professor at UCLA. It's his son that I'm after."

Cumberland nodded and turned back to his computer. He typed, and clicked, and seemed to flash through several websites. Then he shook his head. "If the address is, you know... published anywhere, it's not obvious where to look. If he bought the house in the last twenty years, I think I'd find it."

"I think it's been in his family for decades."

He nodded. "There's probably other ways to search, but I guess I don't know how house ownership works."

Josie thought about it. "Houses are identified by parcel numbers. When the assessor is charging real estate tax, they use those parcel numbers."

Cumberland nodded. "Where's the assessor?"

"The assessor works for the county."

"So the county has a list of property parcel numbers." It was a statement, not a question. "What county are we talking about?"

"I'm pretty sure Topanga Canyon is in Los Angeles County."

"Los Angeles County would be a big list."

Josie nodded. "One of the bigger counties in the country."

"So the property records have to be computerized." Cumberland went back to his computer. A few minutes later, he said, "But they haven't put those records online for the public to look at."

"We can't get to them?"

"I didn't say that. Much of the information available on the internet is in private databases."

"You mean like UCLA. I log on with my password to get what I need. But the public can't look at the records."

"Right." Cumberland did not look up. He typed continuously, his fingers in constant motion. Then he used the mouse to drag some files, resize some graphics. Soon, his screen was filled with computer code, inscrutable numbers and symbols. It was a foreign language to Josie. She could only see that he scrolled and searched and made some keystrokes that looked like copying and pasting.

Computer code flowed up the screen, a river of numbers and letters and symbols.

In another minute, Cumberland said, "What do you know about the property?"

"Nothing."

"But you said you thought the owner's name was Tom Silver."

"Well, yes, I knew that. But nothing else."

"Lot size?"

"I have no idea."

"Number of bedrooms? Bathrooms?"

"No idea," Josie said again.

"You said it was up Topanga Canyon."

"Right."

"So you know more than you think."

Josie realized Cumberland was right. He wasn't being snarky. He was just pointing out a fact. "Okay, let me reconsider," Josie said. "I think Silver said the cabin had been in his family for seventy years. He didn't identify the property as land. So that suggests that the cabin is the main feature, more important than land size. And the cabin was probably built seventy years ago or more."

Cumberland nodded. He typed as she spoke.

Josie continued. "I saw a picture of it. It's near the ridgeline. I saw a pointed rise that may be near the Topanga Overlook. Or near Mulholland Highway. And you can see the Pacific from the cabin. Or at least from very near the cabin." Josie didn't understand how Cumberland could search for anything based on what she was saying.

Cumberland was still typing.

A topographical map appeared on another screen next to him. Josie could see that the topo lines on the map were similar to the ones on the canoe map of the Quetico 2000 miles away.

"Got it," Cumberland said.

"Got what?"

"The cabin. I'll print the address." A printer whirred. A piece of paper came out.

Josie picked it up. It showed the street and number, Tom Silver's name, the parcel number, the assessed valuation. "I thought you said the parcel information was private."

"Right." Cumberland now had a satellite photo on the screen.

"So how did you get into the database?"

"That's how I, um, earn money. Breaking into systems that are supposed to be secure. This one was easy. But there are two Tom Silvers up Topanga Canyon. One is a plumber in Thousand Oaks. Yours is the professor at UCLA."

The printer whirred again. Out came satellite photos of the canyon, four different pictures at ever-closer scales. Next came topo maps with the cabin superimposed on it.

Cumberland picked one up. "This is a useful scale. This little N symbol is north. But that won't help in the field if we don't know which way we're facing."

Josie took the paper from him and set it down on the only

open spot on the table. She pulled out her phone, turned on the phone's compass as Samantha had shown her, and set the phone on the paper.

"My daughter taught me about the compass and which mode to use. A wilderness guide showed us how to navigate. You set the compass on the map so the N symbol on the compass ring is the same place as the N symbol on the map. Then you rotate the map and compass until the compass needle aligns with both. Now your map is aligned with the territory."

"Cool trick," Cumberland said. "I've never been in the woods. My world is just in this studio."

"You must have been in the woods at some point. A school field trip or something."

He shook his head. "A kid I know went camping when we were young. He got a severe case of Poison Oak. He looked like an alien creature. Giant blisters oozing yellow pus. It was beyond gross. I was, like, no way, I'm not doing that. The woods are dangerous."

"But you're willing to go there with me now?"

"Are you going to bring the dog?"

"Yes."

"Good. 'Cause, she will protect us."

Maybe he saw Josie looking insecure.

He added, "Or maybe just comfort us. Just tell me what to do."

Josie's eyes flooded with tears. She wanted to respond, but couldn't make words come.

"Okay," she eventually said. "I have my car," Josie said. "Is it okay if you ride with me?"

Cumberland frowned. "I don't drive."

"Of course. Sorry."

Cumberland picked up the papers and toolbox and light bar. He walked up the stairs and out the front door. Josie followed. "Should I lock the door behind me?"

Cumberland stopped and looked back at her. His face, in the yellow driveway lights, looked confused. "Just shut it. After dad left, mom lost her key. I never had one."

Cumberland stood next to Josie's Prius. "I read about these. Only a nine kilowatt-hour battery on the plug-in version, right? Better than nothing, I guess."

Josie didn't know what he meant. She just bought the car because it was cheap to drive and possibly less polluting. She let Unknown in back and got in. "I have to stop at my office to get some things," she said. "Is that okay with you?"

"You're in charge."

"Right." Josie drove off and worked her way over to UCLA. Because it was late at night, she pulled into the service entrance at Bunche Hall. "We can park here without getting towed. We'll get a few things out of my office."

THIRTY-FIVE

Josie led Cumberland and Unknown past the trash dumpsters, through a metal door, and up the stairs. They were in her office in a few minutes.

Josie opened the door and flipped on the light. When she dropped Unknown's leash, the dog walked over, jumped up on the table, and went into her kennel. She lay down on the dog bed. She didn't relax her head, but watched Josie and Cumberland.

Josie picked up the model crossbow she'd constructed for her dissertation sixteen years before. Cumberland's eyes were wide.

"That is what you brought to class last spring," he said. "It looked smaller in the lecture hall than it looks here." He reached for it. Josie handed it to him.

"I built it to three-quarter scale based on the most common crossbows of the thirteenth century."

"How does it work? I'm sorry. I know you told us in class. But I was, um… I'm not a very attentive student."

Josie was worried about losing time, but she thought that Cumberland would be more effective help if she engaged with him in some depth. That way, he wouldn't feel like his only purpose was to be her hired hand.

She spoke quickly. "You know how a regular bow and arrow works? You hold the bow in one hand and pull back the string in the other. You fit the rear of the arrow on the string. It's called nocking the arrow. When you let go of the string, the arrow flies."

Cumberland nodded.

"This is a similar principle. But the bow is much smaller

and stiffer, and so it is harder to draw the cord back. Instead of pulling the cord with your arm, you turn this crank. Each crank pulls the cord back a little bit. The leverage allows you to put enormous tension on the cord." She pointed. "This ratchet holds that tension. When you get the cord pulled all the way back to this point, it is fully cocked. Then you take a bolt and set it in this groove."

"What's a bolt?"

Josie reached over to a shelf and lifted a metal object out of a wooden quiver. "It's similar to an arrow. But of course it's much shorter—about eight inches long—and it's made of iron."

"It's really heavy," Cumberland said. "My friend has a railroad spike. It's kind of like that."

"I worked with a blacksmith to make six bolts. Once you have the bolt in position on your crossbow, you're cocked and ready to aim and fire. Aiming is a lot like aiming a rifle. You just point it at your target. When you pull the trigger, the ratchet lets go of the cord, it snaps forward, carrying the bolt with it, and the bolt flies like an arrow. Except it has a lot more energy than an arrow. You don't want to be hit by a bolt."

"Is that worse than being shot with an arrow?" Cumberland asked. "Because, from what I've seen in movies, having an arrow stick through your body is really severe."

"It is. And a bolt is even worse than an arrow."

"What next? How do you see this playing out? Are we going to this cabin so you can shoot the guy dead or something?"

Josie paused. "I haven't figured this out. I'm operating by feel. If I can save my daughter without hurting anyone, that would be best. But I'll do whatever it takes to save her. If you come with me, you could be in great danger. You should have a weapon for self protection."

"What's that mean, 'have a weapon?' I'm not the kind of guy who carries a weapon."

"You don't have to. But you probably should."

"What kind of weapon? Are you thinking of a crossbow? Because I would, you know, probably shoot myself with it."

"Then let's keep it simple." Josie walked over to the corner of her office. There was a small wine barrel cut in half. In the barrel were perched several weapons reminiscent of canes but with heavy metal tops, mostly blades, and a few heavy points. They all leaned into the wall corner. Josie pulled one out and handed it to Cumberland.

"This is a war hammer. If you swing it at someone, no amount of armor will protect them. And no amount of strength can deflect it."

Cumberland took the war hammer with both hands and hefted it. "Whoa. I have a neighbor who is a climber. He has an ice ax that looks vaguely like this. But this is twice as long as an ice ax. And it's really heavy. I don't know if I can swing it."

"Sure, you can. Most of the time, you just hold it in front of you at an angle. Like a shield. You only need to swing it if someone is attacking you."

Cumberland nodded. He carried the war hammer over behind Josie's desk and sat down in her desk chair, the lengthy war hammer across his lap. Cumberland looked across the room as if surveying the world.

"So this is what it feels like to be a professor," he said. "You are queen of the kingdom. And if some pesky student crosses you, you pound him into submission with your war hammer."

Josie smiled. She'd never before sensed any humor from Cumberland. For a very short moment, life wasn't completely bleak.

Cumberland looked at the bookshelf next to him. "What are these?"

"Those are caltrops. They're four-pointed devices, kind of like a three-D star. If you throw Caltrops, no matter how they land, one point always faces up. So they're a very nasty way to stop people and horses and—in the modern era—cars, too. The same blacksmith who helped me make my crossbow bolts also made those caltrops."

"Should I bring some with us?"

"Maybe you should. But they are tricky to carry. You can put them into a heavy leather bag. Or as a last resort, you can tuck two of the points between your belt and your jeans, but you have to be careful not to bump your arms against the points that stick out."

Cumberland did as suggested, one caltrop on each side of his belt buckle so that the fourth point projected forward.

"That could work," Josie said. "But be aware that if you bend forward, the points poking into your jeans could stab through the fabric and into your belly. They're really very dangerous."

"I'd still like to try it, if it's, you know, okay," Cumberland said.

"It's fine with me."

Cumberland noticed a photo frame on the corner of Josie's desk. He picked it up.

"Is this your daughter?"

"Yes. Her name is Samantha. She's fourteen."

"She looks smart."

"Yes. She is. Very."

"With a professor mom, she's probably one of those super students."

"No, not at all. But she's a good kid."

As Cumberland set the photo frame down, a small school-sized version of Samantha's photo fell out of the back of the frame onto Josie's desk. Cumberland picked it up. "Is this an extra?"

"Yes. I was the proud mom and gave them away to people I know. I didn't realize there were any left."

"Can I take it? It would be like, um, a motivator."

"Of course."

Cumberland put it in his shirt pocket. He stood up, holding

his war hammer. The front of his jeans seemed to bristle with the caltrops. "Let's go save her," he said.

Josie gathered the crossbow bolts and put them into her shoulder bag. She picked up the crossbow and turned to Unknown, who was still in her kennel.

"C'mon, Unknown. Let's go."

The dog turned and looked at her. She didn't move.

"Unknown," Josie said again. She patted her hand against her thigh. "Come."

Unknown stood, came out of her kennel and jumped down to the floor. Josie picked up her leash, and the three of them left her office.

When they were at Josie's car, she let Unknown in the back seat and set the crossbow in next to Unknown.

Cumberland got in the front, adjusting the caltrops so they didn't puncture his legs or abdomen, and propping the war hammer from the floor up to his shoulder. He picked up the sheets of paper he'd printed at home and left on the dash. "We should look at these topo maps and, you know, memorize the slopes near the cabin. We can't see much in the dark. But any knowledge would be helpful, right?"

Josie understood his point. She reached up to the car ceiling and switched on the map light. "Also, we don't dare turn on the map light when we're parked up near the cabin."

They went over the topo maps and compared them to the satellite photos. Josie pointed out some features, Cumberland noticed others. They discussed the pros and cons and made a plan.

"Ready?" Josie said.

Cumberland nodded.

THIRTY-SIX

J osie drove west on Wilshire to the Pacific Coast Highway and turned right. A half dozen miles out toward Malibu, she turned right on Topanga Canyon Blvd, and started up the canyon. Scattered raindrops started hitting the windshield. Josie turned on the wipers.

"Not far now, right?" Cumberland said through gritted teeth. "I remember a Rambo movie where Stallone is going to attack the bad guy's stronghold at night. So he straps on all his weapons. And he memorizes the maps and the terrain. He uses mud to darken his face. That's like us. But I don't feel like Rambo. I feel like I'm going to be sick. I haven't even darkened my face. At least, you don't have to worry about that. You'll blend into the night. I'm just going to be like a white whale. That low life's gonna shine a spotlight on me and shoot me with a harpoon or a spear gun."

Josie was struggling with the driving, trying to see, trying not to let her own panic and anxiety overwhelm her.

"Stop, Cumberland! That's crazy. This whole mission is crazy. I have to try to save Samantha. And I need your help!"

Josie went around a curve too fast for comfort.

"I'm sorry," Cumberland said. "My dad always said I was a whiner. I'll try to be useful. Tell me how to help."

"Help me see," she said, trying to focus, trying to give Cumberland something to concentrate on.

"What should I, you know, look for?"

"Just watch to make sure I don't hit a deer. What if a pedestrian is on the road? I can't see a thing through these wiper smears. And my glasses are fogging. If I go any slower, it'll be morning before we find that cabin. The guy's probably already left with Sam. If he's the guy who killed Clarice, he's going to kill Sam and dump her body on a dark rainy night like tonight." Josie choked and coughed and wiped away tears.

Cumberland leaned forward, to see better out the windshield.

They climbed about ten miles up the canyon. Josie gripped the steering wheel as if to pull it off.

Josie hated driving at night, she hated driving on twisty mountain roads, and she hated driving in the rain. Usually, she relied on Samantha to help her see.

Cumberland saw their turnoff before Josie did.

"There," he said, pointing. "Up on the right. That's the little spur road we found on the map."

Josie turned off, drove about 100 hundred yards in, pulled to the side, and parked. She turned off her headlights.

"It's raining harder," she said, trying to keep the fear out of her voice. "I can't see anything. We'll never find the cabin."

Cumberland shined a tiny flashlight on the map. He pointed at the paper. "This is where we are. A little farther up, the road ends. But we saw the foot trail on the satellite photo. Or maybe it's an old Jeep trail. All we have to do is walk to the end of this road, and we'll come to the trail."

"And it will lead up along the ridge that goes above Silver's cabin," Josie said, focusing on the mission.

"Right," Cumberland said. It was just one word, but still his voice cracked. "Your plan is, um, good. The only question is if we're brave enough to go."

"We are," Josie said. "All we have to do is think of Samantha held captive in that cabin. We're the liberating army."

Cumberland touched his shirt pocket where he'd put the photo of Samantha. "Maybe you should remind me of what we do next."

"We hike down the ridge trail watching off to the side," Josie said. "We watch for signs of the cabin. Lights. Or voices. Maybe even wood smoke. It's freezing up here in this canyon. If the cabin is heated with wood, he might have a fire going. Once we determine the cabin's location, we go in close enough that you can set up your electronic gear. Once that's in position, we hide in the woods and activate the sound show."

"There's just one problem. Electronics can't be out in the rain. It would die in a minute."

Josie felt desperate, as if the plan was collapsing before it had even begun. She shut her eyes hard, took a deep breath, and fought the anxiety. Samantha's voice came to her. 'You're a professor, Mama. You think and analyze. So think it through.'

"What would it take to make this work?" Josie said.

"Some kind of shelter. Like if we could carry it in a waterproof container and then set it up under a roof or something."

"I've got dry cleaning in the back. Would those plastic bags work?"

"Probably. If they don't have holes."

"There's enough to wrap them around your gear a few times. So they might protect it even if there were a few little holes."

"Worth trying," Cumberland said.

"Okay, I'm going to get out and reach in the back door for the dry cleaning. I'll pull the plastic bags off. You could be ready to take the bags, open the hatch, and wrap your electronics fast before they can get wet."

"Will do," Cumberland said.

"Remember not to stab yourself with the caltrops."

"Right."

They both got out of the car, Cumberland still holding the war hammer.

He leaned the hammer against the side of the car and went to the hatch.

Josie slipped her clothes out of the plastic bags and handed the bags to Cumberland. He reached into the hatch back, wrapped the gear, and held it under his arm. He picked up the war hammer.

"Can you still carry your war hammer?"

He nodded. "Are you bringing your dog?"

"I'm still trying to decide."

"I think you should. Dogs are good at finding stuff, right? Maybe she can find the cabin with Samantha. And the dog could maybe scare the bad dude."

Josie didn't want to say that she didn't think anything could scare Robert Silver. He was a psychopath who had no emotions like fear or empathy. "Maybe she could distract the bad dude," Josie said, using Cumberland's phrase.

Josie unhooked Unknown's leash. She knew the danger was that Unknown might get lost or purposely run away. But Josie feared a worse scenario where Unknown's leash could get caught in the underbrush. Or Robert Silver could grab the leash and hold Unknown captive as well.

"You stay near, okay?" she said to the dog, petting her.

Josie picked up her crossbow and her shoulder bag with the bolts and locked the Prius.

"My eyes are bad," she said. "Can you lead the way?"

"Yeah, I guess," Cumberland said, sounding depressed.

"And we should whisper from here on out. Especially when we get close. And no use of flashlights unless it is absolutely necessary. There's nothing that will alert him to our presence faster than flashlights."

"Right," Cumberland whispered. He marched off.

Josie followed. She couldn't see Unknown in the dark. Especially when she looked down toward where she thought the dog was. But when she looked in front toward Cumberland, she sensed movement below in her peripheral vision. It seemed as if Unknown was staying close. Whether it was force of habit or training or dog fear, Josie didn't know.

Cumberland walked quickly. Maybe his eyes were good enough to see that the path was clear. Or maybe having long legs made him go faster.

Josie struggled to keep up. She was out of breath. And her crossbow seemed much heavier than she remembered.

After several yards, they came to what seemed like the end of the road. The darkness became denser and blacker. There was nothing to see. Josie's senses seemed limited to hearing, although, perhaps, she could smell and feel enough to be helpful in a way.

Cumberland continued on, stepping quietly. In a short time, branches and leaves seemed to be brushing Josie from both sides.

They walked in silence for ten minutes, hearing nothing but the rain. Josie's arm and shoulder grew so tired from carrying the crossbow and bolt bag that she switched the loads to her other side. She had to stop to make the change. Cumberland kept walking, getting farther in front of her. As she started forward to catch up to him, Josie sensed that Unknown had stopped.

Josie whispered, "Cumberland." He kept walking. "Cumberland!"

Josie couldn't see him, but, as with Unknown, she sensed that he'd stopped.

"What?" he whispered.

"Wait up. Unknown stopped. She smells something. Or hears something."

Josie bent down and spoke in a soft voice. "What is it, Unknown?"

Unknown growled, soft. Josie didn't know the nuances of what dogs mean with various sounds. But she thought it seemed more like an alert than a warning of aggression. Josie pet the dog. "Good girl. What do you mean? Do you smell Samantha?"

Unknown didn't make any more sounds. It was too dark to tell if Unknown was looking or listening in a particular direction.

Josie straightened up and whispered to Cumberland. "I don't know what to do."

"Maybe she just wanted us to know that we're close to people or a mountain lion or something. I think we should keep walking."

A sound came through the trees. A soft thud. Like a door closing.

"I'm scared," Cumberland whispered, even softer than before.

"Let's keep going until we can tell where the cabin is. Slow and silent."

Maybe he nodded in the dark. Maybe not. Josie couldn't tell for certain.

Cumberland turned and walked. Josie followed. She thought she could sense Unknown just in front of her.

They crept along. After forty or fifty steps, Josie walked into Cumberland's back. She choked back a gasp.

Cumberland turned and whispered so quietly that Josie could barely hear him. "The cabin is right through those trees. To your right. Move your head back and forth and you can see the glow of a light coming from a window."

Josie did as he said. The glow was very soft, but it was obvious once she saw it.

She pulled Cumberland's head down so she could whisper in his ear.

"I'm going to sneak into the woods to the right. You go to the left and try to circle around and come up to the cabin. I'm hoping you can find someplace to leave your equipment hidden. So when the kidnapper hears the sounds, he can't find the source."

"Now I'm terrified," Cumberland said.

"Me too," Josie said. "Good luck. I'll wait for your vibration signal."

She physically turned Cumberland and gave him a soft pat

on his back for encouragement. Then she turned and pushed into the trees.

She hadn't gone more than a few feet when her crossbow got stuck on branches. It seemed to Josie like it made a great deal of noise. She tried to find how it was caught, but all she could feel was a bunch of small branches around it and in its cord. Then, she realized that she'd forgotten to cock it with a bolt. But her second thought was that the oversight was fortunate, because it probably would have gone off, making a loud snap and alerting anyone to her presence. And as with any weapon, an unaimed weapon can shoot friend as well as foe.

Josie backed up almost to the trail. That seemed to untangle the crossbow. She held it closer to her body and tried moving into the trees from a different spot. That seemed to work. Wet, soggy branches dragged at her arms and shoulders and head, and weapon, too. But she was able to move forward. She tried to keep her eye on the glow of light coming from the cabin. But it was a fractured glow, the light split up into multiple points by the rain on her glasses. For a moment, it got much brighter and then went dark. Had she simply moved in and then out of a good viewing perspective? Or had someone opened a drape or a door and then shut it?

Josie moved by feel. She could no longer see any glow or any other indication that the cabin even existed. The branches hitting her made enough noise that she couldn't hear Unknown, or the rain, either. But it still fell, pelting her head and face. A sense of dread came over her. She felt like she was back in the Canadian wilderness, being hunted by a killer. She stopped, took a deep breath and reminded herself of the difference. The woods were like the wilderness, but this experience was different. She was the hunter. And she was hunting the killer.

After she'd gone what seemed like a sizable distance, she changed her direction as if to come in behind the cabin. Some unseen branches scraped at her skin. Then they snapped away.

Nothing else touched her. Everything looked exactly the same, which was to say she still could see nothing. There was only blackness. Because of the rain clouds, there were no stars. It was an uncomfortable feeling to sense nothing. She could have been on an alien planet with no forest or roads or cabin. Just rain.

Josie thought she'd come far enough that she must be near the cabin. It would be a good time to load her weapon.

She positioned the bow end on the ground and slowly turned the ratchet. With each revolution of the crank, the cord was pulled back an inch or so. Unfortunately, the ratchet that kept the cord from snapping forward made little clicks. In the past, Josie had never thought of it as noise. But out in the woods at night, it seemed very loud. She turned to face away from where she guessed the cabin to be. That might make the clicking sound project away from the cabin instead of toward it.

She kept turning the crank. Click, click, click. Even the rain noise seemed insufficient to dampen the sound. But Josie couldn't think of a better approach. The only way to load and fire the crossbow was to cock the drawstring. And the crank and ratchet mechanism was the only way to do that.

A light came on through the trees. Josie's heart, thumping hard before, raced. The light seemed to point toward the drive. A motion light. Maybe Cumberland had triggered it. Enough light spilled through the trees and brush to partially illuminate Josie. She looked around. There was no place to hide. She could only hope no one was looking her way. She kept cranking the crossbow.

Click, click, click.

After what seemed like a very long time, the draw string was pulled all the way. Josie pulled a bolt from her bag and fitted it by feel into the groove with the point of the bolt facing forward and the back of the bolt against the draw cord. She was lifting the crossbow up into position, when the phone in her pocket vibrated.

Cumberland was signalling that his electronic gear was in position.

Josie shifted the crossbow so she could reach into her right pocket and press the lock button. She felt around, found the button with the indentation, and pressed it.

Josie couldn't hear anything, but presumably there were now kitten meowing sounds just outside of the cabin.

As she pulled her hand out of her pocket and grabbed onto the crossbow with both hands, Unknown growled low and loud. The noise made Josie jerk. A blinding light pierced the rainy night. The light beam washed over her.

There was an explosion, a brilliant flash of light and a deep cracking boom that shocked and numbed her ears. But the sound and light was nothing against the red hot fire that stabbed through her left calf muscle and made Josie pitch face first to the dark ground.

THIRTY-SEVEN

The impact of light and sound and fire-like pain shocked Josie. It took several moments for her to realize she'd been shot. But she was still alive. She saw a light beam flashing in the bushes and trees above her head. Whoever had shot her was coming to make certain she was dead. As quickly as she could make her muscles work, she tried to crawl away on her elbows and the knee of her right leg, which hadn't been shot. It felt like a panicked scramble that, nevertheless, only moved her at the speed of a crawling bug. Josie still gripped the crossbow. It was obvious that if she let go of it, she'd be able to get away faster. But she felt lightheaded. Probably she was bleeding so fast that she didn't have much time to live.

Then came a sound that only Josie would instantly recognize.

"Mamaaaaaaaaa!"

Samantha was here! Samantha was alive! It was possible Samantha could still be saved.

"SAM!!" Josie shouted as loud as she could, realizing too late that she had just let her shooter know that she was still alive.

A third voice called out. The person holding the flashlight. "I can't let you take my boy, Josie. He's all I've got. He's made some bad mistakes. But I have to help him."

Tom Silver.

His voice was coming from over by the wavering flashlight beam. He was getting closer.

Josie realized that her only chance for survival was to hang onto the crossbow. She kept crawling. Away from the wavering flashlight beam.

"You know the law, Josie. A man has a right to defend his castle. Once Robert disposes of your daughter's body and then escapes, it'll just be me explaining to the police how my fellow history professor must have been deranged by her daughter going missing. So she came up here to break into my cabin. I didn't know who was out there. But what choice did I have when someone was threatening me?"

Josie got an idea. She crawled a little farther, dragging herself under a large bush. She reached into her bag and pulled out her little flashlight and, leaving it off, held it in her left hand. She shifted the crossbow so the trigger was near her right index finger.

"I can't believe you shot me," she called out to the darkness. "We could have worked something out, you and I. But now I…" She feigned a terrible coughing and gagging sound. "I can't breathe. I… Oh, God… Blood is coming out my chest. My ears are ringing." She mumbled, "Mother Mary is… is… Mother… I don't think I…" She stopped talking and lay still.

After a bit, she heard movement.

Branches rustling. Footfalls. The snap of breaking wood. The flashlight beam went left and right in a search pattern. Apparently, Tom Silver wasn't exactly sure where he'd find Josie's body.

With each sweep of the light beam, he came closer. He would be on her in a few more steps. Hopefully, he thought she was already dead. Or, at least, unconscious. But once he found out otherwise, he would quickly fire another few shots to be certain Josie was dead.

Josie was shaking with fear. She'd come to face the worst evil, only to find that it was the man whose office was down the hall from hers. She had a brief moment when she thought she might reason with him. Tom Silver was smart. He'd always been sensible. If he could just step back and get a larger perspective.

Then Josie remembered what Samantha had said. In the

movies, whenever the bad guy gets away still alive, he keeps on killing.

The light beam briefly swept over Josie. It stopped. Came back.

Josie hit her own flashlight switch with her left hand. She could see Tom Silver, his grand mane of silver hair illuminated against the night. He brought up his pistol.

Josie fired the crossbow.

The crossbow kicked back hard, driving Josie's arm down into the dirt with such pressure that it felt like she'd been stepped on by a horse.

She kept her flashlight on the man. She saw that the bolt had entered his right eye and buried its entire length in his brain.

THIRTY-EIGHT

A moment after the crossbow bolt hit Tom Silver, he pitched forward and hit the dirt face first. His flashlight flew to one side, his gun out in front of him.

Josie stifled a gasp at what she'd done. She nearly retched.

Then she remembered that Robert was at the cabin, and Robert had Samantha.

Josie reached into her left pocket for the fob that controlled the police sounds. She felt the fob, found the concave button, and pressed it.

This time she could hear the sounds. Sirens grew in the distance. Red and blue strobe lights flashed up in the woods. A horn beeped. More sirens. A car door closing hard. A megaphone came on.

"This is the LA Sheriff! Your house is surrounded! Drop your weapons and come out with your hands up. If you don't come out, we will shoot stun grenades and break down your door. You will be taken, dead or alive!" The recording was so convincing, even Josie started to think it was real. Then she remembered it was her own setup. Cumberland was out there in the dark. Samantha was inside the cabin with her kidnapper.

Josie crabbed her way out from under the bush. She pulled with her arms and pushed with her one good leg. Then she reached back, got hold of the crossbow and pulled it. It wouldn't come. She directed her flashlight at it. The cord that fired the bolt was snagged on the fork of a branch. She twisted sideways, turned so she was sitting, then reached out and unhooked the crossbow cord.

Josie jerked as something wet touched her cheek.

Unknown.

She reached out and touched the dog. It was reassuring to know she wasn't alone out in the cold, rainy woods.

The motion light turned off.

Josie pushed up onto her hands and her right knee.

Josie's bag was still strapped over her shoulder. She reached into it, feeling for another bolt so she could reload her crossbow. The bag twisted. The flap wouldn't open up. She scraped at it with her nails, trying to catch the edge. It felt like a ridiculous struggle trying to reach into her bag. Why didn't she have pants with cargo pockets?!

In the distance, the recorded cop sounds continued.

Josie finally freed the bag flap and pulled out another bolt. But she didn't know how she could load the crossbow in the dark with one hand while she held the flashlight with the other.

Josie realized she could hold the flashlight in her mouth. But the killer could see the flashlight from the cabin. So she turned onto her hands and knees, then pushed up so she was kneeling on the ground, facing away from the cabin, her body shielding the flashlight from view. Her calf muscle burned like it was on fire. She knew that she could be bleeding to death. But there was no point in worrying about that now. She didn't have any easy way to put a tourniquet around her leg. It would have to wait.

Still facing away from the cabin and holding the flashlight in her mouth, Josie cranked the crossbow tension. The ratchet once again made clicking noises as the cord pulled back. Maybe the killer could hear that in the cabin. Josie didn't know of a way to muffle the sound. She turned the crank faster.

When the cord was pulled all the way, Josie fitted a bolt into position. The crossbow was now loaded, as deadly a weapon up close as any.

She looked through the dark, trying to sense the shape of the cabin. The rain increased, running down her glasses and into her eyes, obscuring her view of everything.

It looked like the cabin sat up above the ground. Josie guessed that there was a deck across the front of the cabin and maybe at the ends, as well. There would be steps somewhere, leading up to the deck. She'd never get up steps on her knees. She needed to see if she could stand up. She briefly shined the light across the ground, looking for some kind of stick she could use for a cane.

Ten feet away was a thin, dead branch that was bent in the middle. It was longer than a cane. But maybe it would work. She turned off the light, crawled over, and felt around on the ground. Her fingers brushed the branch, and she picked it up. By feeling the branch up and down, she found it had a fork where she could hold it. She stuck the other end of the branch into the dirt and pushed down.

It was relatively easy to lift her good leg, plant the foot, then stand up, holding her wounded leg off the ground. Gradually, she planted the foot of the wounded leg and put some weight on it. Pain, like a knife, stabbed her calf muscle. But all she needed to do was think of Samantha being held prisoner in the cabin, and the pain seemed minor.

Josie kept the flashlight turned off and held it with the same hand that gripped the branch cane. She carried the crossbow with her other hand. Moving slowly and tentatively, she put weight on her wounded leg, took a step through the dark, and repeated the motion over and over. She sensed a dark shape in her peripheral vision and thought it was Unknown at her side.

The rain seemed to come harder, the drops making noisy splatters on the ground and leaves of trees. The wind blew hard enough to whistle. The recorded sheriff sounds seemed overwhelmed by the storm. But still the blue and red strobe flashed in the woods.

Josie came to steps. It took great effort to go up each one, stepping up with her good leg, then pulling the wounded leg up.

Josie was near the top step when Unknown made a low growl. Josie stopped, leaned against the railing, and raised her crossbow. She held the flashlight but left it off.

A door opened. "Outside!" a man's voice shouted in a whisper. There was a sound of footfalls on deck boards.

A flashlight came on at the deck door.

Josie saw the vague shape of a large man holding onto a tall skinny kid.

Samantha!

Unknown growled and sprinted across the deck. The dog charged the man, stopped two feet back, and growled furiously.

A third shape charged in from the side. Josie turned on her light. She saw Cumberland swing the huge war hammer. It struck the big man on his arm. He let go of Samantha as he screamed.

The man let out a primal, guttural howl of rage. He held his wounded arm at his side as he raised his other arm. The pistol was shiny in the beam of Josie's flashlight. She took careful aim with the crossbow and pulled the trigger.

The bolt struck him in the abdomen. He made a gagging sound as he bent over and sunk to the deck boards.

He still held the gun in his good hand. Once again, he raised it slowly as if trying to decide on his target.

Samantha took two steps and swung her arm. Josie couldn't see what happened in the dark. But she heard a loud thud, and the man slumped forward and fell to the deck.

Cumberland ran over and kicked the killer's gun out of his limp hand and off the edge of the deck.

Samantha ran over to Josie. They hugged. "I don't know how you did it, Mama. I heard a gunshot. I was so scared and worried." Josie sagged down, pulling Samantha with her until they were sitting on the deck. "But you did it. You found me." They hugged, a long hard grip with tears falling onto Josie's rain-soaked clothes.

Josie heard Cumberland talking. She realized that he'd called

911.

Unknown came over and swiped her paw at Samantha, then sat next to her.

As Samantha shifted her grip to rub Unknown, her other hand touched Josie's leg. Josie jerked in pain.

"Mama, you're hurt. What happened?"

Josie was feeling very shaky. She forced a deep inhalation. "Tom Silver shot me."

"You're wounded?! Oh, Mama. How bad is it?"

"I don't think it's life threatening. I think it just went through the back of my calf. But I will say..." Josie paused to breathe again. "It really hurts."

"Mama, we have to do something. You could bleed to death! I'll go find something to make a turniquet. Wait, I can use my windbreaker."

Samantha pulled it off. Cumberland turned on a flashlight and shined it on Josie's leg. Her pant was wet and dark with sticky blood. Samantha bunched the jacket into a loose rope and wrapped it around Josie's leg. She twisted the jacket to tighten the wrap.

Cumberland periodically shifted the light beam. It took Josie a moment to realize he was checking on Robert Silver, the killer who had a crossbow bolt in his abdomen. The man was motionless, lying on his side in a pool of blood.

Cumberland brought the light back to Josie's leg, then he approached. "We're supposed to put direct pressure on a wound, right?"

"I think so," Josie said.

Cumberland pressed down where Samantha's jacket wrapped over Josie's gunshot wound. His touch was very tentative.

He said, "Are you both, you know, okay? I mean, I know you're not okay. But should I do anything?"

"I think you can push harder," Josie said.

Cumberland nodded and pressed hard.

Josie winced.

"We'll be okay, eventually," Samantha said. "You and Mama saved me. Whoever you are."

"I'm, um, I'm one of your mom's students. My name is Cumberland.

Samantha let go of Josie, and leaned over and hugged Cumberland.

The sound of real sirens rose in the distance. The flashing blue and red light from Cumberland's light bar was replaced by light from an ambulance and patrol vehicles.

They all sat in a huddle in the dark, Josie on one side of Samantha, Unknown on the other. Across from them was Cumberland. A short distance away lay the unmoving killer.

Josie couldn't stop her tears. "Cumberland hit him in the arm with the war hammer. I shot him with a bolt to the stomach. But he didn't drop until you hit him with something. What was that, Sam?"

"Remember, Mama? What you taught me about a lethal weapon anyone can make?"

"No, Cap'n, I don't remember." Josie was struggling to breathe.

"I found one of those heavy glass holders for votive candles. It was practically like a rock. You said a person can bring down anyone with a Rock in a Sock."

Unknown stood up, turned toward the approaching medics, then turned back to Samantha. The dog was just visible in the red and blue strobe flashes.

"Look, Mama." Samantha said.

"What?"

"Unknown is wagging!"

EPILOGUE

J osie spent the next day in the hospital. They kept her under sedation, more to help her rest and sleep, she thought, than cope with pain. They did some minor surgery on her leg. The bullet had gone all the way through, and no bone or major artery had been hit. She was told to do only gentle motions for the next week. They said that while she could expect a full recovery in most ways, she would probably always have a tightness and discomfort in her leg.

Josie knew that Samantha had much more to deal with than mere physical injury. The trauma of kidnapping would leave permanent emotional scars. As Samantha tended to Josie's wound, it seemed that Samantha was finding purpose in being useful. Josie had noticed in the past that the more Samantha struggled with her own issues, the more she focused on helping others.

"We should tell the sheriff," Samantha suddenly said the next morning while they were drinking coffee.

It took Josie a moment to realize who Samantha was referring to.

"The sheriff in the canoe country wilderness," Josie said.

"Yeah. Sheriff Denser. He will be worried about our little sweetie." Samantha looked over at Unknown. "We should tell him that she's good and that we caught Bill's killer, too."

"You're right. Do you want to do the honors?"

"Me call him?"

"Yes. You know everything I know, and you're closer to Unknown as well."

At the sound of her name, Unknown lifted her head and

looked at Josie and then at Samantha.

"Look, Mama, she really knows her name, even though it's probably not the name she was given when she was born."

Josie nodded. "She's a smart dog. What do you say about calling the sheriff?"

Samantha paused, then found the sheriff's business card and dialed.

Josie listened with pride as Samantha did a very articulate job of explaining what had happened and how the sheriff might want to know that Bill Masenrud's killer was caught and Bill's dog Unknown was now eating well and had even wagged a couple of times and liked walking the Beach Walk in Santa Monica.

Josie could hear the sheriff saying a few things but couldn't make out the words.

"Yeah, it was a little scary at the end," Samantha said. "I got kidnapped by the killer, and Mama got shot." Pause. "What? Medieval techniques? Oh, you remembered what we did out on the island. Well, yeah, our friend used Mama's war hammer, and Mama had her medieval crossbow. Now the killer's in some kind of security hospital. They say he might never get out of jail. Of course, it's a moot point if he doesn't wake up." Another pause. "Oh, Mama had to shoot him with a crossbow bolt to the stomach, and I knocked him out with the rock-in-a-sock technique." Pause. "You don't know it? It's another medieval skill. If you ever spend time in L.A., you should take Mama's class." Pause. "Okay. Just wanted you to know that your county doesn't need to worry about the killer anymore." Pause. "Thanks again."

Samantha clicked off. She looked at Josie. "You want to know what he said?"

"Yes, please."

"He said if I ever want to work in law enforcement, he'll give me a job."

Samantha made a big grin, and Josie thought that, despite

the probable coming nightmares and questions and worries, Samantha was going to be okay.

Two days later, they had a picnic on the Santa Monica beach. Samantha had found a backpack that was the right size to carry Unknown. She thought the police might not have a problem with dogs confined in backpacks. She set the pack down on the sand and had Unknown stay in it with only her head sticking out. Samantha sat cross-legged in the sand next to her, and Unknown rested her jaw on Samantha's knee.

Shuluwish sat nearby, and across from them sat Cumberland.

"Shulu," Josie said, "this is Cumberland Durand. Cumberland, please meet Shuluwish Ojai." Neither made a move to shake hands, making small nodding movements instead.

"Josie told me about you," Shulu said to Cumberland. "You are the man who used a war hammer on the killer, and you created the cop-sound deception. Very impressive."

"Um, it's real easy." Cumberland spoke toward the sand, too shy to actually look the woman in the eye. "You just download whatever you want and then play it back."

"I've heard of downloading, but I don't really know how it works. I don't have a computer."

Cumberland's eyes widened. He didn't have a response.

"She's an artist," Samantha said. "Paints on canvas. No tech needed."

"Anyway, you helped save Samantha," Shulu said.

"And you gave Mama the right support to come and save me," Samantha said.

Samantha turned to Shulu. "Did she tell you that the cops asked her how she was brave enough to go after two killers? She told them she got spiritual support from a Chumash shaman."

Shulu turned to Josie. "You didn't tell them I said you should kill the bad guy?"

Josie said, "I didn't think that was the best way to categorize your help."

Shulu made a long, single nod. "I worried you might get in trouble."

Samantha guffawed. "When they found out what had happened to me, they practically gave Mama a medal."

"Good," Shulu said. "I saw that the Times called it Citizen Heroism."

Shulu reached into her pack and pulled out a rectangular package wrapped in kraft paper. She handed it to Samantha.

"Because you're worth saving, I wanted to commemorate it with a small gift."

"For me? Oh, my God, that is so nice of you!"

Samantha pulled off the wrapping.

"Mama! Shulu gave me her painting of the Great Horned Owl!" She held it up so the others could see. "It is so beautiful. I remember this is the Chumash goddess. What is her name again?"

"Hutash."

Samantha stood up, handed the painting to Josie, then knelt down next to Shulu and hugged her.

Shulu reached one hand around and patted Samantha on the back.

"I'm so thankful to you, Shulu. You helped Mama and Cumberland save me. Now I'm going to thank Hutash every day." Then Samantha reached over to Unknown and hugged her. "And Unknown helped save me, too."

About the Author

Todd Borg and his wife live in Tahoe, where they write and paint. To contact Todd or learn more about the Josie Strong thrillers or the Owen McKenna mysteries, please visit toddborg. com.

A message from the author:

Dear Reader,

If you enjoyed this novel, please consider posting a short review on any book website you like to use, such as Goodreads and Amazon. Reviews help authors a great deal, and that in turn allows us to write more stories for you.
Thank you very much for your interest and support!

Todd

Made in United States
Troutdale, OR
01/03/2025

27601652R00171